RISING HEAT

ELIZABETH HOLLOWS

Rising Heat
ISBN # 978-1-83943-787-8
©Copyright Elizabeth Hollows 2022
Cover Art by Kelly Martin ©Copyright April 2022
Interior text design by Claire Siemaszkiewicz
Pride Publishing

RISING HEAT

Chapter One

Neil Farris had never seen the point to relationships. They only seemed to breed drama and boredom. Why choose one person to sleep with when the options for many were only a bar trip away?

His co-worker Denise often joked that he could find a fling in a haystack. He took it as a point of pride. He didn't need to settle down into monotony when he could be the envy of many with a few well-placed flirtations. Sex was what he was after, not some white picket fence.

Yet despite her remarks, Neil hadn't expected to have much luck at his yearly manager's meeting. Not only did he know better than to sleep with his colleagues if he wanted his flings to *remain* flings, but the last three years had been the same boring routine.

He managed a men's clothing store that specialized in affordable formal and stylish casual wear. Hardgroves was a leader in the industry with twelve stores in Queensland alone, and they wanted to maintain their foothold in the market. He'd driven the four hours down to Brisbane with the plan to check into his hotel and catch up with the few other managers he liked.

Instead, he found a mistake in the booking culminating in his lost reservation. Thirty minutes of back and forth with the company and he had alternative accommodation in a different hotel twenty minutes across town.

When he finally arrived, tired and annoyed, the last thing he'd expected was a lobby full of eye candy. A dozen muscled men were carrying duffel bags and chatting in small groups. Some were tanned, and some had tattoos. There were a few women with them, but Neil only had eyes for the guys.

Let it be a convention for gay singles.

He didn't know where to look, but Neil quickly found his attention grabbed by a man at reception. His upper body had an attractive V-shape, his arms were muscled without bulging and the view only got better farther down. Neil crossed the lobby to stand behind him. The man's khaki pants hinted at a firm bottom and taut thighs. He was a head taller than Neil with short black hair that was spiking at the top. He was compact in a way that showed he was no stranger to working out.

Now that's a man I'd happily show a good time.

Neil would have continued his admiration if the man hadn't stepped backward and turned. He nearly collided with Neil but jerked away in time.

"Sorry," he apologized. "I didn't realize someone was there."

The man's eyes were as blue as the sky, and his smile was friendly. Neil swallowed down three pickup lines.

"Don't worry about it."

The man flashed another grin before taking a better grip on his bag. He walked over to a group congregating farther inside the hotel. They welcomed him with laughter, backslaps and familiarity. Neil forced his attention to the reception desk rather than the man's biceps. The young woman behind the desk gave him a knowing smile.

"Annual fireman's training," she explained. Her eyes flicked toward the men before back to Neil, and she lowered her voice. "It gives us the best view in the city for the next week."

"I suddenly don't mind being in a different hotel from my colleagues."

"Ooh, you get all the firemen to yourself. Well, half of them." She winked. "I want my share, too."

Neil laughed. He glanced at the men again, lingering on the one who'd almost bumped into him. He was just Neil's type. Being a fireman only added to his appeal.

When Neil turned back to the receptionist, he matched her grin.

"How about you get the straight ones and I'll get the gay ones?"

"Perfect!" They shared another smile before she cleared her throat. "Now, how can I help you?"

"I've got a reservation."

She took a few minutes to sort everything out, but Neil soon picked up his small suitcase and headed to his room. The hotel wasn't the height of luxury, but it was well-maintained. The two-story building had a bar off the lobby, along with a small restaurant. His room was on the ground floor and down a hall just past reception. It had all the standard amenities with a decent-sized bed. He placed his suitcase on the luggage rack and opened it. Originally, he'd planned to order room service and relax, but the firefighters changed things. Pulling out a nice dress shirt and jeans, Neil headed to the bathroom. It didn't matter that it wasn't a club. He needed to look his best if was going to catch anyone's attention. A quick shower helped Neil feel refreshed, and he double-checked his reflection in the mirror. His sandy-blond hair looked naturally tousled and fell just below his ears. The shirt he wore was white with a subtle pattern of small palm trees. The leather bracelet around his left wrist partially obscured his tattoo of a sun. He grinned at the mirror, knowing he looked good.

Grabbing his wallet, room key and phone, Neil slipped them into the pocket of his jeans and stepped out of the room. The hall was empty, but when he reached the lobby, he noted that there weren't as many firemen as there had been before. Neil was quick to spot the one from reception. He was at the bar, ordering drinks with four others. It only took one more once-over for Neil to make his choice. He crossed the room and took a place leaning against the bar two stools down from the group. His chosen firefighter glanced at him, his blue eyes locking onto Neil's green. Neil smiled. He held the man's gaze, feeling a thrill go through him. Neil knew the game well, and he was certain there was interest in the fireman's eyes. Neil only looked away when the bartender approached.

Once his beer was poured, he glanced back at the man and subtly listened to the conversation. They were talking about the upcoming training course and their travels to get to Brisbane. Three of them were from the same town but the other two were from different parts of the state.

It sounded a lot like Neil's own management meeting. He took a sip of his beer and glanced at the men again. His blue-eyed fireman was already looking at him. If they had been at a club, Neil would crook his finger and gesture the man over. Or maybe he'd turn on his stool, sprawling his back over the bar and making it easy for the fireman to step between his open legs. However, with the man surrounded by his friends and colleagues, Neil knew it would be better to wait. He settled for smiling again before taking his beer and heading into the attached restaurant.

Neil selected an empty table with a good view. The group from the bar plus nine more firefighters entered the restaurant for dinner. There were attractive men wherever Neil turned, but he found his gaze kept falling back to the same man. He was watching Neil, too. They exchanged glances throughout dinner, and that found anticipation and desire sparking through Neil. He felt confident enough to move back to the bar after his meal. He ordered another drink and waited. A few of the firemen left to return to their rooms, but the one Neil cared about was soon stopping at the bar stool beside Neil's.

"Mind if I join you?" he asked

"Not at all." Neil shifted to better face him and held out his hand. "I'm Neil."

"Scott," he replied.

Their palms lingered together for longer than necessary and a noticeable tension was thrumming through the air as their gazes stayed locked. It didn't take a genius to realize the guy was interested in him, too.

Gay, hot and only meters from my hotel room. Could this be any more perfect?

When they dropped hands, Scott took a seat on the stool. He angled his body close enough that their shoulders brushed. Neil's desire grew from that small touch.

"I didn't think there would be anyone else here," Scott said. "I thought we'd have booked out the hotel."

"Seems I slipped through the cracks," Neil replied. "Lucky me."

When the bartender came over, Scott ordered a matching beer. Neil had another sip of his but kept his gaze on the fireman. Scott was lightly tanned and had a cluster of three small moles on the side of his neck. Neil wanted to mouth at them until the skin surrounding them was red and flushed. This was the type of fireman who'd be perfect for their famous, shirtless charity calendars — only Neil wanted him removed of *all* his clothes.

"So, what brings you to the hotel?" Scott asked, dragging Neil's attention from Scott's neck.

"Annual manager's meeting," he said. "There was a mistake with my booking, so I ended up here." Neil openly ran his gaze over Scott. "Not that I'm complaining. In fact, I'm going to take advantage of my good fortune."

Because if a one-night stand was practically falling in his lap, he wasn't about to ignore it. Lately, it took more effort and drinks for Neil to get into someone's pants. Right now, Neil felt he could score before they reached a second glass.

"Sounds like a good plan to me," Scott said, his attention dropping to Neil's mouth. "A lot of the guys are having an early night." He caught Neil's gaze again. "But I figure that I'm in a new city, and I should have some fun."

There was a suggestive note to his voice that filled Neil with eagerness. He held out his glass for a toast.

"To a night of fun, then."

Scott brought their glasses together with a soft clink. They never broke eye contact, and Neil already knew they would have sex by the end of the night.

In fact, if he played his cards right, Neil was certain it could happen within the hour.

* * * *

They spent fifteen minutes at the bar. Scott mentioned the city, the hotel and the hot weather. Neil played along as they sipped their beers and waited for the rest of the firefighters to leave. None of them tried to talk to Scott or join them at the bar, and once the last man had left, Neil stood and tipped back the rest of his drink. He let his hand trail absently over Scott's shoulders, skimming his fingers under the edge of the man's collar.

Scott swallowed before pushing out from his stool. He left his beer unfinished, and Neil felt a private thrill at being more desirable than the drink. He wanted to push the man against the bar and kiss him, running his hands underneath Scott's shirt as he chased the taste of alcohol on the fireman's tongue.

But Neil hadn't missed Scott's focus on their small talk. If he had an appearance to keep up with his colleagues, Neil could respect that.

Giving a subtle nod toward his section of the hotel, Neil walked out of the restaurant and across the lobby. Scott followed eagerly, but the moment they were in the hall, Scott touched his arm. Neil turned and Scott gently backed him up against the wall before kissing him. Neil's surprise made way for a pleased groan. Burying his hands in the fireman's short hair, Neil pulled Scott closer until he was all but caged against the wall. Scott cupped his waist, and Neil dropped one hand so he could brush that cluster of moles on the man's neck.

This really is turning out to be my lucky weekend.

When the kiss broke, Neil tilted back his head, trying to catch his breath.

"Which room is yours?" Scott asked, trailing his lips over Neil's jaw.

His touch was hardening Neil's cock with every second his mouth traced Neil's skin. But he wanted the fireman naked on his bed more than getting a hickey in the hall.

He pushed at Scott's shoulder to separate them. When the man stepped back, he gripped Scott's arm and led him to his room. Neil pulled out his key card and opened the door in a rush. When it shut behind them, Scott cupped Neil's neck and pulled him in for another kiss. Scott's touch set his body aflame. The desire that had been simmering since he'd first seen the firefighter was only becoming stronger.

Wrapping his arm around Scott's neck, he stepped close and slotted their bodies together. Scott parted his lips and the kiss deepened. Scott slipped his fingers under Neil's shirt, brushing Neil's stomach and making him shiver. They separated and Scott nibbled on his neck.

"Do you have a preference about how we do this, Neil?"

"No," he answered, feeling impatient. "I don't care."

"Me, either," Scott replied. "Should we flip a coin?"

Neil rolled his eyes and pushed Scott back. "I'll save us the effort. You can top."

He went to unbutton his shirt, but Scott caught his hands and stilled him. Neil frowned but Scott smiled and took over. He worked slowly as he popped every button.

"It might just be some fun," Scott said, "but that doesn't mean we can't do it right."

Neil's confusion deepened. One-night stands were his typical Friday night. He'd gotten it down to an art form and could almost predict every motion they made. For starters, his flings wanted him naked and on the bed without chitchat or foreplay. Scott's behavior was more reminiscent of something people did after a date. It was odd.

When Scott finished with the buttons, he pushed the shirt gently off Neil's shoulders. Wanting to get things back on track, Neil grabbed the hem of Scott's and pulled it over his head. He took a moment to admire him. Scott was *fit*. His job clearly didn't leave him any time for slacking off. There were a few freckles, but they only added to the masterpiece.

Good thing this isn't a club. This guy is way out of my usual league.

Neil knew he was attractive, but he wasn't stupid, either. Scott was the kind of man who could get any hunk or twink he wanted.

Yet, the man was looking at him with open desire and, damn, did Neil like that.

After tugging his soon-to-be lover into another kiss, Neil kept their mouths connected as he started edging them toward the bed. He turned them at the last moment so that Scott's legs hit the mattress. The fireman maintained his balance but the kiss broke. Scott slipped his fingers beneath the waistband of Neil's pants.

"We should get these off."

Scott started undoing the buttons of his jeans, and Neil arched into the touch but needed Scott to go faster. Placing his hands on Scott's pants, he popped the button and undid the zip. Neil could see the hard shape of Scott's erection beneath the thin fabric of his boxers.

Their clothes needed to go.

After kicking off his shoes and socks, Neil shimmied from his pants. Scott followed his example and Neil pressed his hand to Scott's shoulder, encouraging him to get on the bed. Scott complied, and the moment he was on his back, Neil was climbing on top of him.

Finally.

He bent down to kiss the man as he straddled his hips. The friction to his cock had him groaning against Scott's mouth. Scott cupped Neil's thighs, directing him to roll his hips, which he did.

"Maybe I should top from the bottom," Scott said when they parted for air. He slid his hands to Neil's ass and gently squeezed. "You look good sitting there."

Neil paused his hands over Scott's stomach. It was one more peculiarity. He'd expected to get flipped over and taken from behind—no emotions, no strings, just a quick, fast and harmless fuck. But he did like Scott's idea. There weren't a lot of men who would give up their control so easily. If Scott was offering, why would he refuse?

"Yeah, okay," Neil said.

He climbed off Scott and went to his luggage. He always came prepared, but this was the first time his supplies had come in handy at a work conference. Neil pulled out the lube and a roll of condoms before walking back to the bed. He dropped the items on the mattress and kneeled in front of Scott. Grabbing the man's boxers, he pulled them off in one quick motion. It gave him his first look at Scott's hard cock.

Lucky, lucky me.

Scott's cock wasn't the biggest he'd seen, but it was thick and long. Neil already knew it would feel terrific inside him. Judging by Scott's fitness, he'd likely have great stamina, too.

After reaching for the lube, he poured a small amount into his hand. He then grasped Scott's cock and stroked it, wanting to get it to full hardness. Scott moaned and tilted back his head, rocking his hips forward with every touch.

Satisfaction mixed with Neil's desire. He'd always enjoyed being the one to call the shots. This was the best of both worlds. Leaning forward, Neil pressed a kiss to Scott's stomach, feeling it quiver. He trailed more kisses up the man's chest to reach his throat. There was a hint of roughness, and Neil adored the tingle it gave his lips. He didn't stop stroking his lover's cock as he nipped and mouthed at Scott's skin, finally kissing those three moles he'd admired at the bar.

He didn't leave any marks, knowing how these things went, but when he shifted away, there was a nice pinkness from his attention. Neil eyed the rest of his lover. Scott's face remained angled away, and his skin was flushed. Neil knew he could make Scott come easily, just by doing this. He only needed to speed up his strokes, twist his wrist and things would be all over. But that would be a waste.

He let Scott's erection go, making the man give a displeased groan. Neil ignored it to pull off his boxers and throw them to the ground. He placed more lube on his hand and stroked his own dick. It felt amazing. He was already aching with need. The only thing that kept him from stroking off was his desire for a cock inside him.

"Damn," Scott murmured.

Neil glanced up to find Scott resting on his elbows. His pupils blown wide with lust.

"You look so hot," he continued.

"I suppose you'd know all about heat."

Scott gave a startled laugh.

"A fireman joke?" He smiled. "I've always liked funny men."

Neil smiled in return, enjoying the praise to his body and wit. He almost wanted to make a show of it and let Scott look his fill as he worked his aching cock to the peak and over.

But he *really* wanted a good fucking.

He let go of his cock and picked up the condom. Neil ripped it open before straddling Scott's thighs. He rolled the condom onto Scott, hearing the man hiss at the touch. When it was in place, he grabbed more lube and arched his back. He knew how to take a cock and had done it without prep before, but if Scott wasn't complaining, he was going to make it as good as possible. Every second he worked open his ass, he found sweat beading on his body. He kept thinking about how it would feel to have something thicker inside him.

When he was ready, Neil applied more lube to Scott's cock and positioned over the man's erection. Scott brought his hands to Neil's hips to help balance him. Grabbing the base of Scott's cock, Neil guided his ass toward it. He closed his eyes at the first brush of Scott's head to his pucker. He didn't pause before taking it inside. Scott groaned and gripped Neil's hips tighter, but he didn't guide or force him, which Neil appreciated. The firm, bruising feel of his hands was a useful distraction from the stretch and burn as he was slowly filled. The feeling of being penetrated was its own kind of pleasure. He knew the bliss that would follow, and it kept him bottoming frequently. His breathing was heavy as he took more of the cock inside. When he finally reached the base, Neil let out a breathless moan.

He could feel how tense Scott was as he refrained from moving.

So considerate.

It was better than Neil had come to expect from flings.

I've definitely picked the right fireman.

When Neil was ready, he rewarded Scott's patience. Neil pulled off the man's cock before dropping back down in a slow, perfect drag.

"God," Scott groaned.

Neil opened his eyes and grinned. "No. I'm Neil."

Scott's neck had been arched back but he jerked his head forward to look at Neil. Surprise quickly made way for amusement.

"That was lame...*ah!*"

Neil smirked as he clenched around Scott's cock. Scott's eyes had fallen closed, but he soon opened them.

"Unfair," he said, still looking amused despite the complaint.

"All is fair in comebacks and sex."

Scott took a better grip on Neil's hips. "Let's get back to the sex, then."

He shifted his legs and thrust up into Neil, making his back curve as he moaned. After that, they stopped talking. The only thing on Neil's mind was establishing a rhythm for maximum pleasure. When Scott hit his prostate, Neil fell forward. He had to brace one hand on Scott's chest for support while the other went to his cock, stroking it frantically.

Neil closed his eyes and bit hard on his bottom lip. Scott was panting beneath him, letting out the occasional groan as he thrust deeply. They worked in a perfect motion that found Neil's pleasure rising faster than he'd expected. His orgasm was approaching, and Scott's movements were speeding up as he arched into Neil. He hit the right spot every time, and Neil was so close. He just needed a last shove over the edge.

Neil perfectly timed the next strike to his prostate with a twist and squeeze just below the head of his cock. It was all it took. Neil came with a hitched cry, his body tensing as his orgasm pulsed through him. Scott moaned shortly after, thrusting into Neil a few more times before his own climax overtook him. Neil collapsed forward, leaning heavily against Scott. His breath escaped in harsh pants as he recovered from the pleasure.

He forgot about everything but the tingling in his limbs. When Scott gently touched his back, Neil startled. He opened his eyes and quickly realized that the position couldn't be comfortable for Scott. He lifted off the fireman, groaning softly as Scott slid out of him. Neil dropped onto his back beside his lover. Scott reached for the condom then pulled it off and tied it. He then climbed off the bed and went to the bathroom.

At least that is typical one-night-stand behavior.

Neil felt too satisfied to care about Scott's eccentricities. The fireman had given him a better orgasm than anyone had in the last few months. Neil didn't want to move, but his release was drying on his stomach. He got up with a small grimace and followed Scott.

He found the fireman wrapping the condom in some toilet paper and dropping it into the bin. The modest action was almost cute. Neil didn't care if people knew what he got up to, but it seemed Scott was a little more private.

It was almost a shame that Scott would probably avoid him in the coming days. Neil didn't take reoccurring lovers often, but he would have been willing for the fireman.

Grabbing one of the spare face towels, Neil wet it and wiped up the mess on his stomach. He saw Scott had some of it on him, too. He handed over the towel when he finished, and Scott flashed him a smile.

Washing up in the bathroom should have been awkward. Usually, Neil would have already kicked his latest man to the curb, but he felt oddly at ease.

Probably because I'm not at my apartment or his. This is as casual as you can get, short of doing it in a bathroom stall.

When they stepped back into the room, Scott pulled on his clothes and Neil tugged on his boxers. It was only when Scott was dressed that a hint of awkwardness filled the air.

"You said you're here for the weekend?" Scott asked.

"Yeah. I go back the day after tomorrow."

Scott looked hesitant. "Maybe we could have another drink tomorrow night?"

Neil's eyebrows rose.

"You mean you want to…" He gestured at the bed. "Again?"

"Yeah," Scott agreed. "If you do, too."

Guess that's the perk of anonymous hotel sex, Neil thought wryly. *A gorgeous fireman wants to bed me twice.*

It made sense. No strings. No prospect of a relationship. They could have two carefree nights of sex without fear of commitment sneaking into the situation.

"I should be back by six," Neil answered.

Scott smiled and it struck Neil, not about how handsome he was, but about how *genuine* the smile looked. Most of his flings preferred the sexy smolder. Scott grinned like it wasn't a game they were playing. He just looked genuinely happy for another chance to be with him.

"See you at the bar at seven?"

"Seven it is," Neil agreed, still feeling off-kilter.

There was another uncertain moment where Scott didn't seem to know what to do. He surprised Neil by stepping close. He cupped Neil's neck and kissed him. It was edged with barely quenched passion as they brushed tongues, sending fresh desire rushing through Neil. It was a promise of what tomorrow would bring. Neil nearly chased after Scott's mouth when he pulled away, already wanting more.

"Night, Neil," Scott said and let him go.

Neil squashed the urge to drag Scott back into another one. He never did second rounds. It was odd enough that he was doing a *two*-night stand.

He kept his voice firm as he replied, "Night, Scott."

Scott opened the door and left with a nod and a grin. When the door shut, Neil walked back to his rumpled bed. It still looked and smelled like sex, and he surveyed it with a smug grin. He'd just gone to bed with a hot fireman, and he would do it again tomorrow night.

His weekend was turning out far better than he'd expected.

Chapter Two

The meetings included games and group activities designed to get everyone excited while keeping them engaged. Neil tried to stay focused and show enthusiasm, but he kept thinking about what awaited him at the hotel. How could motivating staff and maximizing sales be more appealing than a naked fireman?

When they finally finished, his fellow managers invited him out for a drink, but he declined and headed back to his hotel. He arrived early and walked into the lobby at five-thirty rather than six. There were already a few firefighters present, and he spotted Scott among them. They saw Neil before Scott did. They nudged Scott in the side, smirking and gesturing at Neil. It seemed they weren't oblivious as to what had happened the previous night.

Scott looked up and smiled. Neil felt uncertain about how to respond, but when Scott's friends prodded him again, the fireman rolled his eyes before coming over. Neil stayed where he was, unsure what to expect.

"Sorry," Scott said, quickly reaching Neil. "The squad worked out what happened last night. They've been teasing me all day."

Neil stiffened, remembering how Scott had tried to be discreet.

"Teasing?"

"Nothing bad!" Scott assured him. "It's more about how I" — he awkwardly rubbed the back of his neck — "'scored'."

"Oh," Neil murmured.

It wasn't the response he'd have predicted from a crew of firemen, but it was a lot better than a negative alternative. Neil still didn't know what to say. He rarely ran into a one-night stand outside of a club. He hadn't thought this part through when accepting another night with Scott. The silence stretched, growing more awkward by the moment.

"You got back early," Scott said, breaking the quiet.

"Yeah," Neil agreed. "The traffic was better than I thought."

"That's good."

Neil nodded. He tried to think of something to say. This was why he was better with drinks in his hand and sex on the menu.

"Hey, Scottie!" a fireman called, making Scott look over his shoulder. "We're going to have dinner." He gestured behind him where the other firefighters were taking a seat at a long table. The man's gaze darted to Neil. "Why don't you ask him to come, too?"

"I'm sure he has other things to do," Scott rebutted, sounding exasperated.

Neil frowned. It wasn't his usual move, but then, everything with Scott wasn't typical for him. Besides, he needed to have dinner, and he wasn't about to look like an idiot sitting alone after turning down an invitation.

"Not really," he said. Scott turned to him, seeming surprised. Neil quickly added, "I was going to have dinner at the restaurant, anyway."

"You don't have to join us," Scott insisted. "They're nice guys, but they're not above playful ribbing." He rubbed his neck again. "I don't want you to be uncomfortable."

More of that same consideration.

It reignited Neil's confidence.

"I don't mind being there, if you don't." Neil smirked. "And I can handle myself."

Slowly, Scott smiled. He seemed pleased. "Okay."

He turned and Neil fell into step beside him as they walked to the restaurant. There were nine people at the table already, only two of them women. Everyone nudged each other and grinned at him and Scott.

"Hey, guys," Scott began. "This is Neil."

A chorus of 'hellos' followed, and Neil responded in kind as he took a seat beside Scott at the end of the table. He was facing the fireman who'd invited him to join. The man was tall and broad-shouldered. He was older than both Neil and Scott with a well-maintained beard with flecks of gray. He held out his hand across the table.

"Name's Paul. I work with Scott back home."

"Nice to meet you," Neil said, shaking the man's hand.

When they let go, Neil placed his arms on the table. He could feel discomfort waiting to surface but he refused to feel unnerved. He'd slept with Scott once, but everyone would know it was a casual thing. While he might feel like he was 'meeting the friends', it wasn't real. He needed to get back into the mindset he'd adopted for customers and clubs.

It's worth putting up with his co-workers for another round of sex.

"Scott says you're here for a manager's meeting?" Paul asked.

"Yeah," Neil answered. "And you're here for the annual fireman's training. How's that going?"

"A lot better when we can get to the training!" One man farther down the table complained, gaining grunts and emphatic agreement.

"We don't like being forced to sit around all day watching presentations," Scott explained. "We want to get to the exercises."

"Scott's the only one who's had any exercise so far!"

It earned a few laughs while the back of Scott's neck colored. He sent the fireman who'd spoken an annoyed look before turning to Neil with apologetic eyes.

"Sorry."

Neil chuckled. "If that's the worst they've got, I'm disappointed. I was expecting at least one innuendo about a fireman's hose."

Paul and the other fireman around them snorted or outright laughed.

"Well, the night's still young," Scott told him, the words both a warning and a tease.

Neil grinned. "I'll prepare my comebacks. I always give as good as I get."

"Yeah, I worked that out last night," Scott replied, a grin catching at the corner of his mouth.

Neil winked, feeling the tension leave his body as he relaxed into the lighthearted conversation with Scott. It was like what they'd shared last night. The addition of the other firemen was different, but nothing Neil couldn't handle.

It might even prove a fun story to recount to his assistant manager when he got home. She'd be jealous enough that he bedded a handsome fireman but adding that he sat down to dinner with more of them would only make her groan with additional envy.

And judging by the way Scott was looking at him and brushing their legs together under the table, Neil would also groan soon — only for a much better reason.

* * * *

Dinner was fun, to Neil's pleasant surprise. There was the occasional teasing quip, but mostly the firefighters spoke about the upcoming training, along with embarrassing or funny stories from previous events. Neil had little to add, but he threw in the occasional droll retort to make everyone laugh.

It was almost disappointing when it came to an end. Scott was funny, he kept Neil included and he explained any fireman terminology that Neil didn't understand. His colleagues seemed like the kind of people who would be fun at a party.

When everyone finished eating, Paul shook Neil's hand and the other firefighters waved or said their goodbyes and wandered back to their rooms. It left Scott and Neil sitting together at an empty table.

"That probably wasn't the evening you expected," Scott said with a wry smile. "Thanks for putting up with them."

"It was fine," Neil said. "Better than dining alone." Neil shifted in his seat to rest closer to Scott. "A lot of things get better when you're not by yourself."

"That's true," Scott agreed, desire darkening his blue eyes. "Nothing worse than being lonely, especially at night."

Neil hummed. "Absolutely. I hope you'll fix that for me, Scott."

"You asking me to come back to your room?" Scott asked, yet his smile said he already knew the answer.

Neil placed his hand on Scott's leg, making his intentions plain. He held the man's gaze and asked, "Do you need me to be any more obvious?"

Scott laughed. "No, I think you've made it clear."

He stood up and offered his hand. Neil quirked an eyebrow but accepted and was helped to his feet. Their palms lingered together in a parody of intimacy. Neil pulled away first, not wanting it to continue. Scott was a nice guy, but Neil didn't do relationships and affectionate gestures. Tonight, he'd have sex with Scott. Tomorrow, he'd pack his bags and never see the man again.

Tilting his head in a gesture for Scott to follow him, Neil left the restaurant with Scott at his side. Each step closer to his room found the sexual tension brimming. It wasn't as heady as it had been the night before, but anticipation still coiled inside Neil. He wanted Scott's mouth and body against his again.

This time, they didn't kiss in the hall. They waited until they were inside the room before Scott was tugging their mouths together. Neil eagerly responded and pressed Scott back against the door. They deepened the kiss as Neil slid a thigh between Scott's legs. Scott slipped his hands into Neil's hair, tugging softly on the strands and making him moan. The kiss ended too soon, but they lingered close, catching their breath.

"If only we'd met somewhere else," Scott murmured. "I've liked this."

Neil swallowed, feeling uncomfortable. Normally, if a fling made allusions to a relationship, he was out of the door or telling them in no uncertain turns that it *wasn't* on the table.

But Scott was nice.

While his confession didn't miraculously make Neil want to have a boyfriend, he felt flattered. An attractive firefighter wanted him for more than just sex. It was a nice ego boost and, frankly, he *liked* Scott. He didn't want to shoot the guy down and ruin his weekend.

It won't matter in the long run. How much could it hurt to play along?

"Yeah," Neil answered. "It's been good."

Scott looked like he was going to say more, but Neil silenced him with another kiss. He would entertain a fantasy relationship to be nice, but he didn't want it going any further. He didn't want to know where Scott lived or have the fireman offer to date him. Right now, Scott was sexy and fun. Anything else was opening a box better left sealed.

No attachments. No strings. The Neil Farris way.

When the kiss broke this time, Neil trailed his mouth over Scott's jaw before reaching his neck. He sucked gently on the skin, making the man shiver.

He moved his lips to Scott's ear, tugging at the lobe before continuing from earlier, "But, this will be good, too."

Scott slid his hands over Neil's hips and up to his sides. They moved to his chest, and he gently thumbed Neil's nipples through his shirt. Neil leaned into each teasing stroke.

"You going to top this time?" he asked.

Neil chuckled and shook his head. "I'm not the one with intense training tomorrow. You can top."

Grinning, Scott kissed Neil before whispering against his lips. "Thanks for the consideration."

"You better make it worth my while," Neil responded.

Scott's smile spread wider. His were eyes alight with humor.

"Yes, sir."

A thrill raced down his spine at the words. He'd always enjoyed games in the bedroom and some light orders, followed by Scott's obedience, would be divine. But those kinds of things required discussions. He wasn't patient enough for another conversation.

Moving away from Scott, he headed to the table by the bed where the condoms and lube from last night were resting. He grabbed them, but when he turned, Scott was behind him. He took the items in one hand while he cupped Neil's neck with the other and drew him into another kiss.

Neil hummed. He then dragged his hands through Scott's hair and down his back before scratching his nails against Scott's skin. Scott moaned when their lips separated, and Neil used the opportunity to suck on Scott's neck. This time, he planned to leave a mark. If Scott's colleagues already knew what they were up to, then why not give them even more to talk about?

"Damn," Scott breathed. He was running his hand through Neil's hair while keeping him in place.

Neil happily used his mouth and lips to keep Scott occupied while he slid his hands around to Scott's stomach. He caressed the muscles before locating the button of Scott's pants. Scott's cock was hard and straining against the material. Neil smirked and pulled down the zip before sliding his hand inside to cup the warm, hard flesh.

Scott shuddered and tried to jerk his hips forward but gained little friction. Neil continued stroking Scott's erection, making his lover roll his hips with more constrained effort.

"*Neil,*" Scott groaned, his voice thick with frustration and arousal.

Neil's cock throbbed, desperate for the man's touch. He pulled away from Scott, feeling satisfied that the hickeys would remain for a few days. He gave Scott's cock one last squeeze before removing his hand. Neil enjoyed seeing the high-flush in Scott's cheeks and the desire in his eyes.

"You going to make me do all the work, Scott?" Neil teased. "Thought you wanted to top?"

Scott huffed a laugh, amusement overriding any exasperation. He tugged Neil forward by the shirt until they were inches apart. Scott let go of the material quickly in order to undo Neil's belt. It sent a fresh bolt of desire through Neil. He'd already seen hints of how useful Scott's fingers could be.

This time, I want them inside me.

Desperation was flooding Neil, and he didn't want to waste any more time. He started unbuttoning his business shirt, but Scott stopped him by capturing Neil's hands in his own.

"Let me."

He tugged Neil toward the bed, not stopping until Neil was lying on his back on the mattress. Scott kneeled above him before bending down to kiss Neil, slowly and sweetly. Neil heard the condom and lube land on the bed, but it was a secondary focus to Scott's hands. He undid the buttons of Neil's shirt, and the feel of Scott's fingers brushing over him was a delicious caress that Neil arched into. Yet, it was too light to be satisfying. Neil grabbed Scott's pants and boxers, pushing them down until they were around his thighs and his cock was free. Scott allowed it, but he pulled back with raised eyebrows.

"Feeling impatient?" he questioned.

Neil didn't answer out loud. Instead, he wrapped his hand around Scott's cock. Neil pushed up from the bed, their lips almost brushing.

"I've been patient all day," he murmured. "Now" — he squeezed just behind the head — "I want my reward."

Scott gave a low moan, his eyelids falling closed. Neil gave him two more strokes before letting him go, having made his point. Scott pulled away just long enough to strip off the last of his clothes. Neil did the same but didn't bother to look where their clothes went. All he cared about was Scott pressing a kiss to his shoulder and guiding him to lie on his side. When Scott's hand came around Neil's waist to grasp his erection, he moaned. Scott had coated his hand with lube and each stroke felt like heaven. Neil thrust into the touch as Scott pressed in behind him, his cock brushing Neil's ass in a teasing whisper. He pressed back against it, wanting it harder. It made Scott's strokes falter.

Neil tipped his head back, resting it against Scott's shoulder. His breath came in low pants. Scott's other hand slipped between their bodies, brushing teasingly between the cheeks of Neil's ass. Neil threw a leg over Scott's thigh, trying to encourage the man to breach him. Scott laughed softly.

"It's not the best position, Neil." His fingers continued to trace his cheeks. "You want to be on your back or front?"

Neil didn't need long to decide. He wanted the man pounding into him from above, Scott holding his hips with strong hands and rocking Neil into the bed. His arousal throbbed. Neil didn't bother with explaining. He pushed out of Scott's hold in order to get onto his hands and knees, making his preference obvious.

Scott shifted on the bed, moving into place behind him. He stroked a hand over Neil's ass and Neil clenched the sheets. When Scott first touched him with a slick finger, Neil let out a sigh and relaxed his muscles. Scott slipped it in, and Neil closed his eyes. Scott's fingers weren't as long as his, but they were thicker and just as dexterous as he'd hoped. Scott pressed inside and started thrusting gently.

Neil hummed and rocked his hips. "Another."

Scott complied and slipped a second finger inside. Neil braced one arm on the bed so he could reach down and palm his cock with the other. He clenched around the fingers inside him.

"Scott," he groaned, pressing back against the digits.

Scott kept thrusting, stretching and searching. Soon, he found Neil's prostate. The first touch sent a bolt of pleasure through him, and Neil moaned loudly. He slumped farther against the bed and had to let go of his cock, not wanting to come too early.

"Scott," he demanded, "enough."

"You can be very bossy," Scott commented, sounding entertained.

He pulled his fingers out, so Neil let the comment go. The condom ripping open followed and Neil rested more of his chest on the bed while arching and spreading his legs a little wider. He was open and ready for Scott to take. Neil pressed his face against the sheets, the fabric cool against his flushed cheek. When he felt the blunt head of Scott's cock at his ass, he bit his lip. The stretch was as perfect—as it had been the previous night—and he couldn't stop from gasping. Scott was tightly gripping his hips, and Neil wanted to push back and take more. It felt so damn good. It was everything he'd spent the day longing for.

Neil panted as Scott slowly pushed inside him. He clenched the bedding, ignoring his aching cock to focus on the feeling of being filled. When Scott slipped inside completely, Neil was trembling. It only got better when Scott slid out and thrust back into him. Neil moaned and rocked back against Scott, meeting each thrust but already yearning for the next.

Scott shifted his hands on Neil's hips, pulling Neil onto his cock at the same time as he drove inside. He had the angle just right and Neil cried out at the first firm strike to his prostate. Once Scott knew the spot and the angle, he was relentless. He gave hard thrusts that shook the bed and left Neil at his mercy. Neil could only gasp into the bedding and writhe beneath Scott's onslaught. His cock was hard and brushing his stomach. It leaked with arousal.

"Scott," he whimpered.

Neil moved a hand under his body, grabbing his cock and pumping it. His body rocked with each thrust and his spine arched with every bolt of pleasure. He felt overwhelmed with sensation. Scott's weight, the heat of him against his body along with the sounds of his pleasured pants all drove him closer to the edge.

"Come on," Scott whispered. "Come on, Neil."

Neil's strokes increased. His hand seemed a blur on his cock. When Scott nailed his prostate again, it was all he needed. His orgasm whipped through him, and Neil cried out. Scott kept thrusting, spilling inside the condom moments later.

Neil felt boneless. Scott's hold on his hips was all that kept him from sliding down onto the bed. When Scott pulled out, Neil only rolled to the side enough to avoid the wet patch. Scott dropped down beside him and, somehow, Neil ended up with his head half on Scott's shoulder and his arm against the man's chest as he caught his breath.

They lay there for at least a minute before Scott moved. He shifted away and Neil squinted open his eyes. Scott looked apologetic. He'd pulled the condom off and had it in his hand.

"Need to get rid of this."

He climbed off the bed and headed for the bathroom. Neil stared after him, admiring the naked lines of his back and ass. It was a damn pity he had to give Scott up so soon. It was the best sex to happen to him in a long time.

Coming to a decision, Neil left the bed and headed for the bathroom. Scott was just coming out and they almost bumped into each other.

"Sorry," Scott said.

He had a wet washcloth in his hand, which drew Neil's attention.

Did he plan to clean me up?

It was one more sweet consideration, and it further cemented Neil's decision. It was his last night in the hotel. Tomorrow, he would go back home sans one sexy fireman.

"Do you want to use my shower?" Neil asked. He placed a hand on Scott's chest and stepped closer. "Do you want to share?"

Scott's eyes widened. "Um."

"The other firefighters already know what you're up to. Why not stay a few hours?" Neil shifted even closer and offered a flirtatious smirk. "Why not stay for round two?"

Scott looked tempted. "I have an early morning tomorrow."

"So do I," Neil replied. "But there's still plenty of the evening left."

He stroked Scott's chest, circling a nipple before rubbing it with his thumb until it hardened. It was still too soon for either of them to get truly aroused, but if they gave it enough time, that could change.

Scott caught his wrist. "That's an unfair tactic."

"Is it working?"

Scott stroked a thumb over Neil's tattoo before tugging him forward.

"Yes," he whispered, just before their lips met in a kiss.

Neil closed his eyes. It was a languid brush of mouths that Neil saw no reason to deepen. Neil had kissed a lot of men, but Scott was the first to make him want to take his time and explore what made Scott moan.

When they pulled apart, Neil smiled and pushed Scott toward the shower. His lover gave him no more complaints.

It was a tight squeeze when they got inside, and they couldn't fit under the spray together. What should have been annoying somehow wasn't. Neil liked Scott grabbing his hips to balance them or chuckling against his ear and complaining about not getting enough water.

There was rarely a moment where they weren't touching. Neil especially enjoyed running his soapy hands over Scott's muscled back then having Scott return the favor. They even kissed under the spray, exploring each other.

Neil knew he would never see Scott again after that night. He never *wanted* to see Scott after their fling. But, despite knowing better, Neil still found a part of him disappointed that he couldn't have a few more nights of sex before they went their separate ways. It was rare for him to desire someone more than once—so of course it happened with a man he'd met far away from home.

Chapter Three

They climbed out of the shower after long minutes of kisses, flirtatious murmurs and trailing touches. Scott grabbed the towels before Neil could. He didn't give one to him—instead, he surprised Neil by throwing one over Neil's head. He then used the other to *dry* him. The material was soft and firm as it rubbed over his body. He tugged the towel off his head to stare. Scott was naked, dripping wet and *had* to be colder than him.

So, why is he drying me?

The question was on his tongue, but Scott grinned at him. He also took the same towel and ruffled it over Neil's still-dripping hair. It startled him and made Neil bat at the towel and Scott's hands. His lover laughed but removed the towel. Scott then brought it to his body and started drying his skin. He didn't stop grinning. Neil watched him, feeling puzzled.

Is this some kind of foreplay? It feels…fun.

"You never said what you manage," Scott remarked.

Neil's gaze had drifted, watching the towel swipe over Scott's legs but focusing more on his soft cock. He already wanted to coax it back to life. He cleared his throat and paid attention to the conversation. Neil hoped their talking wouldn't last for long.

"Clothing. Men's clothing."

Scott grinned. "That makes sense. You seem fashionable."

It pleased Neil that Scott had noticed his attention to his wardrobe. He was *also* happy when Scott finished with his towel and moved to hang it up. Neil threw his mostly unused one in the sink. He also closed the distance to slot his naked body against Scott's back. His lover stilled and pulled in a breath. Neil pressed his lips to Scott's shoulder and lightly rocked his hips, letting his cock slide against Scott's ass in a tease of skin.

"I'm very fashionable," Neil murmured. "But I like us better *out* of clothes."

"We just got clean," Scott replied, but he was already rocking back against Neil.

Neil slipped his hands around Scott's chest, tracing his defined muscles and circling his nipples. He nipped lightly at the junction between Scott's neck and shoulder.

"We did. But I think we also spoke about 'round two'?"

"And here I was, trying to get to know you a bit better," Scott said, his voice already turning rough with desire.

Neil thought Scott's attempts were...sweet. Misguided, maybe, but still nice. Getting dried by a towel had been odd — but made him feel warm. Having Scott clean him and invite him to dinner with the other firefighters? It was all really...sweet.

Neil wasn't a relationship person. He sure as *hell* would have run for the hills if this was happening back home. But he was in Brisbane and having a fling. He could be a little reckless.

"I like the color blue," Neil said, trailing kisses over Scott's shoulder. "I've never liked fruity cocktails." His thumb found Scott's nipple and he lightly ran his nail over it. "I think you're *very* attractive, and I'd like you to fuck me again."

Scott groaned, and when he shifted, Neil loosened his hold. They became chest to chest and Scott cupped his cheeks and kissed him. Neil kissed back greedily, already eager for more time on the bed with Scott.

Unfortunately, the man broke away and looked down at him. He seemed almost wistful.

"I really do wish we'd met somewhere else," Scott said.

He rubbed his thumb over Neil's cheek and Neil felt a strange sensation in his chest, along with a clenching of his stomach. The weirdest part of it all was the way he *didn't* want to pull away. He wanted to roll his eyes and kiss Scott until he stopped being so *sappy*—but even that was unusual for him.

He decided not to think about it. He also decided, like before, to tell Scott what he wanted to hear. There was no point in wrecking a chance for future sex by telling Scott that temporary, anonymous club or hotel lobby pickups were his preference.

"Yeah," he said, hoping he sounded genuine. "If only we had."

He must have managed it, as Scott smiled softly. He also bent down and kissed Neil again. It was a little less heated, and Neil felt that awkward clench in his gut again. He shuddered for a reason that had nothing to do with desire or the cold.

It was why he quickly tilted his head and slipped his hands into Scott's damp hair. He pressed his tongue to Scott's lips and was relieved when his lover responded.

He was much better with sex, and Neil was more than eager to turn their attention back to *that*.

Thankfully, Scott complied, and he was able to drag the man to his bed. The second round was *just* as good as the first. Scott took Neil from behind, thrusting into him slowly and making it last. They both moaned their pleasure loudly, and once their orgasms were wrung from them, they collapsed on the mattress once more.

Scott rolled off him and lay at his side as they caught their breath. When Scott removed the condom and climbed off the bed, neither of them spoke. Scott didn't mention 'could have been's' and Neil didn't mention staying the night.

Neil followed him into the bathroom, and they cleaned themselves in silence. Scott then changed back into his clothes while Neil pulled on his boxers. They both knew it was officially over. Despite that, Scott lingered by the hotel room door.

"I had fun, Neil."

"Me, too."

They fell quiet again before Scott made a frustrated sound and ducked in to kiss him. Neil closed his eyes and kissed back. The intensity seared his skin and left Neil gasping when they broke apart.

Scott looked at him with indecision, and for a moment, Neil thought Scott was going to ask him for something.

Another round? My full name? My phone number?

Neil's heart thumped, feeling an emotion he didn't know how to name, but settled on fear.

But all Scott said was a quiet, "Travel safely."

Neil's gut twisted again. He refused to believe it was anything but relief over avoiding a clingy fling.

"Thanks," he said. "Have fun at your training."

Scott nodded. He then pressed a final, lingering kiss on Neil's lips. When he leaned back, he still looked disappointed, and Neil felt a matching twinge.

What about round three?

But before he could suggest it, Scott turned and left. Neil didn't stop him.

Instead, he shook off his unusual dissatisfaction and walked over to his bed. He kicked the ruined sheet away and got comfortable on the side that didn't have a wet patch.

There goes my sexy fireman. Time to file him away as an A-class one-night stand.

Yet, even as Neil thought about it, he knew Scott wouldn't be forgotten so easily. He was a damn good lay, but he'd also been nice. When Neil closed his eyes, he saw the man behind his eyes — the way he'd smiled and the warmth he'd felt as Scott had dried him from the shower.

Neil trailed his fingers over his chest as he thought about the man he'd met by accident. Neil already had a feeling that Scott would be the memory that all future one-night stands would be weighed against.

He couldn't say it wasn't well deserved.

* * * *

The next morning, Neil had checked out while trying not to search for Scott. There had been a few firemen around but no sign of his lover. He'd actually slowed his steps as he'd walked out of the lobby, but there had been no calls of his name. He'd shaken his head as he'd climbed in his car, not sure what had come over him. Good chemistry had never been enough to make him hesitate before, and he wouldn't let it be the same now.

A relationship, even a 'friends with benefits' one, was not something Neil desired. It was better to find a constant, rotating source of sexual release back home.

Despite resolving to push the memories of Scott aside, Neil still regaled his assistant manager with the weekend's events on their next shift. Denise had been envious, like he'd expected. But it had also disappointed her that he hadn't gained Scott's number. She'd wanted him to look Scott up on social media, but he'd ignored her suggestions. He hadn't learned the man's surname or where he lived for a reason. When all her attempts to convince him to track Scott down had failed, the subject had been dropped and their standard routine of flirting with customers had returned.

In the blink of an eye, nearly a week had passed and while Neil hadn't been able to forget Scott like he'd planned, he'd stopped using him as fantasy fodder. Neil knew he needed to wipe the slate clean and have sex with someone else. He was just waiting for his next day off.

Unfortunately, a quiet day in the shop was not helping to distract his preoccupied mind. He wanted to be thinking about what bar he'd visit, but instead, thoughts of hook-ups kept leading him back to Scott. It wasn't even the sex that his mind was fixating on. Instead, it was what had happened before and after. He hadn't mentioned Scott's behavior to Denise, but the man's careful touches and that damned towel drying were like a splinter on his mind, keeping Scott at the forefront.

Why can't I get my mind off this guy? The sex was good, but, Christ, it's like every stray thought leads back to him.

Neil was redressing a mannequin to get his mind off the fireman. Denise should have been on the other side of the shop folding shirts, but she suddenly brushed past him.

"Hot guy alert," she murmured. "I call first dibs."

Neil grinned. He loved working with Denise. She was always a source of entertainment, especially when they were trying to beat each other to the more attractive customers. Neil looked over his shoulder, wanting to size up the newest man to catch her attention. He froze upon spotting familiar blue eyes and styled dark hair.

Scott.

He hadn't spotted Neil yet and Neil felt the sudden, unfamiliar urge to flee. But he didn't react fast enough...then it was too late.

"Hi. How can I help you today?" Denise inquired.

Scott turned, a polite smile on his face, but it fell when he looked past her and saw him. Scott's eyes widened.

"Neil?"

Neil swallowed around a dry mouth.

What the hell do you say to your two-night stand who walks into the clothing store that you manage?

Normally, he had no problem ignoring or dismissing the men he'd bedded when they met outside an apartment or hotel. But he'd already been feeling off-kilter about Scott. Having the man appear when he wasn't expected had Neil feeling like a fish out of water.

"Scott. Er...hi."

The shop suddenly felt awkward. Denise didn't make it any better.

"Wait. This is hot-fireman Scott?" she asked.

Neil nodded while Scott gave an uncertain smile. Denise laughed. She then walked over to Neil and took the clothing from his hands.

"Now you *have* to ask for his number," she insisted.

"I'm not asking for his number," he whispered.

"Yes, you are," she insisted. "Never in three years has 'Mr. Suave' stumbled over his words. This guy has to be worth dinner, even if it's just for another chance at getting him naked."

She walked behind him. When he didn't move, she elbowed him in the back, and it jolted him forward. Neil glared over his shoulder, but she was ignoring him to work on the mannequin. Feeling frustrated and cornered, he walked over to the fireman. He stopped a polite distance away, not sure what to say.

"I didn't realize you lived here," Scott said. He gave a jerky shrug. "Small world, huh?"

"Yes," Neil agreed.

He struggled for another response. It had been so much easier at the hotel. There had been a single, simple goal, and all he'd needed to do was flirt.

"So," he finally asked, "how was the training course?"

"Fine," Scott answered. "Good."

They descended into another uncomfortable silence. Neil just wanted to cut his losses and walk away. Their good chemistry had clearly been limited to that hotel in Brisbane. He was seconds from palming him back off to Denise when Scott surprised him be letting out a frustrated breath.

"Okay. This was unexpected, but it doesn't have to be weird." Scott smiled. "We said, *'if only we'd met somewhere else'*, right? Well, now, we have. Do you want to get a coffee?"

Neil's lips parted with shock.

I did not say...oh. Oh, fuck. I did say that.

He'd been humoring Scott, and now it was biting him in the ass. Neil's knee-jerk reaction was to give Scott a flat no and explain that he didn't do relationships, but unexpectedly, he hesitated.

I haven't been able to get him off my mind. Maybe this will finally get him out of my system? We'll meet up, have a date or two. I'll get to have a few rounds of sex and he'll soon realize that we're not compatible and stop calling me.

It was win-win, and Neil relaxed for the first time since Scott had appeared.

"All right," Neil agreed. "When do you want to have coffee?"

"I'm free the day after tomorrow?"

"I'm working," Neil admitted.

"Why don't you take an extra-long lunch break?" Denise piped up, obviously eavesdropping. "I'd be happy to cover for you, Neil."

He looked over his shoulder to find her with a wide grin. She winked, unconcerned with his glare. When he turned back to Scott, the man just looked amused. It was that same natural, easy-going nature that Neil had enjoyed at the hotel. While he would have preferred an opportunity that could lead to sex, he wasn't about to take back his agreement.

"Well," Neil said, "apparently, I can do coffee."

"Sounds great," Scott agreed. "When do you take your break?"

"One o'clock."

"Then, I'll meet you here."

"Okay," he said, feeling bemused, "it's a date."

My first one in years.

"Great," Scott said. "Although," he said, laughing, "now I probably need *two* dress shirts."

Neil immediately felt back on even footing.

Flirting and selling clothes. Now we're in my area of expertise.

"I do like a man who dresses up."

He looked Scott up and down. He was in jeans and a loose black shirt. Scott looked good, but Neil could always improve it.

"Why do you need a dress shirt, other than to impress me?" he asked.

"Engagement party for one of the guys. We're on strict orders to 'dress nice'."

"Well, I can help you with that," Neil replied. He gestured for Scott to follow him farther into the shop where folded shirts were on display. "What color would you like and do you need anything to go with it?"

"Any color," Scott answered. "And I've got pants at home."

Neil shot him an unimpressed look. "Define pants."

Scott laughed. "Dark blue jeans."

"Hmm," Neil hummed before picking up three shirts. Black, deep purple and a white one with small gray sparrows printed on it. "We'll start with these."

"You're very demanding," Scott remarked, but he followed Neil to the dressing rooms without complaint. "Haven't had our first date and you're already ordering me around."

Neil stopped in front of the first door and raised his eyebrows at the fireman.

"I've been ordering you from the start — or have you already forgotten?"

"No, I remember," Scott said, chuckling softly.

He stepped closer and started taking the shirts, their hands brushing as he did.

He held Neil's gaze and added, "I liked it."

Neil abruptly remembered Scott murmuring, "*Yes, sir*," at the hotel. His mind flooded with images of Scott lying naked on the bed and following his demands.

I wonder if he'd let me tie him to the bed?

Neil's desire was spiking, and he cleared his throat and pushed open the door to the change rooms.

"Go put one on."

Scott smirked, and as if reading Neil's mind, he replied, "Yes, sir."

Neil's fingers twitched with the urge to drag Scott into a kiss. He resisted, and Scott stepped into the change room and shut the door. The moment he was out of sight, Neil ran a hand over his face. Scott was stripping out of his shirt less than a meter away. All Neil wanted was to yank open the door, step inside and be the one undressing him.

But this wasn't a one-night stand. He was at work, for Christ's sake.

"So, how long have you worked here?" Scott asked.

It successfully pulled Neil from his thoughts.

"A bit over three years."

"And do you enjoy telling men what to wear?"

"When they cooperate and listen to my advice."

Scott laughed, and a moment later he was pushing open the change-room door. He was in the white shirt. It fitted him well, and Neil dragged his eyes over the man's front. Scott was still doing up the last button, but when he finished, he spread his arms and turned, giving Neil a complete view. Neil itched to smooth down the creases in the shirt.

"It looks good," Neil said. "How does it fit? Not too tight?"

"It's comfortable." Scott moved his arms, checking his flexibility. "I like it."

"Good," Neil answered. He nodded back at the room. "Try on the next one."

Scott grinned and re-entered the changing room. Neil fought down his own smile. It was rare to meet a man who let him take control, especially after having topped him. A lot of men saw it as an insult to their masculinity, but Scott seemed a lot more self-confident and secure. Granted, Neil's experience with men post-sex was a small pool to draw from.

Most of them thought Neil had more personality flaws than attractive qualities. He'd always been forthright and goal-oriented. While he was happy to take the back seat if he was in unfamiliar territory, when he knew what he wanted, Neil wasn't shy about taking it. Scott's acceptance of that was more attractive than he'd expected.

When Scott opened the door, he was in the black shirt. Neil shook his head instantly. "No."

"Why?" Scott asked, looking down at his clothes.

"You look like you're going to work. *No*."

"You and I have different ideas of what a uniform looks like," Scott said, sounding amused.

He still dutifully closed the changing-room door. Neil frowned, feeling perplexed by the continued lack of anything, even half-hearted complaints. He was never so forthright with his customers, but Scott had asked him out. It meant he got Neil as he was — no holds barred.

I doubt it's a good way to get back into his bed.

"If you like it, I'm sure we can accessorize to make it less corporate."

He turned, planning to look for a jacket.

"Nah," Scott said, making him pause. "Don't worry. If you say it doesn't look good, I'll take your word on it."

"Really?" Neil asked, looking back at the closed door. "You're very trusting of my opinion."

"You've always looked good, and you work in clothing," Scott answered. "So, you must know what you're talking about."

Neil felt flattered. "Thanks."

Scott stepped out of the changing room in the purple shirt. He looked much better. In fact, he looked *gorgeous*. The cut of the shirt accentuated his defined muscles without clinging. It would have been perfect if Scott's collar weren't folded incorrectly. Neil moved without thinking and brought his hands to the material, uncurling and smoothing it out.

He could feel the warmth from Scott's skin, and when he caught the man's gaze, his hands stilled. They were almost chest to chest and his fingers were brushing Scott's neck. He'd kissed and marked that tanned skin only a week prior. Neil would only have to lean in a few inches to kiss Scott. The temptation was fierce, and the look in Scott's eyes said the action wouldn't be unwelcome.

The sound of a male voice made Neil look away as they pulled apart. A new customer had entered the shop. Denise was assisting him, but the man could walk toward the changing rooms at any moment and see them. Regretfully, Neil let go of Scott's collar.

"I like this shirt, too," Scott said, his voice sounded lower than normal. Neil caught the man's gaze. "I'll get both."

"Okay," Neil agreed. "Do you need anything else?"

Scott ran his gaze over Neil, a smile curving his lips.

"Not until the day after tomorrow, but I'll come pick that up."

Neil laughed and the tension of the moment was broken.

"That was terrible."

"But it made you smile," Scott insisted. "So, it was worth it."

Neil shook his head and pointed at the changing room.

"Go get dressed."

Scott looked ready to say something, but the other customer approached them with shirts in his arms. Scott slipped back inside, and Neil walked back out into the store. Denise met his gaze and grinned.

"Well?" she asked, walking over to him. "As charming as you remember?"

"Yes," Neil admitted. "I don't appreciate your interfering but...I will need that extra-long lunch break."

Denise let out an excited noise and raised her hand for Neil to high-five. He rolled his eyes and refused to respond.

"It's a date, Denise — one that won't even end in sex. I'm already running at a loss."

"Ugh," Denise grumbled. "You have a date with a sexy fireman and you're *complaining*?"

"I don't do well on dates."

"He already likes your attitude," Denise dismissed. "You'll be fine."

Scott appeared carrying three shirts before Neil could disagree, which was probably for the best. He'd never gone into the specifics of why he avoided relationships. It would take too long to explain, and Denise probably still wouldn't understand. It was better for everyone if he just played along until Scott realized the mistake he was making.

Meeting Scott, he took the clothing and walked over to the counter. He put the black shirt to the side before ringing up the other two.

"Where do you want to have lunch?" Scott asked.

Neil paused mid-fold, running through the options. He worked in a shopping center and there were several choices, but he wanted somewhere they could have some kind of peace. Screaming children were predominate in the food court.

"Just down from the store is a café called Toasted Beans. We can go there?"

"Sounds great," Scott agreed, barely glancing at the price of the shirts before tapping his card to the machine. "I'll meet you here."

"Yeah," Neil agreed, ripping off the man's receipt.

He paused over the bag.

Oh, what the hell.

He grabbed a pen and wrote his number on the paper before putting it in the bag with the folded shirts. Scott raised his eyebrows.

"In case you need to cancel," Neil explained.

"I won't," Scott insisted. "Not unless there's a fire."

"Hopefully there won't be," Neil said before handing him the bag.

Scott allowed their hands to brush as he took it.

"I'm really glad we met again, Neil," Scott told him.

"Yeah," Neil said. "Me, too."

Scott gave him another smile before he turned and left the store. Neil watched him go, letting his gaze linger on the man's ass. Scott was hot, but that didn't account for what had just happened.

Why did I do any of that?

Neil couldn't answer that question. Yes, Scott had burrowed under his skin and distracted him for days, but to agree to a date where there was no possibility of sex? It was out of character for Neil in every way.

Since when do I entertain anything but a fling?

Neil felt uncomfortable, and it soured his mood and left him snappish and short with Denise and his customers. He tried to get his attitude under control, but the discomfort remained. When he finally had his break an hour later, he was tapping his foot impatiently as he waited for the microwave to heat his food.

He checked his phone and found a new text from an unknown number. His stomach twisted, and his immediate expectation was a cancellation.

No fires yet, but now you have my number.

Neil almost smiled.

Are you expecting me to use it?

You're using it now. And I'll be happy with anything you'd like to talk to me about, Neil.

Neil snorted.

Sap.

He didn't realize he'd stopped feeling uncomfortable, not until he was sitting down with his meal and waiting for Scott's next response. The moment he did, Neil's grin faded, and he looked at their chat with a fresh churning in his stomach.

Shit. Don't tell me I actually care what this guy thinks of me?

Unfortunately, no answer contradicted the sinking feeling in his stomach. It left Neil with the horrible suspicion that he was looking forward to seeing Scott, and it wasn't because of eventual sex.

* * * *

They messaged throughout the next two days. Neil had been wary to encourage their conversations, but Scott was funny and never minded if Neil's retorts were on the harsher side. He learned that the man was a local, his surname was Fields and that Scott had a sense of humor that often surprised him.

Neil found his anticipation growing the closer it came to their date, which only left him more conflicted. It was never more obvious than as he waited in Hardgroves for one o'clock to arrive.

"Eager to see your fireman?" Denise asked, grinning smugly at him.

"I'd be more eager if I had a higher chance of getting him naked," Neil countered.

"Nice try," Denise said, not looking fazed. "But if you didn't care, you wouldn't have fixed your shirt three times in the last hour."

Neil's hand froze on his collar. He lowered it, feeling annoyed with his behavior.

"It's just a means to an end," Neil said. "You know I don't do relationships."

"Uh-huh," Denise remarked. "Well, even if it is all about the 'end goal', it doesn't mean you can't enjoy your date."

"There isn't much to enjoy."

"So, that's why you've been glancing at your phone every few minutes for the last two days?"

Neil glared. "I haven't."

Denise continued to look amused. She even grabbed her phone from her pocket, fluttering her eyelashes.

"Oh! Another text." She gave a mock scowl. "I must pretend to be uninterested in my sexy fireman's fun personality. I must remain 'Mr. Suave'."

"I will remind you that I am the *manager*," Neil grumbled. "I am in charge of your quarterly review."

Denise slipped her phone away but was back to grinning.

"Aw, don't take out your frustration on me." She waggled her eyebrows. "Wait to take it out on him in a few nights' time."

Neil scoffed. "You spend the conversation trying to convince me to focus on the date. Now, it's all about the sex?"

"I work in customer service. I know when to tell someone what they want to hear."

"Why do I even like you?" Neil muttered.

"Because I can be just as much of an asshole as you are," Denise said cheerfully.

She also walked up to him and fixed his collar. Neil felt relieved. He'd wanted to straighten it but hadn't wanted to look overeager.

"It's okay to be excited about the date, you know," she said quietly. "You won't lose any points or respect from me."

Neil grimaced and looked away.

"It's not about that," he muttered.

Her hands paused. "Then what is it?"

I've never wanted a relationship. I should feel annoyance and boredom, but I'm not. It isn't right, and I don't know what to do with it.

Although Neil would rather walk over glass than admit the tremulous state of his emotions, he did feel a need for advice.

"He wants to date me," Neil said, "but I don't date."

"So, why did you say yes?"

"The prospect of sex," Neil answered, but it sounded unsure.

"If that's all it was," Denise pointed out, "you wouldn't care about anything but getting him into bed."

"That *is* all I care about."

Denise rolled her eyes and lowered her hands.

"Deny it all you want, Neil, but if you *do* find him interesting, don't blow it. Experiment a little. Give dating a chance. Worse thing that will happen is you end up back where you were. We both know a shortage of willing men has never been your problem."

"So why am I doing this, then?"

"Because maybe it's time to stop looking for a refill and focus on the glass in front of you!"

Neil frowned. "What does that even mean?"

"It *means*," Denise said, sound exasperated, "that you have a sexy fireman who wants to date you. Don't start planning for the next guy. Plan for date number two with him instead."

Neil turned away from her. He felt like it had placed a spotlight on his poor relationship history. His constant stream of men had never bothered him, but her earnest words had all kinds of thoughts pin-balling through his mind.

What do I even want from Scott?

The sex was his obvious goal, but the towel drying crossed his mind just as quickly. Closing his eyes, Neil pinched the bridge of his nose. He needed to get his thoughts under control.

"I'm going to order the racks," he finally said.

He lowered his hand and stepped away from Denise. She let him go without comment, and he was grateful for the chance for some peace. Denise even talked to any customers that came in, giving him time alone. Neil spent the next few minutes ordering the shirts via size. He did glance at the entrance every few moments, and it meant he was the first to notice Scott arrive.

The man was in a casual gray shirt and jeans. He lifted his hand in a wave, and Neil felt a sharp, excited thrill. Neil left the clothes. He brushed past Denise with a murmured goodbye before leaving the shop to meet the fireman.

"Hey," Scott greeted.

"Hi," Neil said. His gaze traveled over Scott. "You look good."

"I thought I should put in a bit more effort. Can't upset my date's sense of style."

Neil grinned. "If you upset it, I'd just make sure to take over and improve it."

"I do like it when you order me around," Scott replied.

Neil intensely wished they were at a bar. He had a dozen responses he could give that would lead to the bedroom and getting Scott naked underneath him.

But this was a *date*. He had to play by different rules — the kind he'd always failed at conforming to.

"Well," Neil said, struggling to keep his response only mildly flirtatious, "I'll keep that in mind."

Scott chuckled and they began walking in the café's direction. Toasted Beans was tucked into a small corner of the shopping complex and could almost be missed if you didn't know it was there. The center wasn't overly busy, but Scott still moved nearer to him until their arms were brushing.

"How has your day been?" he asked.

"Fine," Neil replied, the hairs on his arm standing on end at the contact. "Retail is retail. What about you? It's your day off?"

"Yeah," Scott said. "I get a few off a week."

"Does that mean you're not on call?"

"They can call me in if it's an extreme situation, but we're not meant to work when our shifts have finished. We have on-call firefighters for back-up."

"That makes sense."

He was curious to know more, but Neil doubted 'extreme fires' would be a lighthearted topic, so he changed the subject.

"How long have you been a fireman?"

"A long time," Scott replied. "I volunteered when I was old enough and did that for a few years. I was lucky enough to get a full-time job when one became available."

The enthusiasm practically radiated off Scott. His smile was contagious, and Neil found a small grin curling his lips.

"You clearly love it."

"I do," Scott agreed. "I enjoy helping people and keeping the community safe. It's a tough job, but it's worth it."

It highlighted a stark difference between them, which amused Neil. He'd never had such passion for a job, and his involvement with the community was nonexistent. Occasionally, he dropped his spare change into donation boxes. That was it.

"You must have loved your training course."

"I did," Scott answered. "I caught up with people I hadn't seen in years and met new recruits. Did you enjoy yours?"

"I preferred my time at the hotel more."

Scott grinned. "Definitely hard to compete with our time at the hotel."

Scott's gaze had barely masked heat, and it made Neil want to kiss him. He wanted to drag Scott somewhere private and make the fireman moan again.

He *really* wished they hadn't decided on lunch in the middle of the day. Scott looked away first.

"Do you like working with clothes?"

I prefer taking them off.

Neil swallowed the response down. Scott either wouldn't appreciate it, or he'd flirt back and they'd end up finishing lunch with hard-ons and frustration.

"I've worked in worse places."

Scott frowned. "That's not the same."

"No, I suppose it isn't," Neil agreed.

It was hard to switch off the usual nondescript answers he gave a one-night stand, but he found a desire to offer Scott more than the bare minimum.

"I like clothing, so it's not a bad place to work. I've just never been picky about my jobs," he explained.

"Well, there's nothing wrong with that," Scott said. "Not if it works for you."

"I'll never be out of work in retail," Neil said. "And I can advance through the company if I put the effort in." He ran his gaze over Scott. "And the manager's meetings come with benefits."

Scott laughed. "Make a habit of snagging firemen, do you?"

No, just men.

Neil almost made the quip, but something made him fall silent. He couldn't pinpoint why. He'd never cared about announcing his casual relationships in the past — but admitting it to Scott seemed…uncomfortable.

"You're the first," Neil answered, settling on an easy truth.

"Glad to hear I'm not competing with anyone," Scott teased.

His smile was easy-going and flirtatious. He didn't know how close he was skirting to the truth.

Neil was grateful to reach the café and close down that topic. Scott opened the door and Neil stepped inside. He was a regular, and when he caught the eye of a server, he gestured between him and Scott and held up two fingers. She nodded and pointed at an empty table, which they headed to. The café wasn't overly large, but it had about eleven tables. Toasted Beans specialized in coffee and sandwiches, but they made a variety of other meals, as well as cakes and sweets. The back wall of the café and behind where the baristas worked had a painted mural with aliens drinking espresso and butterflies carrying bags of beans. Potted plants hung from the ceiling, and the lighting was low. It wasn't the type of place you expected in a shopping center. Its continued existence was a testament to its popularity and regulars.

After taking his seat opposite Neil, Scott looked around, admiringly.

"I love the mural," Scott said. "I can't believe I've never heard of this place before."

"It deserves more attention," Neil agreed. "I only found it when I started working around here and needed coffee."

"I'll have to let the guys know." Scott grinned. "Or maybe I shouldn't. That way I can keep it all to myself."

Scott held his gaze and Neil's foot twitched with the urge to press up against Scott's. It was an ingrained response to flirtation. Only, Neil noticed that *this* flirtation wasn't sexual in nature. It was affectionate and teasing. It also proved that he hadn't scared Scott off.

So far.

"Those are strong words after only one visit," Neil said. "Don't want to end up disappointed."

"I haven't been so far," Scott answered, continuing to watch him.

Screw it.

"Keep that up and I might not go back to work after lunch."

"I don't think your co-worker would be happy with that."

"Maybe not," Neil answered, "but I would be."

He shifted his foot, letting it lightly brush Scott's ankle. The same interest that had burned bright between them at the hotel flared to life.

"Planning to seduce me again?" Scott asked, humor in his voice.

"Is there a problem with that?"

"No, but I still want to get to know you." Scott moved his foot away regretfully. "I'd like to know if there's more than just attraction here. Wouldn't you?"

Neil hesitated. He felt like Scott had pinned him to the chair like a bug. *This* was the question he'd been struggling with the closer it had come to the date.

To try or not to try?

But…that same clench from the hotel had formed in his stomach. He'd been enjoying their banter, and his body had reacted from even the smallest touch from Scott. They had good chemistry, and their personalities clicked. Neil knew, if he asked anyone, they would say it was the perfect recipe for a relationship.

Scott was the first one-night stand to *ever* make him agree to a date.

Surely that means something? Surely it's worth a trial?

"I would," Neil finally admitted.

"Good," Scott said with a smile. "So, we get to know each other and take it slow."

"Slow?" Neil repeated, unable to hide all his disappointment and incredulity. "How slow?"

"Well, if you still want to see me after lunch, we can meet again later this week. After that, we'll see what happens."

That meant little chance of sex over the weekend. It also meant nothing but texts between now and the next date. Scott's goal wasn't to get him into bed. It was to work out if they were compatible for a long-term relationship.

Well, this attempt at a dating will probably be rejected by midway through next week. What's an extra few days without an orgasm?

He didn't have high hopes of Scott sticking around. But, as Denise had said, if he played the dating game and it went nowhere, he was no worse off.

"All right," Neil agreed. He pulled his foot back to his side of the table. "Slow it is."

Scott looked delighted, and Neil felt an unexpected fondness that took him by surprise. Neil had never been the type to get emotionally invested.

How the hell does Scott do that?

Before he could dwell on it, Scott suggested, "Why don't you tell me about yourself?"

Scott leaned forward after he'd asked, looking genuinely interested in what Neil had to say. It was mystifying. *"Experiment a little,"* Denise had said. It would certainly be unfamiliar territory to explore all the strange things he was feeling and thinking.

Hopefully, despite going slow, Scott would prove to be fun company. Otherwise, it wouldn't be Scott ending things. It would be him.

Chapter Four

Surprisingly, their date was enjoyable.

They spoke about hobbies, favorite foods and work. Neil learned that Scott considered the firefighters he worked with his closest friends. Paul, the man Neil had met in Brisbane, was a mentor to him. He had convinced Scott to join a local baseball team, and they competed in regional championships when they weren't out fighting fires. Two years ago, they had even made it to the state finals.

Neil, by comparison, didn't have many stories or relationships to talk about. He went out clubbing with people he wouldn't call friends. Some of them, he didn't even know their surnames or what they did for a living. If he wasn't at a bar, he was working five to six days a week or hanging out alone in his one-bedroom apartment.

Scott's life seemed so much fuller. He had numerous friends and was invested in a large community of people. He worked long shifts that required him to stay in the fire station or drive out to places that put him and his colleagues at risk. Despite the intense hours of his job, he seemed to always find time to go to barbecues and get-togethers.

The differences in their lives were stark to Neil but didn't seem to concern Scott. Instead, he always drew the conversations to points they aligned on. They'd grown up watching the same TV shows and movies, which gave them plenty of things to debate.

Neil didn't realize how much time had passed until Denise messaged him asking if he'd gone home with his fireman. He had been due back fifteen minutes before.

"Shit," he cursed, feeling surprised. "I'm late. I've got to get back."

"Sorry," Scott apologized, looking guilty. "I didn't notice the time."

Neither did I. When has that ever happened?

"It's fine," Neil said, still feeling startled by his reactions. "We were having a good time."

It disappointed him to be leaving.

"We'll have to do it again," Scott replied. "Maybe dinner next time?"

Dinner means a possibility of sex.

If Neil had needed any more incentive, that was enough to seal his agreement.

"How's Saturday night?" he suggested.

"Perfect."

Having nothing more to say, Neil stood, and Scott did the same. They headed to the counter together. There was no one waiting, and Neil started to pull out his wallet, but Scott already had his card out and between them.

"I asked you out," Scott said. "I should be the one paying."

Neil couldn't remember the last time someone had actually paid for him. It was one more occasion of Scott being *nice*.

"Okay," he said, lowering his wallet. "But you really don't have to."

"I insist."

After paying, they made their way out of the café, only to linger beside the door. It was a busy area of the center and people were going past constantly. Normally, Neil would use Denise's text as an excuse to beat a hasty retreat without caring about rudeness. But Scott had been great and *nice*. Neil wanted to end things properly. He just wasn't sure how.

"I had a great time, Neil," Scott said, shifting a little closer.

"Me, too," Neil replied. "I'm sorry to have to run."

"It's fine." Scott smiled. "And I'd better not keep you, but I'll message you about Saturday."

"Sounds good."

Scott grinned. He closed the remaining distance and pressed a soft kiss to Neil's cheek. He pulled back but Neil grabbed Scott's arm. The man paused, and Neil held his gaze.

"We're not that chaste, are we?"

Scott leaned in again, and this time, he brought their mouths together. Neil closed his eyes and kissed back. The embrace didn't deepen but Neil found the soft caress oddly charming. His stomach gave a now-familiar clench, but this time, it didn't leave him feeling uneasy.

When Scott drew back, Neil opened his eyes. Scott was smiling and he let the man's arm go.

"Good luck at work."

"Thanks," Neil said. "Enjoy your day off. I'll see you Saturday."

Scott nodded and Neil headed back to Hardgroves before he was tempted to kiss the fireman again. He didn't turn around as he walked. He'd see the man in a few days, and he wasn't about to look besotted or pathetic. After all, a single nice date wouldn't win him over.

Let's see if we make it to double digits.

Because Neil had his doubts that either of them would hold out... Slow wasn't something he was familiar with, and Scott was unlikely to stay interested once he learned about Neil's many failings. Orgasms could mellow Neil's personality quirks but continued conversations might not.

And yet, despite his uncertainty and wariness, Neil was still looking forward to seeing Scott on Saturday. Neil couldn't explain it, but something about the fireman made it impossible to brush him aside.

What makes Scott Fields so different from all the other men I've fucked?

* * * *

The week passed slowly, and Scott's messages became his highlight. But for all they made him smile and laugh, they also caused his disconcertion at his own feelings to grow.

One afternoon, Neil had tried to switch the conversation to a flirtatious comment about Scott's uniform. He'd wanted to get things back on a track that he was familiar and safe with—but Scott had responded with a selfie. He'd worn a dark navy shirt with the suspenders for his pants tucked over his shoulders. Scott's helmet had been on his head and he was flashing the camera a grin.

Neil had saved the picture so fast that he'd almost hurt his fingers.

The picture had been a comforting reminder of what had drawn him to Scott in the beginning — a sexy fireman. The twist to his stomach and automatic smile when Scott messaged him was a glitch in the system.

But Neil still wasn't ready to call it quits.

When Saturday finally arrived, Scott gave him a time and the name of a popular steakhouse. Neil arrived a few minutes early to find Scott already waiting outside. The fireman was wearing the purple shirt he had bought at Hardgroves, along with black jeans. It was a good contrast to Neil's blue button-down and khakis. Scott grinned and they discussed the traffic as they went inside. The interior was dark and intimate, with wooden features that gave it a more rustic look. A server quickly noticed and seated them at a table in the middle of the restaurant. He ordered a drink and Scott did the same. Neil glanced around after she'd left. Families or couples filled most of the tables, but he saw a group of women giving Scott admiring glances. The fireman was oblivious and already had ahold of his menu.

"Hungry?" Neil questioned.

"Starving," Scott admitted. He glanced up with a sheepish smile. "Do you mind ordering early?"

"Fine by me." Neil grabbed his menu and skimmed it. There were several great choices, but he decided on a T-Bone topped with mushrooms. "Ready when you are."

Scott looked toward the bar, searching for their waitress. Neil's gaze locked on the line of Scott's throat. He'd recently shaved, but Neil wanted to press his mouth against it until a red mark appeared.

Slow. Scott wants us to take it slow.

Neil tried to shake off his wandering thoughts. He needed a subject to talk about, and he alighted on Scott's shirt.

"You mentioned you were shopping for an engagement party when you came into Hardgroves. When's that being held?"

"Tomorrow afternoon," Scott answered.

"Is it for a fireman I met?"

"No." Scott shook his head. "Only Paul and I attended from our station."

Neil frowned. "But you seemed to know everyone there?"

"Yeah, we have a lot of meetups and training courses. We stay up-to-date on social media, too. A lot of the smaller stations throughout the state keep in contact."

"You must enjoy the camaraderie."

"I do," Scott agreed. "I'll have to introduce you to everyone at the station. You couldn't meet nicer people."

Neil felt a spike of dread but tried not to show it. The firefighters at the hotel had been easy to handle. He'd been Scott's one-night stand. An immaterial, passing fancy. It would be different to be introduced as something more. He wasn't even sure if he *wanted* that kind of commitment.

"Sounds like fun," he said, hoping his discomfort didn't show. He swiftly moved the conversation away from it. "How many permanent firefighters are at your station?"

"We've got five, including myself," Scott answered. "We're a good group. There are a lot of volunteers, too.

I've known some of the men and women since I first started."

"I didn't realize how close you'd all be. But it makes sense with such a high-risk job."

Neil wouldn't call any co-worker a friend. He liked Denise the most out of any past colleague, but they'd never socialized outside work. Their job was simple and transient, with people starting and leaving all the time. The dangers Scott faced made it inevitable to form strong ties. It had Neil a little uncomfortable. Scott fought bushfires and there was no guarantee he'd come out of them unscathed. He didn't want any firefighter hurt, but imagining Scott injured formed a ball of dread in his stomach.

His apprehension must have shown as Scott leaned across the table and caught his hand. He squeezed it.

"It might be high-risk, but we all want to come home. We don't take unnecessary chances, and we look out for each other."

"It's still dangerous."

"Everything can be dangerous."

"I think your work is a little more life-threatening than mine."

"I don't know," Scott said. "I hear the fashion industry is pretty cut-throat."

Neil snickered. The joke was silly, but it broke the ice. Scott let go of his hand and Neil missed the warmth. Scott's soft smile almost made up for it, but he didn't have long to admire it before their server arrived with their beers. They used the opportunity to order their meals, but when she left them, the table lapsed into silence. The restaurant was loud. Normally, that was annoying after a long week at work, but with Scott, he didn't mind.

What else can this guy make me okay with?

A part of him remained wary about playing along, but the rest was determined to plow through. People had said he was afraid of commitment, but Neil Farris wouldn't be a coward over a *date*. Their lunch had been about learning favorite things and telling stories about friends and work colleagues. There were other blanks they could cover tonight.

"You said you've worked at the station a long time. Have you always lived around here?"

"Born and bred. What about you?"

"Transferred here from Coolangatta. Grew up farther south on the New South Wales coast."

"Surfer?" Scott guessed.

Neil snorted. "Why does everyone always assume that?"

"Could be the blond hair?" Scott suggested with a grin. "The leather bracelets? The faint tan?"

"Everything you just listed is a stereotype."

"True," Scott agreed. "So, you weren't a surfer?"

Neil's lips twitched. "Well…"

"Hah! Sometimes, the stereotypes *do* hold true."

"In my defense, there was this surfer just after high school and I wanted to impress him." Neil smirked. "I turned out to be a better surfer than him. It also turned out I liked the lifeguard a lot more." Neil paused, reminiscing about those two young men. "That was a great summer."

"Sounds like it," Scott said, not a hint of jealousy in his voice, only good humor. "How old were you?"

"Nineteen," Neil answered. "Both of the guys were a few years older. They taught me a lot." He laughed ruefully. "Including how to have flings."

Neil hadn't planned for it to turn out that way. He'd fooled around with Rich for two months before his head had turned. He'd left Rich and walked straight into sex with the attractive and flirtatious lifeguard. It had been his first time. Neil had assumed he'd be wanted the next morning, but he hadn't been. It had stung, but he'd shaken it off and made it a learning experience. He'd ended up back with Rich, but they'd only lasted a few weeks before Rich had broken up with him.

Neil had met a guy at a club a month later. He'd bounced between men ever since with nothing ever lasting longer than those few months with Rich. None of them had ever made him *want* them to last. It had either been mutually casual, or they'd worked out he was an awful choice for 'permanent'.

Scott will work that out soon, too.

Shaking off his pensive thoughts, Neil asked, "What about you? How old were you when you started dating?"

"Fifteen," Scott answered. "I had a high-school boyfriend. We dated throughout school and only broke up when he moved away for university. I was almost nineteen." A fond smile touched Scott's lips. "He's a real great guy. We still keep in touch."

Neil frowned. "You didn't want to get back together?"

"Nah." Scott shook his head. "We knew at nineteen that even if he'd stayed in the area, we'd have broken up. We weren't compatible enough. Besides," Scott said, grinning, "he got married last year."

"Well, I can't say I'm complaining," Neil said with a wink. "His loss is my gain."

"I could say the same for your lifeguard," Scott replied. "He didn't know what he was losing."

Neil smiled and Scott picked up his drink. He held it out for a toast.

"Here's to not making the same mistake as them."

They held gazes as their glasses clinked. The air seemed to crackle with tension. When they lowered their glasses to take a sip, Neil felt a frisson of excitement under his skin. The same interest and desire that had drawn them together at the hotel was thick in the air. Scott's focus darted to Neil's lips and Neil licked them.

Scott asked for slow, but how long will that last?

When Scott looked away and swallowed. Neil took another sip of his beer to hide his smirk.

Maybe dinner won't be the only thing we share tonight?

After that, their meal went quickly. It was interspersed with flirtations and the suggestive brush of their legs. The first time had been an accident, but after that, they were always pressed together. Their conversations moved from their jobs to the meal then to their favorite restaurant experiences.

The intensity between them never faded as they ate and spoke. Neil unbuttoned the top of his shirt halfway through the meal. Scott's eyes fixated on the revealed skin. Neil swallowed some of his beer and noticed Scott track the movement of his throat. The air felt thick with anticipation. They finished their meals and paid before making their way outside. While the evening air was pleasant, it didn't cool Neil's heated skin. There was only one cure for that.

Scott's gaze showed he was craving it, too. Neil touched Scott's arm, intending to close the distance, but Scott caught his hand and tugged him out of sight of the restaurant's windows. The moment there was a sliver of privacy, Scott kissed him passionately.

Neil groaned into the man's mouth. Scott slid his arms around his back and dragged him closer. Their tongues met and Neil's desire skyrocketed. He wanted the man badly. When they broke apart for air, he caught and sucked Scott's bottom lip. Scott moaned and slid his hand down Neil's back to hook in his belt loop. Neil trailed his mouth over Scott's jaw.

It seemed obvious where the night would take them. Neil wanted to confirm it.

"I thought you mentioned going slow?" Neil remarked, flicking Scott's earlobe with his tongue.

"Slow doesn't—" Scott cursed when Neil nipped his ear. "*Shit*. It doesn't mean glacial, Neil."

"Oh?" Neil asked, feeling amused. "So, it means what, exactly?"

Scott pulled away and Neil frowned, feeling worried he'd miscalculated, and Scott was changing his mind. But his lover didn't go far. He merely grasped Neil's hand and caught his gaze.

"Come back to my place, and you can find out."

Neil shivered, his desire building.

This is what I signed up for.

He caught Scott's lips in another kiss, needing to dampen some of the need burning within him. When they separated this time, Neil stepped away from Scott, not wanting to be tempted into kissing him again.

"Lead the way."

"Did you drive?" Scott asked and Neil nodded. "Where's your car? You can follow me back."

It took them five minutes to locate their vehicles and get on the road, but each minute seemed to take an hour. Neil's body was thrumming with arousal. He tapped the steering wheel when he was caught at the lights and shifted in his seat with every moment they were apart. His pants were already tight, and despite being separated, his lust wasn't waning. All he could think about was how good the intimacy between them had been in the hotel.

Will it be better knowing we have plenty of time?

After fifteen minutes, they finally turned into a suburban neighborhood and pulled up at a nice, single-story house with a garage and well-maintained front lawn. Lights were on in a few of the houses down the street, but the ones on either side of Scott's home were dark. Scott opened the garage and parked inside while Neil parked behind him on the driveway. Neil climbed out and locked his car. He joined Scott and they walked up the path to the man's front door. Scott unlocked it, entered and turned on the hall light. Neil followed him inside, glancing around absently, but there was no sign of another person—no extra shoes by the door or shouts of greeting. Scott locked the door behind them and dropped his keys in a bowl on a small table.

They stood in the hallway, a brief awkwardness infusing the air and making Scott glance away. Neil had expected that they'd fall on each other immediately and barely make it to the bedroom. It was how any other evening for him would have gone.

Eventually, Scott cleared his throat and turned on the living room light. Looking around briefly distracted Neil. There was a large TV taking up center stage. A collection of movies and game consoles were on shelves on either side of it, while a leather couch faced the TV. Neil could easily imagine making out on that couch. More disturbingly, he could imagine watching a *movie* with Scott—sharing a bowl of popcorn as their hands brushed and their thighs pressed together.

"Do you want something to drink?" Scott asked.

He gestured toward the kitchen that was off the living room. It seemed Scott's car ride had left him indecisive about his decision.

How many dates does it normally take for Scott to bring someone home?

It seemed if they were going to do this, he'd have to be the one to instigate it.

"I don't want a drink," Neil said, walking up to the man and placing his hands on Scott's waist.

His lover's eyes darkened, and Neil knew his instincts had been right. Scott wanted to sleep with him tonight. He just needed a nudge.

Leaning in, Neil whispered against Scott's ear, "I want *you.*"

Scott let out a soft groan and turned his head. Neil met him halfway. Scott slipped his fingers into Neil's hair as they kissed, and when Neil nibbled on Scott's lip, he was rewarded by the kiss deepening. Their tongues met in slow strokes, each movement fanning the flames of lust. Neil could have kissed him for hours, but he wanted to do it with fewer clothes. He broke them apart.

"Bedroom?" Neil gasped.

Scott nodded, even as he brushed a sweet kiss to Neil's jaw. He pulled back and took Neil's hand, leading him back to the hallway and farther into the house. The handholding bemused Neil but it made him want to smile. It felt…nice.

They passed three dark rooms off the hallway before stopping at one at the end of the hall. Scott switched on the light and Neil got his first glimpse of Scott's bedroom. A double bed was in the center with its headboard to the wall. Matching nightstands were on either side with a white lamp on the right one. A desk was the only other furnishing, which had a closed laptop on top of it. The curtains were drawn, and there was an en suite attached. The bed was made with military precision, and there were no clothes on the floor.

"Bedroom always this tidy?" Neil asked. "Or were you expecting me?"

"Nothing wrong with being neat," Scott answered. He stepped closer and kissed Neil's neck. "But I hoped to bring you back here after a date."

Neil grinned. "Well, let's not waste the opportunity."

He hauled Scott's shirt over his shoulders, tossing it quickly to the floor. Scott then brought his hands to Neil's, removing the buttons before pushing it off his shoulders. Once they were both shirtless, Neil brushed his fingers over Scott's chest, taking the time to admire him. There were more freckles than he remembered. He wanted to follow their path with his mouth, but for now, he focused on Scott's lips. Neil caught them in another kiss and thumbed Scott's nipples, enjoying the way they hardened beneath his touch. Scott groaned into the kiss and moved his hands to Neil's shoulders. He slid them over Neil's back, his nails scratching down Neil's skin and making him shudder.

Scott kept moving, briefly cupping Neil's ass before going to his belt. They had to stop kissing to concentrate as they hurriedly removed the last of their clothes. Scott's cock was already half-hard, and Neil couldn't wait to get his hands on it.

Scott closed the gap between them, pressing their bodies together. He caressed Neil's sides as he kissed him again. It was a slower and more affectionate embrace. The whole move felt intimate. Neil shivered and his stomach gave its now-familiar clench. Scott ended the kiss, but he trailed his lips over Neil's jaw and down to his throat. When he finished and lifted his head, he was smiling.

"Want to be on top tonight, Neil?"

"You asking me to ride you or…?"

"I've always liked it both ways."

He parted from Neil and walked to the nightstand. Scott opened the drawer and pulled out lube and condoms.

"So," Scott continued, coming back and offering them to him, "do you want to top?"

He hadn't expected Scott to switch so easily, but Neil was pleasantly surprised. Twice, Neil had jerked off imagining this scenario. Who was he to deny it when Scott offered it on a silver platter?

"Yeah," he answered, his voice rough with desire, "I'll top."

Neil took the items in one hand while the other cupped Scott's hip. He planned to guide him toward the bed, but Scott took the chance to lean into Neil's body and kiss him. Neil kissed back and wrapped his arm around Scott's waist. He couldn't help noticing how different it was to their last two times together. Scott was almost being passive. Neil wasn't used to it. The rare time he'd experienced a lover who switched, they'd always remained dominant. Neil pulled back from the kiss to eye Scott suspiciously, but Scott looked relaxed and happy.

He followed my directions in the store, too. He lets me get bossy and doesn't complain.

It had been the deal-breaker in the past for reoccurring flings. He hadn't cared about the men, but he had felt frustrated by their refusal to budge. Sometimes, they'd complained about his personality and desires. He wasn't putting up with that for anything, especially sexual conquests.

He didn't want to say Scott was *special*, but he'd bounced through enough men to know when someone was different. The fireman wanted an actual relationship with him, and Neil wasn't so emotionally stunted as to ignore his own cautious interest.

Just play it by ear and see what happens. The rest can be worked out later.

Kissing Scott again, Neil funneled all his desire into the embrace. His following kisses were placed over Scott's neck and shoulder. He gently encouraged Scott toward the bed and only stopped kissing him so they could climb onto the mattress.

Scott lay down on his back and shuffled up toward the pillow. Neil knelt over him, wanting to explore the man. He put aside their supplies and bent down to lick one of Scott's nipples. Neil brushed his lips down Scott's body to a series of freckles over his ribs. As he did, Neil slid his hands down Scott's arms, then jumped over his abdomen before reaching his goal. Neil cupped Scott's cock and stroked it. He was rewarded by Scott's moan. Neil continued to kiss and mouth Scott's chest, moving back up to catch and briefly suck a nipple. He then made his way downward, lavishing attention on every muscle on his way to Scott's glorious, hard cock. Neil sucked a kiss to Scott's thigh, enjoying the twitch of his lover's hips before he licked a path from the base to the tip of Scott's erection.

"Neil," Scott choked out, tightening his hands in Neil's hair.

He didn't force him closer, and Neil rewarded that consideration by taking the base in his hand and sliding his mouth around Scott's cock. He pressed his forearm to Scott's hips, preparing to hold him down. Scott cursed, but despite a small jerk, he stayed in place. Neil tried not to smile.

So well-mannered.

Neil sucked behind the head. He tasted the salty tang of Scott's lust and bobbed up and down, letting saliva coat the man's erection. Scott was cursing and gasping beneath him. Neil had always enjoyed giving head, but rarely performed it on his one-night stands. While it gave him a thrill and a power trip to have someone's orgasm in the palm of his hand — or, rather, the suck of his mouth — he didn't like people thinking they could call the shots and make demands.

Knowing Scott wasn't about to annoy him, Neil closed his eyes. He got lost in the feeling of working Scott's shaft. He sucked and slid his mouth up and down, letting his tongue rub along the base. Scott continued to tug lightly at his hair and moan his name, but otherwise let him do what he wanted.

It almost tempted Neil to reward him with an orgasm, but he wanted to fuck him more.

Neil pulled off and opened his eyes to see Scott's thick cock curved in the air between them. It was flushed red and straining with need. When his focus traveled higher, he saw that Scott's face and chest were equally red with arousal and his lips were parted in pleasure. The temptation to stroke him off and watch

Scott climax beneath him was hard to resist. Scott's release would be glorious, coating his chest and making him look completely debauched.

Next time.

Neil grabbed the lube and poured some onto his fingers. He took Scott's leg and had the man bend it to give him better access. Scott complied eagerly, and Neil brought his fingers to the man's entrance. He lightly teased the pucker before pressing his first finger inside. Scott groaned and bore down to help accept it. Neil watched as his first finger went in to the knuckle. He slowly started to thrust into it, noticing Scott's hole clench. He did glance up occasionally, enjoying the sight of Scott grinding his head against the pillows. Slipping in a second finger, Neil thrust deeper, searching for his prostate. When he nudged it, Scott gave a low groan as he arched. That sent a wave of satisfaction and pleasure through Neil, so he rubbed the spot again, enjoying the way Scott's cock jerked and leaked with fresh pre-cum.

"Neil," Scott moaned, a plea in his voice. Scott lifted his head and caught Neil's gaze. His lover's eyes were wide and dilated with need. *"Please."*

Neil swallowed. His throbbing dick was becoming impossible to ignore. He didn't want to drag this out anymore, either.

"Okay," he agreed.

After removing his fingers, Neil grabbed a condom and ripped it open before slipping it on. Spreading the lube over his shaft, Neil bit down on a grunt of pleasure. He thrust into his hand, needing some friction on his aching flesh. Letting go was difficult, but looking at Scott lying spread out before him was motivation enough. The man looked delectable. His eyes were half-lidded and his cheeks flushed with lust. Neil wanted to be inside him, to feel the way his walls clenched as he came. Neil slipped into position between Scott's spread legs. His lover instantly wrapped a thigh around his hip, pulling Neil closer. Neil positioned his cock and gripped the base of his shaft. They both groaned as he guided the head inside. Neil closed his eyes. His sweat-dampened hair stuck to his forehead, and he trembled as he worked his way deeper. It seemed to take an eternity before he finally bottomed out. Scott was panting beneath him. Neil opened his eyes to find Scott's were squeezed tightly shut. His cock was still curved toward his stomach.

God, he's so hot...so tight.

Neil just wanted to thrust until he came, but he had to make sure his lover was okay.

"Scott?"

"Good," he urged. "*Go.*"

Neil didn't need to be told twice. He pulled out before sliding back in. The drag of his cock sent sparks of pleasure racing up his spine. Scott wrapped his legs firmly around Neil's waist and Neil shifted closer. The position allowed him to thrust deeper and get the perfect angle. Scott moaned loudly and Neil grinned. He bent down and placed a sloppy kiss on Scott's jaw.

"Come on," he panted. "Touch yourself."

Scott's hazy eyes opened, and he chuckled.

"So," he groaned, "*pushy.*"

Neil laughed, feeling something giddy erupt in his chest. Scott sounded *amused.* Neil kissed him again, and Scott smiled. He also snuck his hand down as he'd been ordered. He began stroking his erection in time with Neil's thrusts. They were both panting as their bodies rocked and their pleasure mounted. Neil could feel his orgasm approaching, but he wanted Scott to come first. He focused every thrust on driving Scott to the edge. He ignored his own need. Grabbing Scott's hips, he drove his cock deeper, nailing Scott's prostate with consistent strikes. Scott was digging his teeth into his bottom lip, and his hand was a blur on his cock.

Neil tried to keep his eyes open, but his own release was on the horizon. He was moving his hips in a frantic rhythm, but he needed to hold out a little longer. When Scott squeezed behind the head of his cock and Neil thrust inside, Scott finally gave a choked cry and arched his back. His orgasm made his muscles tighten around Neil's cock. A few last thrusts were all Neil needed, and he was following. His orgasm slammed through him. The ecstasy forced him to bury his face in Scott's shoulder, muffling his low moan of the man's name. Neil shuddered with aftershocks, and he tried to climb down after such a blissful high.

When Scott loosened his legs' hold around him and touched Neil's shoulder, Neil shifted back and slid out of his lover. Neil wanted to collapse on the bed, but he couldn't yet. He removed the condom and tied it. He didn't have long to consider what to do with it. Scott, ever practical, leaned over the bed and picked up a wastepaper bin. He held it out and Neil amusedly dropped the used condom inside. Scott put it back under the nightstand while Neil stretched out on the mattress. He watched with a small smile as Scott grabbed some tissues to clean his stomach before throwing them away.

When he finished, he lay down beside Neil with a soft groan. They were close enough that their arms could brush. Neil thought that would be it, but Scott shifted onto his side. He ran his fingers over the back of

Neil's hand. Neil glanced down and watched the movements. Scott traced his skin for a few moments before taking his hand. He raised it and pressed his lips to the knuckles. Neil repressed a shudder, but gooseflesh still erupted over him.

"Stay the night?"

Neil's gaze snapped to Scott's. His lover was smiling hopefully, and Neil swallowed, feeling his stomach squirm with nerves.

He didn't have to work the next day and had nothing planned. Normally, he would say no on principle. It was easier to go home rather than stay for an awkward breakfast in the morning.

But Scott is different. Maybe, this could be okay.

Neil found it wasn't even the lure of more sex that made him want to agree. It was the way Scott was looking at him.

"Yeah," he mumbled. "Okay."

Scott smiled and he kissed Neil's hand again. The gesture was sweetly affectionate, and Neil's stomach flipped. Scott then leaned across the bed and pressed their lips together in a chaste kiss. Neil responded automatically, but his touches were hesitant as he cupped Scott's cheek.

He wasn't used to lingering in bed after sex. He wasn't used to kisses that were more suited to a relationship than a one-night stand.

Is that what this is? A relationship?

Neil wasn't sure how to feel about that, so instead of dissecting it, he simply ignored it.

Chapter Five

When Neil woke up the sun was slipping through the curtains, bathing the room in a golden glow. Scott was stretching beside him, but he stilled when Neil shifted to look at him.

"Sorry." Scott's voice was rough. "Didn't mean to wake you."

"You didn't," Neil answered.

It was true. He'd expected to toss and turn all night or be unable to settle with someone beside him, but he'd rested peacefully. Hell, the mattress was better than his. Extending his arms above his head, Neil brushed the headboard.

"Want some coffee?" Scott asked.

"Yes," Neil answered eagerly, keen to get caffeine.

Scott grinned before pushing out of bed. He ignored last night's clothes to get fresh boxers from the closet. He also grabbed some baggy gray tracksuit pants.

"Do you want to wear these?" He held them up. "They'd be more comfortable."

"Sure."

Neil sat up and extended his hand. Scott brought them over and their fingers brushed. The small touch stirred Neil's desire. He stroked Scott's hand and tugging him down by the wrist. Morning sex was a definite perk of staying the night. Scott seemed to realize his intention. He leaned in only to pause. Something strange crossed his face, which made Neil frown, but before he could ask, Scott pecked his cheek before breaking from his loose grip and stepping backward.

"How do you take your coffee?" he asked, avoiding Neil's gaze.

"Milk, one sugar," Neil answered, feeling perplexed.

Why did he pull away from me?

"Gotcha. I'll be in the kitchen." He pointed at the closed door. "Bathroom's through there."

"Thanks."

Scott nodded and left without a second glance. Neil felt a sinking suspicion.

Great. Here's that awkward morning after. Neil sighed and scrubbed a hand over his face. *Should have left last night.*

After climbing out of bed, Neil went directly to the bathroom. He flicked on the light. There was a toilet, a large shower, a basin with a mirror above it and drawers beneath. Neil looked at his reflection. His hair was sticking up every which way and he had a pillow crease on his cheek.

At least I won't have to wait for a taxi before I can leave.

Following his splashing water on his face to wake up, Neil also fixed his hair. There was no point walking out of the front door looking like something that the cat had dragged in. He liked to maintain a little dignity when booted out on his ass.

I dated him twice. A few more times would have been nice.

Neil felt a twinge of disappointment but tried to shrug it off. He'd known dating was likely to blow up in his face. At least he'd gained another round of sex out of it.

After putting on Scott's pants, Neil tied the drawstring to keep them from falling down. While they were both of similar height, Neil's waist was clearly slimmer. He padded his way out of the room and down the hall to the kitchen. He found Scott with two white mugs on the counter. A domestic scene might have made him uncomfortable before, but with Scott's current discomfort and the approaching end of their dates, he could only sigh.

It would have been fun to explore this kind of thing with Scott.

Scott finished pouring the coffees and Neil forwent a seat to stand beside the counter. Scott wasn't pushing for him to leave yet, but it was only a matter of time.

He'll probably be polite and let me finish the coffee first — maybe even have a shower.

Neil let his gaze glide over Scott's muscled physique. He felt another unhappy twinge that it would be the last time he'd be able to admire it. Scott pushed the coffee toward him, but Neil didn't take it. He waited, already anticipating the breakup speech.

"Neil," Scott said, staring at his coffee mug and turning it absently, "about last night."

And there it is.

Neil closed his eyes briefly. He'd known it was coming, but unlike the men in his past, hearing it from

Scott actually *hurt*. He opened his eyes, not wanting that ache to show.

"You don't want to do it again," Neil said, keeping his voice even.

Neil was already running through which speech Scott would give him. '*It's not you, it's me*'? Scott seemed the kind to avoid blaming others. Neil didn't expect Scott's head to snap up, his eyes wide.

"What? No! I didn't mean it like that! I just didn't plan for it to go this fast." He ran an awkward hand through his messy hair. "Last night, I wanted nothing more than to get you back into bed." He looked back at his coffee. "I just don't want our relationship to be a solely physical thing, Neil."

Wait. Neil felt incredulous. *He still wants to date me?*

"You regret us having sex? But nothing else?" Neil clarified.

"I don't regret *anything*," Scott disagreed. "I just don't want sex to cloud things. I really like you, Neil, and I want to know our relationship can work outside the bedroom."

Neil felt relief. It startled him how strongly it rushed through him, but their misunderstanding had made the truth obvious. He didn't want Scott to kick him out.

But if Scott were being honest with him, Neil would have to do the same — which meant things could still go downhill. Neil mentally braced for it.

"Look, Scott," Neil began. "I think I should admit something to you."

Scott frowned. "What?"

Neil hesitated, and it was his turn to look at his coffee mug. He tapped his fingers absently on the counter.

"I haven't had much experience with relationships," he explained, feeling uneasy. "Most of the time, sex is the only thing I'm out for. If I do go for more than that, the sex is the major incentive. When that doesn't work and things fall apart, it's usually the other person who ends it."

Scott was silent for long enough that Neil felt a desperate need to grab his things, get in his car and never look back.

"Do you want more than sex with me?" Scott finally asked.

Neil felt conflicted. The question should be simple, and his emotional responses to Scott dumping him should have made it easy, but admitting it out loud? Neil's shoulders tightened with tension. Scott could drop '*I like you*' into conversation with the ease of asking about the weather. He couldn't.

"I like spending time with you." Neil's insides felt as if they were twisting into a ball. "I...enjoy dating you."

Neil was still drumming his fingers in an anxious rhythm. When Scott's hand covered his, Neil stilled. His gaze jerked up to his lover. Scott was smiling.

"You want us to work?" Scott clarified. Neil nodded sharply. "Then we're both aiming for the same thing." Scott squeezed his hand. "We had a connection at the hotel that I think still exists between us and is worth pursuing."

"I don't think sex will ruin it," Neil blurted. Scott blinked. "*Sex*, I know how to do. We're good at it. I don't know why we'd have to stop that."

"You said sex was the main focus of your past relationships," Scott pointed out.

"To the exclusion of all else," Neil explained. "Already this is different. *You're* different." Neil laughed self-consciously. "Do you think I have heart-to-hearts with all the guys I date?"

"I'm guessing you don't."

Scott seemed amused rather than wary or uncomfortable. The latter was what Neil would expect when a potential boyfriend admitted they were shit at commitment and dealt exclusively in flings. Scott continued to defy his expectations. It found Neil determined to keep pushing through the conversation. Neil's skin felt like it was crawling and the knot in his stomach was growing larger, but his stubbornness won out.

"Is this a deal-breaker?"

"No," Scott answered without hesitation. He squeezed Neil's hand again. "Those relationships are in the past. What matters is ours, right? We'll work it out as we go."

Neil felt a fresh wave of relief, and his shoulders slumped forward. Scott came around the counter but didn't let go of his hand. He placed his arm around Neil's waist and pressed a kiss to his temple. Neil closed his eyes.

How does he make me want to stay in his arms rather than run for the hills?

"Still want to stick around for breakfast?" Scott asked quietly.

"As long as you're cooking," Neil shot back.

Scott laughed. He kissed Neil's temple again before pulling away. Neil opened his eyes, already missing the man's warmth.

"Bacon, eggs and toast. How's that sound?"

Like you should cook them for a better boyfriend prospect.

"Perfect," he replied, quelling his thoughts and forcing a grin.

Scott didn't notice his discomfort. He headed to the fridge and started taking out food.

"What are your plans for the day?" Scott asked.

He was acting as if Neil's confession really was easily acceptable—like it really *was* something in the past and couldn't destroy their entire relationship. Neil didn't understand it, and despite feeling like a shoe still needed to drop then be used to kick him out, Neil played along with the conversation.

"Nothing. Just relaxing. What about you? You said the engagement party is today?"

"Yeah, it starts at one," Scott replied, dropping four slices of bread into the toaster. "A lot of people have kids, so it'll only go for a few hours."

"Sounds like a good time. I can be out of here after breakfast."

Scott looked over his shoulder. He was already frowning. "You don't have to leave so soon, Neil."

It surprised him. "You want me to stay?"

"Yeah. Neither of us has anywhere to be. Why not spend the morning together?"

Neil grinned and a flirtation about morning sex was immediately on his tongue. Only, he didn't want to instigate something Scott would misconstrue. Sex was his go-to response for being with someone. Scott was aiming for more.

"Sure," he agreed.

Scott flashed him a smile before continuing to get breakfast ready. Neil took a sip of coffee and watched him. Scott was attractive. It was a simple fact. Seeing all his skin on display made Neil want to press against him, cover him in bites and kisses then blow him against the counter.

Swallowing another mouthful of coffee, Neil racked his brain for a simple, neutral topic to distract his thoughts.

"Is this a normal morning routine for you?" he asked.

"I'd have usually done a run around the block and showered by now," Scott replied. He glanced at the clock. "I'd then have breakfast in front of the TV."

"Oh? What do you watch?"

"News. Maybe catch up on a TV show if there's nothing in the headlines." Scott placed the bacon in the pan. "What would your normal morning be?"

"If I wasn't working, I wouldn't even be out of bed."

Scott chuckled. "Not an early bird?"

"Not if I can help it."

When he'd finished the last of his coffee, he took it to the sink and rinsed the mug. Neil put it on the dirty side and cocked his hip against the counter. Scott was monitoring the bacon while the eggs were beside him just waiting to be cracked into the pan.

Who'd have thought I'd ever be doing something so homey?

"So, what happens when you wake up?" he questioned.

"I stumble out of bed, check my phone, eat something, watch TV and maybe go out later in the evening."

"Sounds like a good day off. I usually spend an evening in with a beer and a classic movie."

"And what are your classic movies?"

"Old black-and-whites," Scott answered. "Gregory Peck, Katharine Hepburn, Jimmy Stewart."

"Never really watched them."

Scott paused his cooking to stare at Neil.

"That has to be fixed," he stated.

Neil laughed. "Well, we have time before you head to the engagement party?"

Scott looked pleased. "We'll watch one with breakfast. I already have the perfect movie. Have you seen *The Philadelphia Story*?"

"Nope."

"We'll start with that."

He turned back to breakfast, rearranging the bacon before moving to grab plates. He put the bread down in the toaster, took butter and some assorted condiments from the fridge. Scott then cracked eggs into the pan. Neil watched him work. Scott was comfortable and at ease. Normally, Neil would enjoy the idea of being waited on, but something he couldn't identify found him wanting to assist.

"Want me to make us another coffee or get the movie ready?"

"I wouldn't say no to a drink, but I'd rather have juice."

"I can do that."

Heading to the fridge, he breathed in the smell of bacon and eggs. He hadn't had a meal like this since he'd lived at home. After opening the fridge, he grabbed the apple juice before being directed to the cupboard that held the glasses. He ended up pouring two of the same. The toast popped as he was finishing, so Neil buttered them and placed them on their plates. Scott finished cooking and dropped the bacon and eggs beside them. They worked together easily.

When they dished everything up, they carried their food and drinks to the living room. Scott put his plate on the couch and searched for the movie. Neil watched Scott with amusement as he took a seat.

He's just the type to prefer a hard copy over streaming. Then again, can you even stream such old films?

When he returned to the couch, Scott sat near enough that their legs brushed. It wouldn't be hard to close the space between them. If he were lucky, they might end up pressed together and sharing a kiss by the end.

Glancing at Scott, Neil realized he wouldn't mind the occasional early morning with the fireman if they turned out this way.

* * * *

The movie was more fast paced than Neil expected, but most of his focus remained on Scott. His lover grinned throughout the film and Neil even caught him mouthing the occasional line of dialogue. It was cute. They'd moved closer once they'd discarded their plates on the coffee table. They were both shirtless and more than once the feel of skin-on-skin completely distracted Neil from the actions on-screen. When the credits rolled, Neil felt disappointed that their time on the couch was over. Scott turned off the TV and turned to him.

"What did you think?"

"It was good," Neil admitted.

"It is one of the best romantic comedies ever made," Scott insisted.

"Is that why you picked it?" Neil teased. "You wanted a date movie?"

Scott laughed. "If I wanted that, I'd have saved it for late at night, not first thing in the morning."

"First thing in the morning doesn't count?" Neil questioned, amused at the distinction.

"It would, but I was trying to right a wrong in your movie education, not get you into bed."

Neil huffed a laugh. "Well, you succeeded at the first, but there's still time for the second."

The flirtation was instinctive. It was only after he'd said it that he realized the mistake. Only Scott didn't look unhappy. Instead, his gaze darkened and his attention darted to Neil's lips. Neil darted out his tongue to lick them. Scott let out a small noise and Neil moved forward before he could think it through. He pressed their lips together and Scott immediately kissed him back. He *deepened* the kiss and Neil groaned and stroked his thumb under Scott's jaw, feeling the growing stubble. Scott shivered and broke apart their lips.

"Neil," he gasped.

Neil had intended to move to Scott's neck, but he paused, remembering their discussion in the kitchen and Scott's earlier request for '*slow*'.

"Do you want us to stop?" he questioned

Scott groaned and Neil tried to pull back and look at his lover, but Scott didn't let him go far. He used his hold on Neil to tug him forward and into a new kiss. It was intense, making Neil moan against Scott's mouth. His lover shifted farther down the couch and their kiss broke as they rearranged. Scott ended up on his back while Neil rested propped above him. Scott's chest was flushed, and Neil ran his fingers over it, circling a nipple and watching it harden.

It wasn't the only thing getting hard.

Their hips were pressed together, and Neil's track pants and Scott's boxers made their lust obvious. Neil wanted to give them what they obviously wanted, but he didn't want to put them back where they'd started.

"Do you want us to stop?" Neil asked again.

Scott swore and tilted back his head.

"Scott?"

"I regret bringing it up."

"Scott—"

"No, that's not true," he interrupted, looking back at Neil. "I don't regret saying it. Because I *do* want this to work. I wanted to know we we're on the same page."

He untangled his hand from Neil's hair and slid it down his back to cup his ass. He pushed Neil's hips forward, making Neil close his eyes and grunt at the friction.

"But I don't want us second-guessing," Scott continued. "I want us to do what feels right whenever it feels right." He shifted up to brush his lips over Neil's. "We've got a bit over an hour before I have to get ready for the party, and I don't want to waste it."

Neil responded by kissing Scott again. He rolled their hips in slow, enticing motions. The kiss seemed to last an age, and pulling back found them both gasping. Catching his breath, Neil enjoyed looking down at his lover as Scott lay prone and flushed beneath him. Neil's mind was already racing with a dozen fantasies of what they could get up to.

"There's a lot we can do in an hour," he murmured.

Scott cupped Neil's hips before sliding his hands toward the waistband of Neil's borrowed pants. Neil sat up, kneeling on either side of Scott's legs and giving him perfect access. Scott untied the strings and tugged them down. They pooled around his thighs, revealing Neil's stiffening cock. Scott licked his lips and Neil's skin prickled with anticipation and desire. He watched with half-lidded eyes as Scott encircled his cock. Neil's eyelids fell to half-mast and he tilted back his head.

Scott's grip was firm, but he stroked slowly. Neil hummed with pleasure and rocked into his lover's touch.

He looked beneath his lashes at their bodies. The sunlight filtered in between the venetian blinds, painting the room in streaks of light and shadow. It was the middle of the morning. If anyone stepped into Scott's yard and looked through at the right angle, they could easily see what they were up to. Neil loved the thrill of it. His gaze moved farther down to look at Scott. The man's attention was locked on his cock. Neil's arousal built as Scott pumped his shaft with intense focus.

Neil rolled his hips with each pump of Scott's hand, grunting and letting out soft moans as his cock reached full hardness. He was soon stiff and aching. When Scott let him go, he barely contained his whine of displeasure. Scott smiled.

"A bed might be better for this," Scott said.

He tried to encourage him to rise, but Neil didn't move. He looked down at Scott, splayed before him with a bulge and wet patch in his boxers. The couch wasn't really big enough, but Neil didn't care. He bent down and kissed Scott deeply. He used Scott's distraction to cup him through his boxers. Scott broke the kiss with a moan.

"Stay here," Neil said with a gentle squeeze to Scott's cock. "Behave and you'll be inside me in a few minutes."

"Shit," Scott hissed. "Okay."

Neil rewarded him with another kiss and a firm rub to Scott's erection. Regretfully, he had to pull back and climb off his lover. He kicked off his pants and paused momentarily to admire Scott.

"Get rid of your boxers by the time I get back," Neil said, his voice already rough with arousal.

Scott's eyebrows rose, even as his hands went to them.

"So bossy."

Neil had to turn away so the sight of Scott's cock wouldn't distract him. He hurried through the house to Scott's bedroom. He found the lube and condoms from the previous night and brought them back to the living room. Scott was where he'd left him, and Neil stopped walking just to admire him. Toned, flushed skin lay spread out before him. Neil's cock throbbed with need. Yet despite how much he wanted to get Scott inside him, another thing caught his attention. His chest was warm. He wanted to kiss Scott and not just as an instigation for sex.

Normally, he'd shake it off, but after their conversation over breakfast, he wanted to prove he could desire more than just a fuck. He closed the remaining distance but didn't straddle Scott immediately. He bent down and brushed their lips together. It was a soft touch, the kind of intimate gesture he normally never bestowed. Scott cupped his cheek and Neil leaned into the touch. It only lasted a few moments, but the warmth in his chest had spread.

Scott stroked his cheek and the affection in Scott's gaze made Neil's stomach clench. Uncertain how to handle the tenderness, Neil turned his face away. He playfully nipped one of Scott's fingers to break the moment. When he glanced back at Scott, the man's pupils were blown wide. Once more on familiar ground, Neil straightened and climbed onto the couch. He kneeled on either side of Scott and offered his lover the lube and condoms. Scott took them and Neil braced his hands above Scott's head on the arm of the couch before arching his spine.

"Get me ready," Neil said, "then I'll ride you."

Scott let out a soft, needy noise but quickly went to work. He dropped the condoms on his chest, opened the lube then poured some onto his fingers. Neil closed his eyes when he felt Scott's hands on his ass. He shivered when Scott's finger teased between his cheeks. Neil tried to spread his legs even wider.

When the tip of Scott's finger finally pushed at his entrance, Neil let out a shaky breath. Scott started easing his way inside and Neil relaxed his muscles to help. His lover wasted no time in pressing in then drawing out of him.

"You look so good," Scott murmured.

Neil opened his eyes to find Scott already watching him.

"I *love* doing this," Scott continued, a second finger coming to join the first. Neil bit down on a groan and pressed back against them.

"You're gorgeous, Neil."

Heat crept up his neck, and it wasn't just from lust. He wanted to shut Scott up or tell him to stop being so *tender*. Despite his uncertainty, he stayed silent.

"So gorgeous," Scott repeated.

Neil shuddered. He didn't know what to say. Scott curled his fingers in just the right way to make Neil gasp as pleasure raced up his spine.

"Oh," he moaned as Scott stroked his sweet spot again. "Ohhh, Scott. *Shit.*"

Scott chuckled. "I could keep doing this — watching you like this for the full hour." He rubbed Neil's prostate again, making Neil's body tremble. "Still got plenty of time to drive you crazy."

"Don't you dare," Neil gasped.

Yet, despite his words, Neil was still pressing back against Scott, only wanting more. His body was at war with his mind. He needed Scott's cock inside him, but he would equally be happy riding his lover's fingers and enjoying each teasing brush of bliss.

Scott chuckled again.

"Okay," he agreed. "Next time."

Scott pulled out his fingers and Neil whined, hating how empty it made him feel. He heard plastic ripping and looked between their bodies. His cock was hard and dripping pre-cum, and so was Scott's. When Scott slid on the condom and coated it in lubricant, Neil's impatience had reached a fever pitch.

"Hurry up," he ordered, his voice thick with need.

Scott nodded and shifted to a better angle. The tip of Scott's erection pressed against his entrance. Scott touched his hip before guiding him down. Neil groaned loudly as he was slowly breached. The angle and the position made him feel each inch as it pressed inside. His arms trembled as he slid down onto Scott's shaft. He felt like he was going to fly apart by the time he was fully seated in Scott's lap with Scott's length inside him.

"Neil," Scott gasped, one hand on his hip, the other on his thigh.

It felt incredible, and while it was probably too soon, Neil didn't care. He needed more. Neil drew partially off Scott's cock before dropping back down. It was on his second attempt that he changed the angle and got filled in the exact way he wanted. He let out a loud moan.

Oh God, yes.

"There," he whispered.

Scott understood. He took a better grip on Neil's hips and together, they started a rhythm that found every thrust aiming exactly where Neil needed it. He was quickly seeing stars and unable to keep his eyes open. It felt too good.

"God," Neil choked out, "don't stop."

"Neil," Scott gasped.

His thrusts were becoming more frantic. Neil could only moan and ride out each jerk of Scott's hips as they drove him closer to the edge. He was desperate for friction on his cock.

"Scott," he whined, "touch me."

He braced his arms better on the couch to more easily meet Scott's thrusts and moments later, Scott curled a hand around his arousal. Neil gasped out a pleased sound as his body came alight with pleasure. He could feel his orgasm approaching and he clenched around Scott while thrusting into his lover's slick strokes.

It took almost no time for his climax to burst over him, blackening his vision and making him cry out. He heard Scott groan and felt him thrust several times before tensing and pushing deep into him. Neil shuddered and finally allowed his trembling arms to slacken. He slumped against his lover, trying to catch his breath.

Neil felt Scott's fingers trail up his spine in a soft caress but didn't bother to open his eyes. He wanted to purr like a contented cat.

"I think we're going to need a shower now," Scott remarked.

"I'm busy enjoying the afterglow."

"You won't enjoy it if you get a cramp," Scott pointed out. "That wasn't the best position to have sex in."

"I got an orgasm, so it was a *great* position to have sex."

Scott laughed softly, but his hand became more insistent as he encouraged Neil to get up. Neil groaned but complied. He carefully levered off Scott, feeling his legs and lower back complain. Scott pulled off the condom and stood.

"Come on," he said, touching Neil's arm. "Plenty of room in the shower for two."

Neil stretched his back but followed along after his lover with a smile.

I wonder if Scott will towel dry me again.

Chapter Six

The shower remained chaste. They kissed a few times and Neil used the excuse of cleaning Scott's back to explore his skin and massage his ass. Scott laughed at him but leaned into his touch, causing Neil to bite down on multiple flirtatious remarks. He also had to resist sliding his fingers between the man's cheeks or cupping Scott's cock. His reward for his restraint was Scott washing his hair. He'd been dubious at first, but the slow motions and gentle massaging found Neil's eyes fluttering shut and a contented sigh escaping.

When they finished, Scott grabbed towels, and just like the hotel, he tossed one to Neil for use on his body, but the second he used on Neil's hair. Neil enjoyed the pampering. Scott's hands were firm yet somehow tender. When he finished with Neil, he used the same towel over his skin. It made Neil want to return the favor—or just push him up against the wall for a kiss. But before he could do either, the sound of a phone chiming pulled their attention to Scott's bedroom. Scott wrapped a towel around his waist and walked into the room. Neil sighed wistfully. While he hadn't expected they'd have another round of sex, he would have enjoyed admiring Scott naked for a little while longer. Securing one of the free towels, Neil followed his lover.

Scott stood beside the bed, drops of water still sliding down his back and over his toned body. He would have looked perfect—if it weren't for the grimace twisting his lips.

"What's wrong?"

"The best man was helping organize the engagement party, but he's down with a cold," Scott explained. "They're asking for help to set everything up."

Scott looked torn over what to do. While Neil liked knowing Scott wanted to stay with him, Neil knew the better option was to have him go. Not only were Scott's friends important to him, but Neil still couldn't shake the feeling that the longer he stayed with Scott, the sooner his lover would find fault in him. It cemented his decision.

"Go help. We didn't have anything planned."

Scott looked surprised. "You don't mind?"

"No. We've had most of the morning together."

Scott smiled. He also closed the distance and wrapped his arm around Neil's waist. He caught Neil's lips in a soft, chaste kiss.

"Thanks, Neil," Scott murmured after they parted. He stroked Neil's waist. "I've got Tuesday night free. Do you want to have dinner again?"

"Yeah," Neil agreed.

"I'm still sorry we have to cut our morning short."

How about you make it up to me?

Neil's desire made a valiant comeback as he pictured Scott whipping his towel away and dropping to his knees. His cock was already hardening with interest. Scott raised his eyebrows, obviously noticing, but he looked amused.

"Or do you have something in mind before I go?" he asked.

Scott's hand turned sensual as it slid over his back before down the towel and over his ass. Neil's hips twitched forward. Scott's other hand came to his thigh before edging toward the knot in the towel. He didn't unhitch it, choosing instead to slip between the folds until his fingers could graze Neil's cock. Neil groaned at the featherlight touch.

When Scott gripped his shaft, Neil's eyes closed. His lover bent down and started placing kisses on his shoulder and neck. Neil gripped Scott's arms for balance as Scott started stroking him in earnest.

"Scott," he groaned.

His hips were pumping in time with Scott's motions. His cock was fully erect, and his body was aching for more friction. Scott moved his lips to his ear, tugging lightly on the lobe before sucking. Neil's breath hitched and his cock throbbed. He *wanted* that mouth on him.

Neil brought his hands from Scott's arms to his shoulders. He pushed lightly and Scott stilled before pulling away. Neil opened his eyes to find Scott grinning.

"Do you want something, Neil?"

Scott's teasing tone found Neil scowling. He pushed with more insistence. Scott chuckled. He let go of Neil's cock but did as directed, slowly dropping to his knees.

"Yes, *sir*," Scott quipped.

Neil's stomach squirmed with anticipation as Scott positioned in front of him. This time, he didn't slip under the towel. It was already loose from his lover's ministrations and Scott easily tugged it free. It pooled around his feet, allowing his hard cock to bob. Neil dug his fingers into Scott's shoulders, but when his lover didn't move forward, he tugged him closer. Scott complied. Scott *followed* his commands until Neil stopped him with his lips right in front of Neil's cockhead. His warm breath was a delicious torment.

"*Scott*," Neil groaned.

Thankfully, his lover took Neil's cock into his mouth. The first feel of smooth, wet heat had Neil tipping back his head with a whine. Scott didn't waste time. He sucked gently before lowering his lips farther down the shaft. Scott gripped the back of his thighs and encouraged him to thrust. Neil didn't need further prompting. His breaths became shallow as he moved in and out. Scott ran his tongue along the base and sucked on the head as he withdrew.

"Fuck," he moaned. "*Scott*."

Scott hummed and Neil dug his nails into his lover's shoulders. His thrusts picked up speed as his climax swiftly approached. Scott opened his mouth wider and let him chase his pleasure. He tried not to push too hard, but his need for release was becoming blinding.

When Scott abruptly removed his mouth, Neil gave a grunt of complaint. He wanted to drag Scott back, but Scott didn't go far. He placed one hand around the base of Neil's cock and stroked. His other moved down behind Neil's balls, pressing and stroking the skin. He then encircled the head and sucked *hard*.

"Oh, *fuck*," Neil gasped.

He gave a few short, jerking thrusts before coming forcefully into Scott's mouth.

Neil shuddered through the aftershocks. His body felt loose and light. When Scott let him go, Neil stumbled backward before dropping down hard on the bed. Scott was still kneeling on the ground. There was a noticeable tent underneath his towel and his smile seemed pleased and a little smug. Neil was still getting his breathing back under control.

"What now, *sir*?" Scott teased.

Neil felt a zing of pleasure run down his spine. He tried not to show it, masking it with a roll of his eyes.

"Get up here if you want me to do anything about *that*."

Scott chuckled but quickly stood and walked toward him. Neil immediately leaned forward and pushed Scott's towel aside. He didn't undo it. In fact, he paused with his hand hovering over Scott's shaft. He looked up at his lover.

"Hold on to your towel," Neil said.

Scott snorted. "What, like hold on to your hat?"

Neil's lips twitched. "No. I mean, don't let it go."

Scott raised his eyebrows but followed the order. He hitched his fingers around the material, keeping it secure. Neil took Scott's shaft and stroked it slowly. Scott's breath caught. When Neil glanced up, his lover's eyes had fallen closed. Neil closed the distance and wrapped his lips around Scott's cock. He mouthed lightly at the head while one hand stroked Scott's inner thigh and the other gently rubbed his balls.

Scott groaned and jerked his hips forward. Neil worked his way down Scott's cock while the hand on his balls slipped backward and stroked between his ass cheeks. He moved farther down the shaft, sucking as he went. He kept his other hand sliding over Scott's body. He swirled his fingers over his left thigh and above Scott's knee. The movements of his mouth and lips remained slow and languid.

"*Neil*," Scott groaned, his voice gaining a hint of pleading.

He could feel the repressed tension in Scott's muscles. His body was thrumming with arousal. Neil angled his head to look up at his lover. Scott's body was flushed, and his hands tightly gripped the towel. Neil felt a surge of delight. It was a small thing, but he enjoyed it when his lovers followed orders. Neil decided to reward Scott by finally taking his lover's cock deeper into his mouth, hollowing his cheeks as he descended.

"*Ah*," Scott gasped. "*Shit*."

His breaths were becoming labored and he was starting to jerk his hips. Neil slid his hands over Scott's ass and thighs one more time before bringing them up to Scott's. He touched his lover's tense fingers and pried them from the towel. Scott let go and Neil moved the man's hands to his head. When Scott tangled his fingers in his hair, Neil moaned his approval.

"Neil," Scott whispered, his voice strangled.

Neil hummed and brought his hands back to Scott's ass, encouraging the man to press deeper inside. Scott's cockhead was nearly at the back of his throat. Neil *loved* it. He closed his eyes and focused entirely on the weight and feel of Scott's cock as he coaxed him the last of the way to orgasm.

When Scott came, he tightened his grip in Neil's hair and Neil sucked for all he was worth as Scott spilled his release. Neil swallowed it all down and slid off Scott's softening cock. Scott's hands remained in his hair but there was no resistance to his movements. When the head cleared his lips, Neil noticed with amusement that the towel which had been struggling to remain around Scott finally fell to the ground.

Scott tilted up Neil's head. He then bent down and pressed their lips together. When Scott pulled back, he had a rueful grin.

"At least we don't need another shower."

Neil chuckled. "I wouldn't complain if we did."

Scott's smile faded. He rubbed his thumb along Neil's jaw. "I'm sorry I have to cut our morning short."

"It was a lot longer than I thought it would be, so don't worry about it."

Scott frowned. "What do you mean?"

Neil stilled. *I didn't think that through*. He'd already explained his previous relationships to Scott but talking about it still made him uncomfortable. It was a testament to how relaxed he'd been that he'd admitted it in the first place.

"I told you about my relationships," he said cautiously. "Neither of us normally wants to stay."

"But you liked staying here with me?"

A fresh knot formed in his stomach. It then moved up to his throat, making speech feel impossible. His skin felt too tight, and he wanted to squirm. He couldn't answer verbally, but he gave a sharp, awkward nod. It seemed to be enough for Scott as his expression smoothed out. He ran his fingers soothingly through Neil's hair.

"Good. Because those other guys aren't me, and I like having you here."

Neil felt the knot of tension ease, and when Scott encouraged him forward, Neil rested his head against Scott's chest and closed his eyes. Slowly, his discomfort faded away.

"If I'm going to go," Scott said regretfully, "I'd better do it soon."

Neil wondered if Scott was giving him a chance to reconsider, but Neil knew it was best to send Scott on his way. He pushed away from Scott, not wanting things to get awkward or strained.

"Yeah. I should change, too."

Neil turned from Scott and climbed off the bed. He collected his clothes from the previous night and tugged them on with quick, practiced motions. He'd long perfected the art of a quick redress. When he turned back, he found Scott standing in front of his closet but with his gaze on Neil.

"Got distracted by the view," he said, grinning unrepentantly.

"You have good taste."

He came to stand beside Scott, but one glance at Scott's outfits had him reassessing his statement. The best three shirts were the one he'd bought from Neil. He *tsked*.

"I take that back. You need better clothes."

"Do I?" Scott asked, sounding entertained.

"Yes."

Neil stepped around him and started flicking through his closet. There were a few decent button-up shirts, but mostly he had cheap T-shirts and jeans. There were even multiples of the same shirt. Neil took one out and narrowed his eyes. He turned to the fireman.

"Please tell me this didn't come out of a packet."

Scott's lips were twitching as he tried to quell a laugh. "Okay, I won't tell you."

Neil gave a pained groan. He hung the shirt back up and found the one with sparrows that Scott had bought from Hardgroves. He selected it and some dark jeans. Neil turned to present them to Scott, only to pause.

I hope I didn't just piss him off.

He'd just hunted through the man's closet like he owned it, as well as blatantly insulted the man's fashion choices. Surprisingly, Scott took the clothes with good humor. He reached behind Neil and grabbed boxers and socks from a shelf inside the closet then started getting dressed.

Feeling uncomfortable, Neil muttered, "Sorry about going through your closet."

"It's fine," Scott said. "I told you that I don't mind you bossing me around."

He glanced over his shoulder and winked at Neil. The gesture made him relax.

"You do follow orders very well."

Scott was buttoning his shirt and Neil stepped forward. He touched Scott's shoulder to make him turn. Scott had finished the buttons, but Neil unfolded and smoothed out the collar. He then slid his hands over Scott's shoulders to remove any wrinkles.

"You look good," Neil complimented.

Scott smiled and the moment stretched. Neil felt a prickling along the back of his neck. He swallowed and turned away. He went back to the closet and selected shoes for Scott. His lover took a seat on the bed and Neil handed them to him.

"Do you know a place called Strings?" Scott asked as he tied them.

"No. Why?"

"They do good food, and they have live music twice a week. It's a great place. We could go there on Tuesday?"

"Sure," Neil agreed. "How about six-thirty?"

"That's great."

With their new date settled and their clothing on, there was nothing left to do.

"I guess I'd better go," Neil said.

"I'll walk you to the car."

Neil nodded and they made their way through the house. Neil had everything he'd brought with him, but Scott grabbed his phone, keys, and ducked into one of the other rooms in the house to collect the engagement present he'd purchased for the couple. They paused outside as Scott locked up, but all too soon, they were walking down the path to Neil's car.

Neil glanced down the street and spotted a middle-aged couple next door. They were sitting on their front porch, eyeing him curiously. After that, he quickly noticed a man was washing his car across the road and another woman was gardening. They glanced at him twice in less than a minute. Neil felt like there was a neon-sign over his head telling the street what he'd been doing with Scott. He tensed without realizing.

"Neil?" Scott asked. "Is something wrong?"

He dragged his gaze back to the fireman. Scott looked concerned.

"I think your neighbors might be putting two and two together."

Scott glanced around. The middle-aged couple waved, and he waved back. He turned back to Neil and gave a helpless shrug.

"Everyone's nice, but some of them can be a little nosy. Don't worry about it."

"You can always tell them a friend stayed over," Neil said, unlocking his car.

"Do you want me to?"

Neil paused with the door open. He looked back at Scott.

"Do *you* want to?"

"I've always been open about my relationships," Scott answered. "I don't want to hide that I'm dating you. I want you to meet the people in my life." He frowned. "Will that be a problem?"

I don't know.

He'd never hidden his sexuality. He'd walk unflinchingly through town wearing a pride flag and flip anyone off who didn't like it. But promoting a *relationship* was different. Neil knew it should be the same or even easier, but somehow it left his stomach squirming and his hands feeling clammy.

Is this the fear of commitment everyone accused me of?

The thought hardened his resolve. He wasn't afraid of people knowing he slept around. Why did it matter if people knew about him and Scott?

"No," Neil said decisively, refusing to second-guess it. "That's fine."

Scott grinned. He also leaned in and kissed him. Neil froze. He felt overly aware of everything — the heat of the sun, the metal of the car door under his palm and the sounds of the suburban neighborhood. He closed his eyes forcibly and kissed Scott back. He felt heat on the back of his neck and hoped to God he wasn't blushing.

I haven't blushed since I was a child.

Neil drew back after only a few moments. He didn't hold Scott's gaze as he sat down in the driver's seat.

"I'll see you on Tuesday, Scott."

"Can't wait." Neil dared to glance at the man, but Scott was watching him fondly. "See you then, Neil."

Shutting the door, Neil turned on the car and reversed out of Scott's driveway with a hint of relief. Scott waved to him, and Neil lifted his hand and returned it, hoping he didn't look too wooden. He could already see the old couple trying to call Scott over.

The neighbors are about to find out Scott has a new...boyfriend.

Neil gripped the steering wheel, feeling a rush of panic that he'd never experienced before. Not even the warmth of Scott's kiss could calm his suddenly racing heart or the lead in his stomach.

He was someone's boyfriend, and he wasn't sure if he should be.

* * * *

Neil tried to avoid his misgivings for the rest of the day. He tried to remember that even if their relationship fell apart, he wouldn't come out of it any worse off. He had to keep thinking of it as an experiment. His feelings were a confusing by-product but nothing he couldn't handle.

The next couple of days seemed to pass in the blink of an eye, and when Tuesday night finally came, Neil felt the same uncomfortable mixture of nerves and uncertainty. He had time for a quick shower and change at his apartment after work before he was heading for the restaurant.

Strings was in a part of town jam-packed with restaurants. Neil preferred the bars and popular single spots. This was a more relaxed *dating* environment. Everywhere he looked, there were couples. Neil parked down the street and lingered in his car.

What am I doing here?

But he knew the answer. Scott kept drawing him back. Their relationship was strange and discomforting at times, but it was *nice*. He still wanted to see where it could go.

Taking in a breath, Neil determinedly got out of his car and locked it. He made his way down the street toward the restaurant. He quickly spotted Scott waiting out front.

"Hey," he called.

Scott turned and grinned. He helped closed the distance and placed a hand on Neil's arm before pressing an affectionate kiss to his cheek. Neil's insides immediately felt scrambled. Scott pulled back but didn't let go of his arm.

"Hey… How was your day?"

"Fine," Neil answered. "The usual." He cleared his throat. "How was the engagement party?"

"Good. It—"

"Scottie?"

Scott stopped talking and they both looked to find who'd called him. Neil recognized the man who had spoken as the older, broad-shouldered fireman from their hotel in Brisbane. He was clasping the hand of a tall, dark-skinned woman.

"Paul," Scott greeted. "Cindy. Hi."

He stepped away from Neil and shook Paul's hand before kissing Cindy's cheek. Neil stood back awkwardly, but Scott didn't let him linger there long. He turned and gestured at Neil.

"This is Neil."

"We met at the hotel," Paul said, a hint of a smile on his lips. He held out his hand. "Scottie mentioned he bumped into you."

"Yeah, turns out we live in the same city," Neil answered, shaking the man's hand.

"What a lovely coincidence," Cindy said, taking and shaking Neil's hand in greeting. "It's a small world after all."

"A lucky world," Scott corrected.

His arm brushed Neil's before Scott caught his hand and linked their fingers. The gesture made it obvious they weren't out as friends. Cindy looked delighted, and Paul's smile spread wider. Neil felt a surge of his earlier panic.

"You boys eating at Strings, too?" Paul asked.

"Yeah," Scott agreed. "It's always good on a band night."

"Excellent. Feel like a drink beforehand?"

"Paul!" Cindy chastised. "We don't want to interrupt their evening."

Paul didn't look repentant and neither did he take it back. Neil glanced at Scott. He already knew his lover would want to accept.

This will prove I can handle this 'relationship' thing.

"I think a drink would be fine," Neil said. "We're not in a rush. Right, Scott?"

Scott smiled and squeezed Neil's hand. He turned back to Paul and Cindy.

"Yeah," he agreed. "A quick drink would be great."

"Excellent," Paul repeated.

They needed no further discussion, and the four of them made their way inside. The restaurant opened onto a large space filled with tables, half of which were already full. There was a bar to the right while the back of the room hosted a stage with musicians setting up. There was an open door on the left, which revealed a quaint beer garden with at least five sitting areas.

"Scottie and I will grab the drinks," Paul declared. "You two find us somewhere in the beer garden."

"White wine, please, Paul," Cindy requested.

"Neil?" Scott asked.

"Just a beer, thanks."

The moment he'd given his order, Paul placed a hand on Scott's shoulder and directed him to the bar. Cindy started heading for the beer garden and Neil fell into step with her.

"I apologize for my husband," she said. "But that's how he and the company are. If they see one another, they always need to stop and chat. It doesn't matter if they were only talking a half-hour prior. They just can't walk away."

"I doubt that's the only reason he wants to talk," Neil pointed out.

Everyone would be curious about him. Scott had told him about the company, and while he hadn't given an outright warning, Neil could read between the lines. If the group were as close as they seemed, potential partners would need to be vetted. He would have to prove he was worthy of Scott—something Neil doubted he'd be capable of over extended periods.

He could be charming and good with people. He had to be in his job. But it was a persona that he couldn't maintain indefinitely.

It's just a drink. You've lasted longer at manager meetings.

"Paul can be protective," Cindy acknowledged, returning Neil's attention to the conversation. "And he's always looked out for Scottie."

"It's nice that Scott has people who care about him," Neil answered. "I can imagine Scott doing the same for his friends."

"Yes," Cindy agreed. "The company would do anything for those they consider family. It's a wonderful group but" — she sent him an apologetic look — "they can be intimidating."

"I'm not easily intimidated."

"Good," she told him. "You'll need to be strong."

Neil frowned. "Why?"

Cindy didn't answer immediately as they entered the beer garden. They were lucky enough to find an empty table toward the back and took seats opposite each other. It wasn't until she'd put down her purse that she returned to their conversation.

"Because you'll need strength," she said, finally answering his question. "It can be hard to date and love a fireman."

Oh.

Neil hadn't forgotten what Scott did, but it felt like a bucket of water had been upended over him. Cindy hadn't given specifics, but Neil's mind was quick to paint a hundred pictures. Fighting fires wasn't a safe job. Scott, and the other men and women in his company, went into the heart of a blaze while everyone else fled for safety. A chill went down his spine. He didn't love Scott. He wasn't even sure *what* he felt for Scott, but it didn't mean he wanted the man in danger.

Neil felt a different twist to his stomach. It also made him want to shift so that he could look into the restaurant and search for Scott. Neil forced the impulse down, not wanting to seem ridiculous. Scott was at the bar. He was *fine*.

But it doesn't mean he always will be.

"It's normal to feel worry and fear," Cindy said when he hadn't responded. "But for every moment you feel that, there will be thousands more filled with joy." She smiled softly. "And Scottie is a wonderful man."

"Yeah," Neil murmured, "he is."

Cindy's expression remained warm and friendly even as she changed the subject. "So, you met Scottie when he and Paul were away on their training course?"

"Yeah," Neil agreed. "I was at the same hotel for a manager's meeting."

"What kind of work do you do?"

"I manage a men's clothing store."

"Oh!" She brightened. "I used to manage a jewelry store before marrying Paul." She chuckled and shook her head. "Now, I manage three children and just work part-time."

"*Three* children?" Neil commented. "Are you sure you stopped working full-time?"

Cindy laughed. "Oh, some days it certainly feels busier than the jewelry store, but I wouldn't trade it. Although" — she leaned in conspiratorially — "when my sister offers to babysit and give us a night off, I don't say no."

Neil chuckled, but before he could reply, Scott and Paul appeared at the table. He was glad to have his lover back, but Cindy's warning still lingered in his mind. On top of that, he doubted Paul would be as easy to appease as Cindy. Scott placed a beer in front of him and slipped into place beside Neil, pressing their thighs and arms together.

"What did we miss?" Scott asked.

"Oh, nothing. We were just getting acquainted," Cindy answered.

She took her wine from Paul and kissed his cheek in gratitude.

"So, Neil," Paul said. "Have you been to Strings before?"

"No, it's my first time."

"You've picked a good night," Cindy interjected, her eyes twinkling with good humor. "They usually have a dance floor on Tuesdays."

"Do they?"

Neil flicked a glance to Scott. The only dancing he'd ever done was at a gay club and that was more of a full-body grind than swaying to music.

"We might leave the dancing to you and Paul," Scott said. He gave a sheepish laugh. "You know I have two left feet."

"Never seen anything wrong with your dancing," Paul disagreed. "Ben's wife always dances with you."

"That's because Ben has all the grace of a newborn foal. Anyone is an improvement."

The group laughed. It was the same easy, relaxed banter from the hotel, but this time Neil could appreciate the way Scott's face lit up with warmth and affection.

"Think you'll be able to tempt Scottie to dance tonight, Neil?" Paul asked.

Neil shrugged. "I can give it a crack, but I can't say I'll be much of an improvement."

"You say that now," Scott said with a laugh. "Wait until you're working with the beat and I've stood on your foot for the third time."

Neil snorted. "I'll have that problem fixed long before we get to three."

"That confident?" Scott asked, still grinning. "Thought you weren't good at dancing."

"Dancing? No. But, I'm good at managing people."

"You mean being bossy," Scott teased.

"You haven't complained yet."

"No," Scott agreed, "I haven't."

Neil's mind drifted back to their time in the bedroom when he'd given Scott an order and he'd followed it without complaint—when he'd let Neil *dress* him. The memory of sex should have been stronger in his mind, but instead, his fingers tingled remembering the feel of Scott's shirt as he'd fixed it.

Neil didn't realize how long he'd been staring at Scott with a small smile until Cindy broke the moment.

"Well," she said, "the music's started. Get to it."

Neil startled. He'd forgotten they weren't alone. He'd *forgotten* that he'd all but agreed to dance publicly with Scott.

"I'm game if you are," Scott said.

Neil knew he could back out and everyone would brush it aside with a laugh.

This shouldn't be any different from what I do in a club. It'll be tame *in comparison.*

Despite his words of confidence, Neil took a mouthful of his beer for added encouragement before standing. He held out his hand and Scott took it without hesitation. They made their way into the restaurant with Paul and Cindy close behind. It was much louder than the beer garden. People were ordering food or eating as the band played in the back. The restaurant had left an open space free of tables to allow a dance floor, but there was no one dancing yet.

They didn't go directly to the floor, choosing to find a table to place down their half-finished beers. Paul and Cindy did the same across the room. Neil could feel the eyes of other patrons on them as they took a place at the edge of the dance floor. Neil's hands felt too large and awkward as he laid them on Scott's hips, and his lover's arms looped around his waist. The lights obscured most of the room from view, but Neil still knew everyone could see them.

"I hope meeting Paul and Cindy wasn't too much," Scott said.

"It was fine. They're nice."

"They like you already. I can tell."

"Do they?"

"Yeah," Scott answered. "I knew they would."

Neil glanced away. He didn't feel comfortable hearing that. It felt like he'd been complicit in a lie. He wanted his dates with Scott to go well and he wanted the man's friends to at least *like* him, but it still didn't feel right when it happened. He was still waiting for something to go wrong.

But he didn't want to ruin their evening.

It was why, instead of answering, he pressed his lips to Scott's in a kiss. He hoped it conveyed something positive, because he didn't know what to say.

Chapter Seven

They danced until the song ended.

Scott rested their cheeks together as they swayed, and by the end, Neil even stopped feeling like a fraud. Afterward, they took a seat at their table and ordered their meal. They talked about music and dancing. Scott told humorous stories about past weddings and social gatherings. Neil steered the conversation away from the times he'd been grinding on a dance floor. When they left Strings, it was late, but Scott took hold of his hand as they paused outside the restaurant.

"Do you need to go home?" Scott asked.

Neil worked in the morning, but it wasn't enough to make him refuse.

"I can stay over."

Scott smiled and pulled him into a kiss. It was more heated than the one they'd shared while dancing. They parted to go to their cars, but Neil's body was already alight with desire. Scott's house was closer to Strings than the steakhouse had been, allowing them to arrive sooner. The neighbors' lights were out, which Neil was grateful to see. There were only the streetlights and stars to illuminate the way. They walked up the path eagerly and the moment they stepped into his house, Scott kissed him. Neil gripped Scott's shoulders and pressed him against the wall. The kiss only rekindled the flames of his desire. When it broke, Neil immediately pressed his mouth to Scott's neck, mouthing at his skin. Scott tilted into his touch, sliding his hands up and down Neil's waist.

"I was going to put on music," Scott murmured, "so we could dance again."

Neil stilled. It had been discomforting to dance in public. He wasn't sure if it would be worse doing it in Scott's home. The intimacy of it was too unnerving. He didn't want to find out if he liked it or not.

"I'd rather be doing something else," Neil said, grazing his teeth over Scott's throat.

He felt his lover swallow. When Scott spoke, his voice came out hoarse. "Well, we can always put music on for that, too."

"I don't want to wait for you to find a good playlist."

Scott laughed. "Fine. No music."

Neil tried not to show his relief, but the darkness of the house made it easier. The streetlights gave them enough to see by but still kept them in shadow. Scott eased him back, but he also took Neil's hand and led him down the hall. Neil felt that same uncomfortable stirring in his stomach, but a warmth in his chest followed it. Neil didn't want to analyze what any of it meant. It was easier to focus on Scott.

When they reached the bedroom, Scott moved to turn on the light, but Neil stopped him with a kiss. Neil cupped Scott's face and used his mouth to distract his lover. Neil felt like he'd been under a spotlight all night, so he found comfort in the darkness. He wasn't searching for anonymity or to pretend he was with someone else. Neil just wanted something simple and familiar. He wanted the ability to hide what he was feeling where nobody could see.

Tugging off Scott's shirt when they split apart, Neil admired the shadowed plains of his lover's chest. Scott started pulling at his clothes and they made their way to the bed, stripping as they went until they hit the mattress. Scott kissed him again while running his hands over Neil's back.

They only broke the kiss to climb onto the bed. Scott grabbed the condoms and lube, and Neil was grateful when he didn't turn on the lamp. Scott slid between his thighs and kissed him. Neil spread his legs wider, making it obvious what he wanted.

Scott didn't draw out the foreplay. He prepared him while placing kisses along his collarbone and neck. Neil curled into his lover's touches, letting out soft groans as the fireman worked. When Scott replaced his fingers with his cock, Neil arched his back and moaned Scott's name. He wrapped his legs around his lover and clutched the man's back as Scott thrust into him. The fireman panted against his jaw, placing the occasional kiss against his skin. He set an easy rhythm and Neil soon wrapped a hand around his cock, stroking it in time with his lover's movements.

When his orgasm crashed over him, Neil groaned Scott's name. His lover continued to pound into him a few more times before he moaned his release against Neil's neck. His lover's weight rested on top of him, but Neil didn't move him. It felt strangely nice.

But all too soon, Scott climbed off him and the bed but he still didn't turn on the lamp. The action had Neil frowning. Scott went to the bathroom and came back with a cloth. He ran it over Neil's stomach, but when he went to leave, Neil reached up and snagged his wrist.

"You're not turning a light on," Neil said.

"You seemed to want them off."

There was no accusation or annoyance in Scott's voice. He just sounded accepting. It made something twinge pleasantly inside Neil's chest.

"And that doesn't bother you?"

"No," Scott said.

He leaned down and kissed him. Neil cupped Scott's neck and pulled him even closer, trying to say without words how much he appreciated it. Scott stroked his cheek and gentled the kiss until it was a languid, relaxed brushing of mouths. Scott then finished it with a kiss on his cheek. Neil removed his hand regretfully so his lover could leave for the bathroom. It felt like too long by the time Scott reappeared.

"Do you work tomorrow?" Scott asked.

"Yeah."

"Want me to set an alarm?"

"Yeah."

Scott grabbed his phone and just like that, Neil was staying another night. Neil would have expected to feel awkward about everything that had happened, but the darkness helped. When Scott slipped between the sheets, he immediately pressed against Neil and wrapped an arm around his waist. Neil relaxed into the embrace, his back flush against Scott's chest. Scott kissed his shoulder and Neil closed his eyes.

"Thanks," Neil whispered.

His voice was so soft that he wasn't sure Scott would hear it. He also didn't know if Scott would understand all it encompassed. But when Scott kissed his shoulder again, Neil hoped he had. It just seemed easier to allow a softer intimacy when nobody could see.

* * * *

When Neil woke in the morning, it was to a hand stroking his chest. He blinked open his eyes and looked over his shoulder. The room was lit by the faint glow of early morning light, and Scott was smiling.

"Morning," he said.

"Morning." Neil rubbed his eyes. "What time is it?"

"Almost seven. The alarm will go off soon."

Neil groaned and buried his face back in the pillow. Scott chuckled.

"Do you want me to make you a coffee?"

Neil smiled, feeling relaxed and content. He didn't second-guess his ease. He turned fully until he was lying on his back and looking up at Scott.

"I hope that isn't a trick question."

"It's too early for trick questions."

Neil's smile widened, and Scott grinned in response.

"I can make you some breakfast, too," Scott added.

Neil was incredibly tempted, especially when he still wanted kitchen sex with Scott, but he also knew it wouldn't work.

"I won't have the time," Neil said regretfully. "I have to get home, shower and change."

Scott sighed. "I wish you could stay longer."

"Yeah," Neil said, feeling comfortable enough to admit the truth. "Me too."

There were a few seconds of quiet where Scott stroked Neil's chest and Neil closed his eyes, almost drifting back to sleep

"Neil," Scott began. He grunted an acknowledgement. "I was wondering how you felt about meeting Paul and Cindy."

Neil cracked open an eye, feeling wary. "It was fine. Why?"

"I was wondering if you'd be okay meeting a few more people this Saturday."

Neil tensed, instantly feeling on edge. Two people had been bad enough.

How many more does he want me to meet?

"Why would I be meeting people on Saturday?"

"My baseball team is playing a game."

Neil felt like a deer caught in the headlights, and unfortunately, Scott was watching his reactions closely. He probably saw his instinctive panic and discomfort.

"Most of your company will be there, won't they?" Neil asked, trying not to sound as uncomfortable as he felt.

"The ones who have the day off, yeah."

Nothing like a chance to screw everything up on a grand scale.

Because it was one thing to meet Paul and Cindy by chance but another to show up at an event where most of Scott's friends would attend.

"We usually play for two to three hours and then we go out for lunch," Scott continued. "I'd like to introduce you to everyone."

Neil felt incredibly self-conscious in a way he'd never experienced before. He also felt *afraid*. Things had been going better than he'd expected. Scott had accepted everything Neil had thrown at him with nothing more than a smile and a laugh. He didn't want to ruin the good thing they had before he'd been able to fully enjoy it.

"Are you sure that's a good idea?" Neil asked cautiously. "We've only been out a few times."

"Does that matter?" Scott asked. "If I want to introduce you and you want to come, shouldn't that be all that counts?"

Neil didn't have an argument. He could either say yes or he could say no. Despite his worries, Neil didn't want to disappoint Scott. He'd already told Cindy that he wasn't easily intimidated. Would he really let a few firefighters scare him off?

If it all turns to shit, it's better it happens now before I get used to this relationship.

"What time does the game start?"

"Ten," Scott answered. "Everyone normally arrives around nine-thirty."

Neil nodded. "All right. I'll come to the game."

Scott beamed. He also ducked in and kissed Neil. Closing his eyes, Neil kissed back. He ran his hand over Scott's back.

It feels nice, making him happy.

The sound of his alarm cut off anything further. They pulled apart and Scott rolled over to turn it off.

Regretfully, Neil pushed into a sitting position, and Scott turned back on his side to look at him, disappointment clear on his face.

"Time to go?"

"Yeah," Neil answered. "I'll be late if I don't leave soon."

"I guess we'll have to get up."

Despite his words, neither of them moved. The sheet pooled around Scott's waist and Neil stroked his chest, moving up to circle a nipple before trailing his fingers up Scott's neck and under his jaw. It was already rough with the start of stubble, and he wanted to run his lips over it and feel the tickle on his skin. Scott caught Neil's hand. He then slipped his fingers down to trace the swirls of the tattoo on Neil's wrist. He traced the circle in the center before stroking each of the curling rays.

"What made you get a sun?"

It was the first time any of his lovers had ever asked that question.

"I wanted to symbolize new beginnings and rising anew," Neil answered. "I'd just turned eighteen and liked the imagery." He chuckled. "I thought it was the height of genius." He sobered. "I came out as gay to my family on the same day."

"How did they react?"

"Ironically, my parents were more upset about the tattoo than about me being gay."

"That's the better thing to be upset over."

"Yeah," Neil said, thinking back to that day. "I'd had a pretty good idea they'd be okay—or have already worked it out. My youngest brother just wanted to get back to his PlayStation."

Scott sniggered, but he never stopped tracing Neil's tattoo. The touch was comforting, and it kept Neil lingering on the bed.

"Do you only have one brother?" Scott asked.

"No," Neil replied. "I've also got an older one." He finally looked at Scott. "What about you? Any siblings?"

"Three younger sisters," Scott answered with a smile.

"And they know?" Neil asked.

It seemed ridiculous that they wouldn't when Scott was so open about his sexuality, but Neil didn't want to assume.

"Yeah. I started telling people when I was fifteen." He chuckled. "And they love that I'm gay. They used to drag me to all their girls' nights and out to bars to look for guys." He shook his head fondly. "But it hasn't happened for a while. One's married now, and the other two are in long-term relationships."

"What about your parents?" Neil asked, curious to know about what had happened. He'd never asked someone these questions. "How did they react?"

"Mum said she'd suspected for a while and was waiting for me to feel comfortable enough to tell her. My dad? Well, he's actually my stepdad. He frowned and declared, *'Well, we need to have a different version of the sex talk. I'll go get a banana.'*"

Neil laughed loudly, imagining Scott's mortified face. Scott laughed as well, and it took them a few seconds to recover.

"He sounds like fun."

"He is. Full of terrible dad-jokes, though."

"Aren't all dads?"

Yet Neil's humor soon faded over his next question. He asked it carefully, unsure if it was a sensitive topic.

"But, if he's your stepdad, what about your father?"

"He died when I was three."

"Shit. I'm sorry."

Scott shook his head. "It's okay. I don't really remember him. Mum remarried when I was six. Donovan, my stepdad, already had a daughter from his first marriage, and I soon got two more sisters. I couldn't have asked for a better family."

Neil relaxed, grateful that he didn't have to navigate an emotional conversation.

"They sound great."

"They are. Some of them might be at the game, actually. They try to come when they can."

Neil felt a cold sweat break out. It was one thing to meet friends and work colleagues, another to meet Scott's *family*.

"Hey," Scott said, obviously noticing his mounting panic, "don't worry about it. You'll be fine."

Neil didn't reply. He could already see a thousand ways it could go wrong. More than that, he felt a growing nausea at being surrounded by people who all expected a *boyfriend*. Everyone loved Scott. What the hell were they going to think when they met *him*?

Scott squeezed his hand, and Neil focused back on the room.

"You don't have to come if it's too much," Scott said, looking concerned. "I want you to have fun. I want you to *want* to be there. Don't feel like you have to attend."

Neil wanted to back out. If he were honest, he wanted to leap out of bed, give an excuse and avoid all Scott's text messages until the whole situation went away. But if he ran, he'd never have another morning with Scott. He'd lose *everything*. Somehow, that was even more distressing than being thrust into a family meeting.

Rip it off like a Band-Aid. Scott's worth the attempt, isn't he?

"I'll come," Neil said firmly.

"Yeah?" Scott asked, excitement lighting up his face.

"Yeah," Neil admitted, admiring the happiness his lover exuded.

Scott kissed him. "You won't regret it."

"We'll see," Neil said neutrally, not wanting to get either of their hopes up. "But, right now, I need to go to work."

He moved away from Scott and climbed out of bed. Scott was quick to follow.

"If you want to get changed, I can make you coffee in a thermos to take?"

"Won't you need it?"

"Not today." Scott grinned. "And it gives me an excuse to come by and see you later." He winked. "Maybe, you'll convince me to buy another shirt."

"Your wardrobe is atrocious. You should definitely let me."

Scott laughed. "Then, I'd better stop by. You take lunch at one, yeah?"

"Yeah."

"How about we head to Toasted Beans again?"

"All right," Neil said, actually feeling excited by the prospect.

"Great. I'll go make the coffee."

He grabbed his boxers, and after giving Neil another peck on the cheek, left the bedroom. Neil watched him leave with a shake of his head and fond amusement. Neil started picking up his clothes and got dressed. When he finished, he went to the kitchen and found Scott filling a silver thermos. He screwed on the lid a few moments later and held it out to him. Neil took the coffee, feeling the warmth seep into his hand. It seemed to go throughout his body and rest in the center of his chest.

Is this what waking up with a boyfriend feels like?

Neil's stomach seemed to do a somersault. *Boyfriend.* He'd never put it into words with anyone, not even Rich. He'd never felt ready to *admit* it. But looking at Scott and planning to meet his *family* made it all too obvious what he was — what Scott wanted him to *be*.

"I have to go," Neil said.

"I'll walk you to the door."

Scott came around and touched his back. His hand was a firm pressure between his shoulder blades, and Neil walked to the door in a daze. He unlocked it and Neil stepped outside automatically. He paused and looked at the suburban neighborhood and the thermos in his hand.

All we need is a dog or a child and I might as well be the husband.

Neil swallowed, entirely unprepared for any of the thoughts or feelings rushing around inside him like a pinball machine.

"I'll see you at one?" Scott asked.

"Uh, yeah," Neil replied.

Scott touched his shoulder and Neil turned. Scott captured his lips in a kiss and Neil closed his eyes. He leaned into Scott's touch, feeling his racing thoughts calm down a little as he focused on the brush of their mouths. When Scott stepped away, Neil didn't want to open his eyes.

When he did, he found Scott leaning against the doorframe, his arms crossed over his naked chest and grinning.

Neil wanted to throw away the thermos, call in sick and fuck Scott against the nearest flat surface. He wanted to kiss him until they ended up back in bed and Neil didn't have to think about what any of this meant.

Resisting the urge to give in to his impulses, Neil smiled and hoped it looked genuine rather than tense. He turned away and walked to his car but couldn't help glancing at the thermos again. No one had ever done that for him nor had anyone inspired so many conflicting emotions.

But then, this was the first time he'd had a boyfriend. So far, even the panic had been worth it. He hoped the feelings would be, too.

Chapter Eight

His lunch date with Scott was just as enjoyable as the first, which helped ease many of his worries. Scott had arrived before one and bought two more shirts, along with a pair of slacks. They'd then bickered about clothing as they ate lunch and, after walking Neil back, Scott kissed him goodbye.

Even Denise's good-natured teasing and questions about their relationship couldn't dim his good mood.

But as the weekend slowly approached, his earlier dread returned. Scott was busy at work, and with one of his co-workers sick, he'd picked up an extra night duty shift. They'd barely had time to text, let alone see each other before the game. Neil's discomfort grew into a lead ball in his stomach. Twice, he got out his phone to message Scott saying he couldn't come, but both times, he stopped at the last moment. He kept remembering Scott's excitement. Neil didn't want to be the one to ruin it.

When Saturday finally arrived, Neil got ready with a sinking feeling in his gut. Arriving at the venue wavered Neil's resolve. There were at least a hundred people. They were parking their cars or milling about and talking in large groups. He hadn't expected such a big crowd.

Since when has baseball been so popular in Australia? Then again, it might just be Scott's team that's popular.

Neil parked his car and climbed out. He felt anxious as he walked closer to the brick club house. Neil was in his usual button-up shirt and slacks. He looked overdressed compared to the sea of jeans and polo shirts.

One more reason I don't fit in.

Neil trailed his gaze over the crowd, searching for Scott's familiar profile. He spotted him standing beside the metal stands overlooking the pitch and talking with four people. Scott was in his baseball uniform. The body of the shirt was dark blue while the sleeves were white to match his pants. It was easy to pick out the rest of his team and the opposing side. A member of Scott's team was standing beside him, along with another man and two women.

No turning back now.

Neil drew in a fortifying breath and walked forward. Scott had been listening to his team member speak, but his attention had also been flicking over the crowd. It meant he was quick to notice Neil's approach. When he did, he grinned.

"Neil," he called, his enthusiasm carrying through in his voice.

The people with him turned to watch his arrival. One woman was smiling widely. When Neil reached them, Scott wrapped an arm around his waist and pecked his lips in a kiss. They slotted together easily, despite Neil's mounting tension.

"This is Russell and his fiancée, Debbie," Scott said, beginning the introductions. "I went to their engagement party on the weekend."

They were both tall, blond and lean. Neil shook their hands. "Nice to meet you."

"This is Lisa, my youngest sister." Scott indicated to the still-grinning brunette before turning to the man in a matching baseball uniform. "And Leslie, her boyfriend."

Neil shook their hands while keeping his customer service smile on his face. He hoped it could hide the apprehension he was feeling.

"It's great to finally meet you, Neil," Lisa said.

"Finally?"

"Cindy mentioned you. I've already punched Scott for not letting me meet you first."

"I didn't do it deliberately," Scott complained.

"No excuse. We had a pact."

Neil looked between them with puzzlement. "A pact?"

Scott sighed, but explained, "We were teenagers. The only way they allowed me to meet and scrutinize their boyfriends was if they got the same opportunity with mine."

"Ah," Neil said, not knowing what else to say.

"Maybe you should do a different pact," Leslie said, seeming to take pity on him. "Like *let's not ambush the boyfriend after only a few dates*?" Leslie sent Neil a look full of commiseration. "All three of them descended on me on the fifth date."

"But where would the fun be in that?" Lisa asked, smirking deviously.

Leslie rolled his eyes, but he also wrapped an arm around his girlfriend's shoulders.

"You're lucky I'm an only child or I would have returned the favor."

Unfortunately, the words turned Lisa's attention back to him and Scott.

"Maybe that's what Scott has to look out for in the coming weeks. Sibling ambushes."

Neil felt a jolt. He'd never even *considered* introducing Scott to his family. He'd never brought a lover home, let alone told his family about one. The idea felt foreign and disorientating to imagine.

"Nah," Neil said, pushing aside his unease for an easier excuse. "I grew up in New South Wales. It would be hard to get my brothers up here on short notice."

"Oh?" Russell chimed in for the first time. "Whereabouts? I grew up in Ballina."

"Kings Cliff, up near Tweed," Neil replied. "But I've been down there to visit the Big Prawn."

Russell laughed while Debbie shook her head.

"You Australians and your 'big things'," she said, a noticeable accent curling her words.

"Sorry we can't be like you English and have big castles," Russell teased.

The group all gave soft chuckles, which made Neil wonder if it wasn't a well-worn topic of discussion. He didn't have time to ponder it as Lisa was quick to pounce on him again.

"So, Neil—"

"Look over there, Lisa," Leslie interjected loudly. He turned toward the club house, using his arm to guide Lisa. "We should go see what they're talking about."

"Leslie!" she complained.

"It looks very interesting," he insisted, continuing to practically drag her away.

He threw a brief look and wink over his shoulder. It was easily translatable as *'you're welcome'*. Russell and Debbie also politely excused themselves to *'catch up with some people'*. It left them alone.

"Sorry," Scott said, looking sheepish. "Lisa doesn't really have a filter."

Neil felt a little ruffled, but it wasn't from Lisa's abrupt nature. He'd known attending the game would come with its share of questions. His uncertainty stemmed from what she'd inadvertently made him picture. Scott meeting *his* family. It was almost more terrifying than meeting Scott's. He forcibly shoved it aside, not needing a new ball of anxiety to unravel.

"It's fine," Neil said. His gaze did dart over the crowd, finding Lisa already watching them. He looked back at Scott. "Did she come here specifically to meet me?"

"No. She was already coming to see Leslie play. She, ah, asked if you'd be attending, though."

"Am I a hot topic among your family?"

"I haven't had a serious boyfriend in quite a while. They want to get to know you." He squeezed Neil's hip. "And I want them to see how great you are."

Neil felt surprised and a little bit flattered. His stomach twisted with pleasure.

"You haven't had someone?"

"No," Scott said. "I was always happy to wait until I met someone I really liked."

Neil swallowed, feeling a lump form in his throat. He couldn't hold Scott's gaze. He focused on the grass at their feet. He didn't know what to say, but he curled his arm around Scott's waist in response. Scott squeezed his hip again. Their embrace somehow became not just affectionate but supportive. Neil found the tension in his shoulders slowly unwinding until he was leaning a little more against Scott. His gaze soon moved from the ground to scan the crowd. Scott hadn't said a word, letting him collect his thoughts and composure in silence.

When Neil spotted Lisa laughing with her boyfriend and a few other members of the team, fresh determination flooded him.

Scott thinks I'm worth introducing. Scott likes me. I'm new to this, but goddamn it, I'm going to give it my best shot.

"Introduce me to everyone," Neil said. "And explain the game to me."

He looked back at Scott, finding the man smiling.

"I'm happy to do that. I didn't realize you knew so little about baseball."

"I don't know much about any sports," Neil admitted with a wince. "I get bored by them."

Scott, rather than being offended, merely laughed. He also unwound his arm, much to Neil's regret, but he took Neil's hand and started walking them away from the bleachers.

"Well, I'm glad you're willing to sit through three hours of *my* game."

"Well, that's different," Neil answered absently. "The game has you."

Scott stilled, and Neil's breath caught as the words registered. So far, he'd admitted nothing definitive. Scott had been the one to drop "*I like you*" while he'd only admitted to enjoying their time together. Confessing that he was sticking around for *three hours* on his day off just because of Scott? It was terrifyingly damning.

Before Neil could panic and try to bolt for the exit, Scott said quietly, "The game's already better, having you here with me."

The matching confession eased Neil's racing heart. He dared to glance at Scott but only found his lover smiling. When Scott caught his gaze, he leaned forward to brush their lips together. Neil closed his eyes, immediately feeling better.

"Come on," Scott said when they broke away.

He squeezed Neil's hand before starting them walking again. They weaved between the groups with Scott gaining waves and greetings. He returned all of them, but he didn't stop. It took Neil a few moments to realize where he was heading. Paul and Cindy were with a group of adults and children. There were picnic blankets littering the area, along with toys and snacks for the children. Paul was in his baseball outfit, along with three others. Cindy noticed them first and waved.

"Neil!" she greeted. "How wonderful you could make it."

A few people glanced at him, but with the children keeping their parents occupied, most of them were soon turning away. Paul had a little girl on his hip who couldn't have been over five. Neil didn't know which of the other children were theirs.

When they got near, Paul held out the hand not supporting his daughter.

"Neil, good to see you again," he said, sounding genuine.

They shook hands while Cindy came over and kissed him and Scott on the cheek.

"Did you have a nice week at work, Neil?" Cindy asked.

"Yeah," he agreed. "Busy, as always." Noticing the curious gaze of their daughter, Neil offered her a smile and a small wave. "Hello."

She waved back shyly and murmured a quiet, "Hi."

"I thought Neil could sit with you guys," Scott said. "My sister's trying to mount a thorough inquisition."

Cindy snorted. "Yes, that sounds like Lisa. I'm surprised you shook her loose."

"I probably owe Leslie a beer for that."

"With any luck, we'll be having victory drinks over lunch," Paul said. He nodded at the other team in their yellow and white uniforms. "I think we're in for a good chance."

"They haven't played well this season," Scott agreed.

"And we haven't been sick this season," one of the other players said, coming forward. "This time last year we had half the team out with that stomach bug."

The other two players gravitated toward their group, nodding and joining in.

"Leslie's the best pitcher we've ever had," another one said. "And we've always had Scott and Jackson as our top batters."

Neil felt a small flush of pride at Scott being one of the best.

"Odds are in our favor," Paul acknowledged, scanning the spectators. "Looks like it's getting time to start."

Neil glanced down at the field where members of both teams were heading. There were nods and words of agreement as the team turned to their families. Paul exchanged a few words with his wife and daughter.

"You'll be all right?"

Neil turned back to Scott. He raised his eyebrows at the man's concerned expression.

"I am a grown adult. I think I can handle watching a baseball game."

"Even if Lisa ambushes you?"

Neil felt a small jolt of anxiousness but refused to let it show.

"I'm not afraid of your sister," he drawled.

"Even without a buffer?"

"I have Cindy to protect me, remember?" He placed his free hand on Scott's chest and caught Scott's lips in a brief kiss. "I'll be fine. Go make home runs — or whatever else it is you do to win a baseball game."

Scott chuckled. "Home runs help."

"Then go make some," Neil repeated.

He patted Scott's chest before dropping his hand and taking a step back. Scott kept their fingers interlaced.

"Do I get a victory kiss if we win?"

"I'll give you one even if you lose."

Scott beamed and he tugged Neil back for one more quick peck before he let Neil's hand go and started walking down to the field. Neil watched him go with a smile curling his lips.

"Neil?"

He dragged his gaze from Scott to look at Cindy. She was sitting on the picnic blanket with her daughter and two boys. One of them looked to be the same age as the girl while the other was older. Cindy was beckoning Neil to join them. Neil took the free spot beside Cindy. Her daughter was sitting between her legs and her youngest son was beside her on the other side. Her oldest boy was at the edge of the blanket, his eyes riveted on the field.

There were more picnic blankets and some fold-out chairs to their left. Neil saw Russell and Debbie take a seat on some green chairs closer to the field. Neil noticed the curious gazes of a few women on him. He was just waiting for Lisa to appear and zero in on him.

"Have you watched much baseball?" Cindy asked.

"My first time," he admitted. "I was never much of a sports person."

"Well, it's fairly simple, but I can explain anything if you're unsure."

"Thanks," Neil said. "Mostly, I just plan to clap when everyone else does and hopefully cheer at the right time."

Cindy laughed. "That works as well."

Neil was about to say more when he heard footsteps on the grass a moment before someone dropped down beside him. It didn't surprise him to see it was Lisa.

"Have I missed anything?" she asked. "Grilled Neil in my absence, have you, Cindy?"

"Not unless you count asking him about baseball."

"I don't count it," she answered cheerfully.

She then pinned Neil with a look. Neil felt a little like he was talking to Denise. He decided to handle it the same way he'd deal with her. He cut to the chase.

"What do you want to know about me?"

"Are you going to break my brother's heart?"

The blunt question startled him, as did the wave of protectiveness the thought brought.

I don't want Scott hurt. I don't want to be the one to do it.

"I'm going to try not to."

"You're in it for the long haul?"

That one was trickier, especially considering he'd barely grazed the subject with Scott. It didn't feel right confessing it to the man's sister before he'd spoken to Scott.

"Neither of us wants something casual," he hedged.

Lisa narrowed her eyes. "Can you handle him being a fireman? You won't break up with him six months down the line claiming it's 'too much'?"

"*Lisa,*" Cindy groaned.

"I can't tell you that," Neil said, ignoring Cindy. "But I'm not oblivious to what his job entails."

"Hmm," Lisa hummed. "Well, at least you're honest."

"I don't see how lying would help me."

Lisa smiled, looking pleased by his answer.

"Well, I think I'll give you a pass for now."

"Really?" Neil asked, feeling startled.

"I like that you didn't suck up to me." She lifted her fingers in a gun gesture. "Straight shooter. Scott wouldn't do well with someone who couldn't tell it as it is."

"Oh," Neil said, still feeling mystified it had been so easy. "Well, that's good for me."

"It is," Lisa agreed. She then turned from him to Cindy. "How are things at work? That junior still being a pain?"

Cindy sighed and immediately regaled them with the problems with the newest staff member. Neil let out a surreptitious breath as their attention shifted away from him.

Was making her like me that easy? Surely, there has to be something I'm missing?

It was still early in the day. Neil wouldn't lower his guard after only one conversation.

* * * *

Surprisingly, Lisa didn't revisit her interrogation, but Cindy pulled him into the conversation about the highs and lows of working in customer service. Lisa worked in real estate and knew how tiresome people could be. They spoke until the game started when they were promptly distracted. Lisa was predictably loud. She stood up, cheered, whistled and shouted her support. Cindy was quieter, but her kids gleefully joined in with Lisa, and toward the end of the match, Neil was standing up and cheering, too. He couldn't help being swept up in the atmosphere, especially when Scott was up to bat.

Once, after a phenomenal home run, Scott had looked into the crowd, right at Neil, and gave a two-finger salute. Neil had clapped fiercely. When Scott's team won, Neil's cheeks hurt from the force of his grin. Scott, Paul and Leslie all came up to them after shaking the hands of the opposing team. Paul's children ran toward him, and Lisa walked up to greet Leslie, but Neil waited with a smile. Scott's outfit had grass and sweat stains. He'd pulled off his cap to reveal his sweat-slicked hair. He smelled and he was filthy, but Neil thought he was gorgeous. Neil cupped his lover's neck when Scott was close enough and hauled him in for a kiss.

Scott cradled his face, softening their embrace as their lips brushed slowly and their tongues briefly touched before Scott shifted and their lips parted.

"Spent the entire game waiting for my victory kiss," Scott murmured.

"You deserved it," Neil said, stroking his thumb along Scott's hairline. "You were great. Congratulations."

"I had a lucky charm with me."

"Oh?" Neil teased. "Four-leaf clover in your pocket?"

"More like a boyfriend on the sidelines."

Neil huffed a laugh. He also kissed Scott again, feeling Scott sigh against him. It didn't last anywhere near long enough as they *were* in public and surrounded by children. Their kisses still warmed Neil all the way through.

When they separated this time, Neil ran his gaze over Scott's uniform. He fingered the collar as a few thoughts ran through his mind. It surprised Neil that they hadn't occurred to him earlier.

"If I'm the lucky charm for the star baseball player, should I also be giving him a special reward for winning?"

Scott caught on and his eyes darkened.

"I would be willing to see what you had in mind," he said, his voice a little rougher.

Neil's smile turned devious.

I wonder if I could get him in his fireman uniform someday?

A baseball outfit could be a good way to test the waters.

"You boys coming to the celebration lunch?"

Paul's inquiry had Scott send him a questioning look. Neil shrugged. It hadn't been as bad as he'd feared. He could handle a little longer around Scott's friends and sister.

"I've got nowhere else to be," he said.

"Count us in," Scott said, turning to Paul.

The man didn't verbally respond. He was helping Cindy corral not only their kids but the others as well.

"I've got to shower," Scott continued, drawing Neil's attention. He stepped back. "I won't be long."

"All right," Neil said.

Scott headed toward the clubhouse. Neil didn't know how many shower stalls there were but considering there were two teams, he wasn't expecting Scott to be back for a while. He wasn't sure what to do, as Cindy was with her husband and Lisa was with Leslie. It left him standing to the side and watching the friendly, familiar interactions between the various men, women and families.

A small tug to his pants leg drew Neil's attention. It was Paul and Cindy's daughter.

"Hello," Neil said. "I don't think I know your name."

"Peta," she answered.

"I'm Neil."

She tilted her head in obvious confusion. "You kissed Uncle Scott."

Neil froze, feeling the back of his neck heat. He tried to figure out how to answer, but Peta was continuing undaunted. "Are you my Uncle Neil now?"

Neil's flush deepened, moving to cover his cheeks.

"Uh," he mumbled.

"Peta!" Cindy called, walking toward them while holding her youngest son's hands. "I hope you aren't bothering Neil?"

Oh, thank God for that.

"We were just introducing ourselves," Neil said, hoping to sidestep the whole 'Uncle Neil' thing.

"Well, you can always talk to Neil later," Cindy said. "We're all going out to lunch. Come on. We need to get everything to the car."

She offered her hand and Peta walked over and took it. She waved goodbye and Neil offered an awkward one back. Cindy smiled at him.

"Will you be fine waiting for Scott?"

"Yeah, don't worry about me," he said. "Go get your family sorted."

"Oh, I'll try," she said wryly.

She'd barely finished the words before her eldest son called for her. He was carrying their blanket, looking moments away from tripping. She hurriedly went over to help him. Paul wasn't to be found, but Neil assumed he'd gone into the clubroom to shower and change, too. He continued to feel out of place as he watched people pack up and leave.

When he spotted Lisa approaching, he turned to better face her, feeling less wary after their commiserative conversations about customer service.

"I won't be going to lunch," she said. "I've got to go into the office, but it was nice to meet you."

"You, too."

"I look forward to seeing you again."

"Yeah, that would be good."

Her eyes twinkled in a way that made him feel like he was missing something.

"Great. Say goodbye to my brother for me?"

"Sure."

Lisa offered him a grin and a wave before she left as well. It left him without a familiar face in sight. He pulled out his phone and checked for any messages. There were a couple from Denise and a forwarded Facebook post from his younger brother. He was so absorbed that when hands landed on his hips, he startled and looked behind him. Scott was grinning.

"Hope I didn't keep you waiting too long."

Neil closed his phone and pocketed it again. "It was fine. Also, your sister said goodbye."

"Thanks. I'm sure she'll message me later."

"With a list of all my pros and cons?" Neil suggested.

"I'm expecting nothing but positives," Scott insisted, drawing back.

He had a duffel bag on the ground, which Neil hadn't heard him drop. He picked it up before offering his hand. Neil felt momentarily bemused, but he took it and they walked toward the parking lot.

"Did you have fun?" Scott asked, a thread of nervousness entering his voice.

My attention didn't drift away from you or the game once.

He didn't feel comfortable saying that. He settled with a more neutral, teasing response.

"Yeah," Neil answered. "I didn't even try to sneak away like I did at my brothers' cricket games."

"Well, I feel special then," Scott replied, keeping his tone lighthearted. "Did you ever play on a team at school?"

"Nope. I was never sport-minded."

"I've always been in teams," Scott said. "Soccer and cricket at school."

"You really were the sports star, weren't you?"

Neil could just imagine Scott as a teenager. He'd be funny and kind, win games for the school and be the one all his classmates crushed on.

I wonder if I would have been able to convince him to make out behind the school sheds?

"Well, I wouldn't say *star*," Scott replied, pulling Neil from his thoughts. "I was good, but I wasn't the best."

"They say you're one of the best hitters on this team."

Scott looked away but Neil could see his flush of pride.

"Well, I try," he said modestly. He also changed the subject. "What are you doing tonight?"

"No plans."

"Do you want to come over for dinner?" Scott asked. "We can order in, or I can cook something."

An acceptance was on the tip of Neil's tongue, but he paused. Scott had been the one pushing things forward and so far, Neil had been warily following along. For once, Neil wanted to respond in kind—maybe even raise the stakes.

"Why don't you come over to my place and *I'll* cook dinner?"

Scott's expression softened into pleasant surprise.

"That sounds great."

Neil felt a small frisson of worry run through him. He couldn't help comparing his compact, impersonal unit with its unwashed dishes and messy bedroom to Scott's neat and welcoming suburban house.

But if I haven't scared him off, I doubt my crappy apartment will.

"So, what's the plan after lunch?"

"Nothing really. But lunch after a game can span a few hours and end with a barbecue at someone's house."

Neil wasn't surprised. He'd seen enough to know that any event that involved Scott's friends or fellow firefighters wouldn't have a quick getaway. So far, Neil had fit in fairly well.

"Well, don't go accepting a barbecue invite," Neil said. "We've got dinner plans."

"And miss a chance to have time with you alone? Not going to happen."

Neil's desire was quick to ignite. His earlier thoughts about Scott in uniform ran through his mind.

His cock gave an interested twitch. But, where Neil's mind had gone to the gutter, Scott's words had been light.

He probably meant just having time in my company.

His fondness for the man almost eclipsed Neil's desire. He let his gaze run over Scott as his lover directed them through the car park, taking care to avoid reversing cars and children. Scott had parked much closer to the clubhouse than Neil. They stopped in front of his car, and he unlocked it and tossed his duffel on the backseat. He shut the door and leaned against the car.

"Leslie said we're going to Hayfield Tavern. Know it?"

"Yeah, I've been there once."

"Next time, I should give you a lift to the game. We wouldn't have to go our separate ways."

"It's not like we'll be apart for very long."

"But I'd rather not give you up for any of it."

Scott's tone was teasing, but Neil's heart still skipped. He couldn't help closing the gap and kissing Scott again. He cupped Scott's waist and slotted his body along his lover's. Scott groaned and Neil deepened the kiss. He rolled their hips together, dragging a gasp from Scott's lips. He gripped Neil's shoulders and briefly arched against him.

Yet, before Neil could shift again, Scott was turning his head away.

"Neil," Scott panted, "we've got to go to the lunch."

Screw lunch. Come back to my place. Neil swallowed down the offer. *This is important to him. I'll get him naked tonight.*

Trying to force his lust back under control, Neil nodded. He forcibly let Scott go and shifted backward.

"Right," Neil said, clearing his throat when it came out rough. "Hayfield Tavern. I'll follow you?"

"Yeah," Scott answered.

Despite being the one to end their kiss, Scott closed the distance and cupped Neil's cheek. He pressed a featherlight kiss to his lips.

"It means a lot that you came, Neil."

Neil shivered but the feeling was pleasant. He also smiled at the soft look in Scott's eyes and brought his hand to Scott's chest, stroking it gently.

"Thanks for inviting me."

Scott smiled and brushed Neil's jaw with his thumb, and they kissed again. Neil wished they were going straight back to his apartment — and preferably to the bedroom. The memories of their last night together played on his mind. This time, he didn't want them in darkness. He wanted the same softness to their movements, only this time with him able to see Scott. The thought sent a thrill of both nervousness and excitement through him.

It was the yearning to experience it that got him away from Scott. The sooner they had lunch, the sooner they could be alone,

"We better go," he said.

Scott nodded, but it was Neil who stepped away. He then headed to his car, not looking back. The car park had a good portion of spots empty now, and he reached his car without delay. He took his seat and turned on the engine. It was only then that a fresh thought crossed his mind, making him freeze.

Do I have anything edible in my fridge?

Chapter Nine

The lunch spanned late into the afternoon. The meal was a loud affair with over half the team and their spouses and children present. They took up almost the entire pub and were lucky that someone had booked ahead. When the meals finished, most of the families left, but everyone else remained to play rounds of pool, have a drink and talk about the game.

Neil got introduced to everyone in a rush of names and faces. He didn't know how he was meant to remember them, but he found a friend in Leslie as they teamed up in a game of doubles at the pool table. Scott was never far from him, touching his waist and getting him a fresh drink. Neil also gained his own victory kiss when he and Leslie won their game.

Neil had a better time than he'd expected. He'd even agreed to a rematch with the guys he and Leslie had been versing. One of them was a fireman, and before he left, he said he'd iron out the details with Scott in the coming days. When Neil and Scott left the pub not long after, it was late afternoon. Scott headed home to drop off his baseball clothes and shower properly while Neil went to the supermarket to buy something for dinner. He settled on the ingredients for a garlic chicken penne. He wasn't the best cook, but it didn't seem like something he would ruin.

When he arrived at his apartment, Neil put the food in the fridge and cleaned up a couple of dirty coffee mugs. Everything else was decent enough for company. He wasn't much of a homebody, and it showed. His furniture was cheap and basic, and there were very few personal touches. Once again, he couldn't help comparing his small apartment to Scott's house. It made him grimace. His place didn't look like a *home*. He hoped it wouldn't remind Scott how different they were.

Not wanting to dwell on it, Neil used his extra time to make his bed. It might have been presumptuous, but Neil was hopeful to get Scott back there in a few hours. He was just straightening the blanket when he heard the buzz of his doorbell. Neil immediately left his bed and headed for the door.

Opening it, he found Scott dressed in another of the shirts from Neil's store. He also had a six-pack of the beer Neil always ordered. Neil grinned.

"I see you've been paying attention," he said, nodding at the drinks.

"When it comes to you."

Neil laughed but opened the door wider for Scott to come inside. His lover gave him a quick peck on the cheek as he passed the threshold. Neil took the beers from him, carried them to the kitchen then tore the cardboard to get out two bottles. He put the rest in the fridge and hunted around for his bottle opener. Neil got the tops off and offered one to Scott, who took it and had an appreciative sip.

"So, what's for dinner?" Scott asked.

"Garlic chicken penne."

"Sounds good. Can I help?"

Neil raised his eyebrows. "I thought I was cooking for you?"

"Doesn't mean I can't help."

Scott stepped farther into the kitchen, placing his beer on the bench and wrapping an arm around Neil's waist. Scott kissed his neck before resting his chin on Neil's shoulder.

"What does Chef Neil want me to do?"

"Chef Neil won't be cooking at all if you keep holding him like this."

Scott chuckled. "So, you're saying it's dinner or you? That's a tough decision."

Leaning back against Scott, Neil enjoyed the way Scott's other arm curled around his waist, encircling him in a hug. The embrace made him feel content. He wanted to stay exactly where they were.

I don't need dinner or sex, just this.

The thought should have had Neil stiffening, but this time, it didn't. Neil didn't want to second-guess his feelings. He just wanted to enjoy sharing a soft and private moment with Scott. He'd spent all day surrounded by the man's friends and family. *This* was nice.

But he knew Scott was at his apartment for more than just a cuddle in the kitchen. He had to provide a meal, especially if he wanted to keep Scott around for the rest of the evening.

"How about dinner first and me later?" Neil suggested.

"Like my own special dessert?" Scott replied.

He trailed his lips over Neil's clothed shoulder. The barely felt touch was a tantalizing tease, and Neil's eyelids fluttered closed. It was like a reversal of their usual roles. *He* was trying to facilitate the date while Scott was edging them toward the bedroom.

Scott placed one firm and last kiss to Neil's shoulder before unwinding his arms. Neil opened his eyes and turned to face his lover. He knew it would be easy to kiss Scott and draw the man into a quickie against the counter. But, for the first time in his life, Neil wanted more than an orgasm from his partner. He remembered the domesticity from their morning in Scott's kitchen. He wanted that again.

Walking around Scott, he grabbed the pasta from his pantry and held it out to the man.

"You can make this al dente."

"Yes, sir," Scott replied, taking the container with a wink.

Neil bit his tongue to keep from saying something flirtatious. He didn't want to indulge in trains of thought that would only end up with him hard and burning the kitchen down because he was too distracted by getting into Scott's pants.

Opening the fridge, he started getting out ingredients. He'd already taken out a pot for the pasta earlier and he heard Scott fill it with water. Placing his items on the bench, Neil pulled up the recipe on his phone and gave it a quick skim.

"Is this a new recipe?" Scott asked.

"I've cooked chicken penne before," Neil answered. "But, if I'm putting in the effort of cooking, I want to try something new."

He didn't mention that this was the first time he'd cooked in over three months. Microwave meals or takeout were usually his preference. The thought of standing up to make something after eight hours on his feet was rarely appealing. When he did cook, it was only on his days off.

"I'm the opposite," Scott replied. "I prefer to cook my favorites. Comfort food, you know?"

"What's your favorite meal to make?"

"Pizza with garlic bread—covered in toppings and with the butter on the bread melting in your mouth."

Neil's stomach rumbled. "Damn. You're making me want that now."

"We'll make it when you're over next."

Neil nodded. He also grabbed a pan and placed it on the hot plate beside the pot of pasta. Neil put in some oil and left it to heat as he seasoned the chicken breast before placing it in the pan. He could feel Scott's gaze on him, but the fireman never spoke a word. He seemed content to simply watch Neil work.

The scrutiny, however, left Neil uncomfortable.

"So, what else do you like to cook if not pizza?"

Scott happily recounted his preferred dishes, and Neil relaxed into the comforting sound of Scott's voice. He listened with half an ear as he fried the chicken, flipping it halfway to make sure it was cooked all the way through.

The pasta finished at the same time as the chicken. Neil told Scott where to find the strainer. Putting aside his chicken to cool, Neil moved on to making the sauce. He saw Scott check the recipe from the corner of his eye. His lover was quick to grab the chicken and start dicing it. Neil paused what he was doing to watch. They were working seamlessly again. It didn't matter if they were in Scott's suburban house or his bachelor apartment, they still fit together. Affection blossomed in his chest, creating fresh longing.

"Scott," he called.

His lover glanced up and Neil gestured him over. Bemused, Scott put down the knife and came forward. He looked down at the phone as if expecting something to be wrong with his preparations. Neil used his distraction to surprise him with a kiss. It didn't last long as Neil didn't want to wreck the sauce.

"What was that for?" Scott asked.

"I just wanted to kiss you," Neil said dismissively.

He turned back to stirring, hoping his embarrassment didn't show.

Talk about being sentimental.

He'd demanded Scott stop working just to *kiss* him. Yet, even as he worked, he noticed Scott smile from the corner of his eye.

"Seems like a good reason to me."

Neil swallowed. His stomach churned and he wanted to kiss Scott again, but he didn't. Neil resolutely stared at the food.

"We have a dinner to make," Neil muttered.

Scott's grin widened. "Does it matter if it takes a little longer? I've got nowhere else I want to be."

Neil snapped his head to the side. Scott took his wrist and encouraged him to take the pan off the heat. He then cupped Neil's cheeks and kissed him. Neil's heart kicked into overdrive, and he clutched Scott's shoulders. Scott held and kissed him tenderly. Neil gave a small whimper he would deny if ever mentioned. There was so much coursing through him that he didn't know whether to pull Scott close or shove him away.

The decision wasn't needed when Scott broke the kiss and rested their foreheads together. Neil swallowed thickly, feeling caught off guard and vulnerable. Neil had never believed in romance, and he'd always scoffed at love. But he was in his kitchen making a meal with his lover. He'd met Scott's friends and family. He'd *kissed* Scott for no reason — not to have sex, not to get him in the mood but because he'd wanted to.

He'd never felt the devotion, infatuation or need that people talked about when they formed a relationship. But the clench to his stomach, skip to his heart and warmth in his chest was all pointing to one very dangerous thing.

Neil had a boyfriend. He was in a relationship, and he didn't want to lose Scott. The swooping wave of terror could have been overwhelming but pressed against Scott and with another chaste kiss being given to him, Neil could keep it contained.

Everything's been fine so far. You can make this boyfriend thing work. Just don't screw up and you'll be able to keep him.

Neil tried to infuse his thoughts with confidence, but he wasn't stupid. Making a relationship work would be easier said than done, and if either of them were going to mess it up, Neil knew it would be him.

They lingered together for a minute, and Neil ended up having to start the sauce again from scratch, but the distraction helped him calm down. The chicken and sauce got added to the cooling pasta, and when they sat down on the couch with dinner and beers, Neil felt better. They channel surfed for a few minutes, but when they found an old crime movie playing, Scott was immediately hooked.

The death scenes were ludicrous and the acting appalling, and Neil would have long changed channels if not for Scott. They spent most of the movie chuckling while discussing the silliness during ad breaks. It had been a long time since Neil had watched a movie the old-fashioned way. After eating, Neil took their bowls away to rinse them in the sink, leaving Scott to stay riveted to an interrogation scene. He could hear it from the kitchen and rolled his eyes at the corny and predictable lines.

When he finished with the dishes, he didn't go back to the couch, preferring to lean against the kitchen wall and watch Scott. His lover couldn't look away from the movie. Neil watched on with amusement. The interrogation scene flowed into the final confrontation and the big conclusion. Scott was leaning forward in his seat, completely oblivious to what was going on around him. Neil quietly pulled out his phone and took a photo.

That's my ridiculous lover.

He didn't even want to tease Scott over the image. Neil wanted it kept next to the one of Scott in his fireman uniform — two sides of the man who was changing Neil's life a little more with every date.

Returning to the couch, he sat down beside Scott. His lover glanced at him, flashing a grin before turning back to the TV. His hand came to rest on Neil's knee, and Neil relaxed back against the cushions to wait. The movie ended ten minutes later, and Scott let out a huff of frustration.

"Something wrong?" Neil asked

"I thought they'd have a more dramatic ending."

The ending had been cliché and very predictable. The only thing missing was a big shoot up. Clearly, Scott wished they'd gone that route.

"That's probably why it was on TV. It was crappy and cheap to run."

"It wasn't that bad," Scott insisted, turning to him. "The gangster's girlfriend was great."

Neil hummed noncommittally. She'd had the best acting out of all of them, but that didn't mean she'd saved the film.

"I'm glad you enjoyed watching it."

He'd meant the words genuinely, but his statement made Scott shift awkwardly.

"Sorry," he said, guiltily. "I didn't mean to get so…into it."

"I wasn't complaining," Neil said. He shifted forward enough to run his hand over Scott's. "Watching you get hooked on it was just as entertaining."

"Still…" Scott insisted. "I'm sorry I ignored you."

Cupping the back of Scott's neck, Neil squeezed it gently.

"If I was bored, you would have known it. I would have turned off the TV or climbed into your lap to make you pay attention. I don't sit back if something annoys me."

"That's true," Scott agreed, starting to grin. "You're too bossy for that."

"You like it when I'm bossy."

"Yeah," Scott answered, his hand sliding farther up Neil's leg, "I do."

Neil's body responded to Scott's deepening voice and tantalizing touch, desire spreading through him in anticipation of what was about to happen. What he hoped *might* happen.

"How bossy do you want me to be?"

"You haven't annoyed me yet," Scott said, turning to better face Neil. "Let's see how far you can go."

Neil slipped his hand to Scott's shoulder and Scott leaned in for a kiss. Neil closed his eyes and wrapped his arm around Scott's back. Scott rearranged, not breaking their embrace, even as he straddled Neil's thighs. Neil arched his hips, allowing their rapidly hardening cocks to brush together through their pants.

The kiss broke and Neil panted. Scott turned his attention to his neck, and he shifted to give his lover better access. Neil's desire rose with every scrape and pressure of Scott's mouth and Scott even pushed aside his shirt to get to his collarbone and shoulder. Neil ran his hand through Scott's hair while the other slipped under his shirt, sliding over the muscles of his back. He was getting uncomfortably erect already. He wanted to rip their clothes off and climb on top of Scott.

We need a bed.

He gave a groan of frustration as he tugged Scott's mouth away from him. Scott frowned with confusion.

"Bedroom," Neil clarified.

Scott's responding smile was almost mischievous. "Yes, *sir*."

Neil stifled a moan and dragged Scott into another kiss. Desire added desperation to his touches, and when they split apart this time, Scott wasted no time in climbing off Neil. He offered his hand and tugged Neil to his feet. Scott kept their hands clasped as Neil led them to the bedroom. The moment they were inside, Scott backed Neil against the wall, kissing him fiercely.

It's been too damn long.

They'd been together almost all day, and this was their first chance to get each other naked.

Or maybe you just didn't want to stop dating him to fuck.

Neil ignored the voice in order to grapple with Scott's shirt. He tried undoing the buttons without breaking the kiss, but he wasn't doing well. Scott soon laughed and helped finish the buttons, getting his shirt open. Immediately afterward, Neil's was tugged over his head. It ended up on the floor, but he didn't push Scott's off his shoulders, enjoying being able to touch Scott's chest with the material on either side of his hands. It made it feel like Scott was a present he hadn't fully unwrapped. Pressing his lips to Scott's collarbone, Neil trailed them down to lick at his lover's right nipple, swirling his tongue over the hardening bud while his fingertips dipped under the waistband of Scott's pants teasingly.

"Neil," Scott groaned, twitching his hips forward.

He smiled and sucked on Scott's nipple one more time before he let it go and straightened, but he kept his fingers hooked around Scott's jeans.

"You know, I did promise you something special for winning your game." Neil chuckled and fingered his shirt. "Too bad you don't have your uniform. I could have stripped you out of it."

"I'll remember that for next time."

"You should wear your work clothes some time, too. I'll happily play '*my hero*' with you."

"I'm *not* wearing my uniform," Scott said, sounding flustered.

"Really?" Neil asked, letting his voice get low and breathy. "Not even if it means me on my knees for my heroic fireman?"

"*Shit*," Scott hissed.

Scott's cock was hardening further at his words, proving at least *some* part of him was keen on the idea. But his face was also bright red with embarrassment.

Taking pity on him, Neil suggested, "Think about it. You might change your mind."

"If anyone will make me change my mind, it will be you," Scott grumbled, but there was no annoyance in his voice.

"I'll take that as a compliment."

Scott snorted. He also leaned closer and nuzzled Neil's jaw.

"Of course, you would."

Scott tilted his head just enough to kiss Neil again. They traded slow brushes of their lips that were at odds with the lust burning within Neil's blood. All too soon, he needed more.

Neil deliberately brought their pelvises together. He moved his hands to Scott's hips and ground their arousals, making them both moan. Neil broke away and pressed his forehead against Scott's shoulder. He concentrated on rolling his hips in slow motions. It gave some temporary relief to the tightness in his pants, but Scott didn't seem satisfied.

He stepped back, forcing Neil to loosen his grip. When Neil lifted his head, Scott's cheeks were flushed and desire had blown his pupils wide. He grabbed Neil's pants, immediately popping the button and pulling down the zipper. Neil shuddered. Scott's fingers felt so good against him, even when they were barely touching him.

"Let's get these off."

"I thought I was giving the orders."

"Haven't heard any yet," Scott remarked. "You might have wanted to boss me around for a while, but you don't seem that good at it."

Neil glared at Scott. The challenge ignited his blood and made him bat away Scott's hands.

"On the bed, on your back," Neil commanded.

Scott raised his eyebrows, surprise mixing with amusement. Neil wasn't sure if he'd obey, but he kicked off his shoes and toed off his socks before doing exactly what Neil had demanded. Neil's mouth went dry. Scott lay in the center of his bed, his muscled chest on display as he waited for more. He was aroused, relaxed and at Neil's command.

Neil suddenly had *no* idea what to do. He'd fantasized about this situation, but he'd never thought it would happen. The few times he'd been bossy in bed with past lovers, it had been *during* sex, not as a precursor.

Walking to the side of the bed, Neil then trailed his fingers over Scott's inner thigh. He swallowed when Scott opened his legs in invitation. His gazed stayed on Neil's face the entire time. His expression was soft, and his lust hadn't wavered. Watching Scott offer his body gave Neil a rush he'd never experienced. He wanted to kiss Scott. He wanted to *reward* him.

Neil traced his fingers higher, tracing Scott's inseam. Scott had a prominent bulge in the front of his jeans. Neil cupped it, squeezing gently until Scott groaned and tilted his hips forward. Neil grinned.

"What am I going to do with you?" he asked.

"Have sex with me?" Scott suggested.

"Eventually," Neil said, removing his hand.

His pants were still undone from earlier, and he shoved them off, along with his boxers, shoes and socks. He was naked when he climbed on the bed. Scott's gaze locked on his cock. He straddled Scott's thighs, putting his cock on display as he reached down and started to stroke it. Neil's eyes closed as he felt his desire building. He really needed lubricant, but the opportunity was too good to waste.

"*Neil,*" Scott groaned.

Neil opened his eyes. Scott's hands were twitching like he wanted to touch him.

Is he waiting for permission?

Neil felt a little jolt. He licked his lips.

"You can touch me," Neil said.

Scott instantly gripped Neil's hips. It wasn't what he expected Scott to do, just like he didn't expect Scott to tug him up the bed. He shuffled forward, feeling his heart pound and his cock twitch. Scott kept encouraging him up the mattress until it positioned him with his cock right above Scott's head.

"Scott?" Neil asked.

Scott curled his hands around Neil's thighs, brushing the curve of his ass. He held Neil's gaze as he caught the tip of Neil's cock in his mouth, and Neil moaned before tightly gripping the headboard of the bed. Scott sucked on his cockhead before sliding farther down Neil's shaft. Neil's breath was shaky, and he had to concentrate to keep from thrusting toward the delicious heat on his cock. Scott kept taking him farther inside, using his hold on Neil's hips to guide Neil in and out of his mouth in a punishingly slow rhythm. It was heaven. It was *hell.* Scott mouthed at his cock like it was his favorite dessert and he was trying to savor it.

"Fuck," Neil gasped. "You're going to kill me."

Scott chuckled and the vibrations made Neil curse and thrust forward instinctively. Scott took it. He opened his mouth wider and rode out Neil's thrust. Scott took almost all of Neil's cock inside, swallowing around him and making Neil cry out. He jerked forward again, and Scott hummed with pleasure. Neil tried to stay gentle, but Scott kept encouraging him to thrust deeper. Neil knew he was going to come if they did this much longer. He could already feel his pleasure building. One more minute and he'd be finished before Scott had even pulled off his pants.

It took monumental self-control for Neil to pull away from the compelling heat of Scott's mouth.

He almost came when he glanced down and watched his cockhead slide out from between Scott's lips. They were red and puffy from working Neil's cock, and he licked them as if relishing the taste.

But all too soon they were turned down in a small frown.

"Why'd you stop?" he asked.

"I was going to come."

Scott grinned and tried to encourage him back.

"I thought that was the point?"

Neil's cock gave a twitch of interest. The thought of seeing those lips stretched around him again was almost enough to destroy his resolve, but stubborn determination kept him from giving in.

"I'm the boss," Neil insisted, putting on his best manager's voice. "I get to call the shots."

"Surprised you're not trying to take what I'm giving." His eyes twinkled. "*Sir*."

Neil nearly threw in the towel and gave in to Scott's suggestion.

I'm never going to be able to hear 'sir' again without getting hard.

"Right now, I want something else," Neil said gruffly. "Right now, I want you out of your pants. Then I want your fingers inside me, followed by your cock."

Scott groaned and clenched Neil's thighs before releasing.

"Shit," he said. "Shit. Yeah, okay. Where's the lube?"

Neil shifted off Scott's thighs. He opened the nightstand and grabbed both the lubricant and the condoms. He felt Scott moving and glanced to the side to see him hurriedly shrugging down his jeans and boxers. They caught around his knees, but Neil stopped him from doing anything further. He liked the idea of Scott half-clothed. Neil straddled him again, this time over Scott's stomach. He arched his spine and gave Scott the lube. His lover wasted no time opening it and bringing his fingers to Neil's ass. Neil's eyes fluttered closed and he grunted as the first finger pressed against him. He relaxed his muscles and let out a shuddering breath as it pushed inside.

"Good," he groaned. "Scott. More. I need —"

Neil cut off with a gasp as a second finger pushed in to join the first. He hummed and pressed back against Scott, loving the feeling of Scott thrusting in and out of him. The rush made his desire heighten. He didn't need much preparation. Hell, he was almost willing to take it without. There was something about a fast, messy, rough coupling that appealed to him. When Scott crooked his fingers just so, Neil jolted and almost collapsed on Scott's chest. He stayed upright, but he was beyond ready.

He pressed his hands to Scott's chest and insisted, "Enough. Get the condom on."

Scott's fingers left his ass, and when Neil heard the plastic rip, he looked over his shoulder. Scott hissed as he rolled on the condom and spread some extra lube along it. Neil was quivering with anticipation.

"Hold yourself," Neil demanded while shifting to line his entrance up with Scott's cock.

The head brushed his ass and Neil pushed back against it. He gasped but it was quickly drowned out by Scott's moan. Neil pushed down, taking more inside him. He squeezed his eyes shut and breathed shakily, but Neil didn't stop until he reached the base. He panted, getting used to Scott's thick girth inside him. Scott grasped his hips and Neil blinked his eyes open. Scott's head was thrown back and his chest was rising and falling in harsh breaths.

Neil rocked his hips and Scott dug his nails into his skin. Neil loved feeling Scott underneath him, completely at his mercy. He pushed up before sinking back down onto Scott's cock. Scott groaned and tried to spread his legs wider, but his jeans restricted his movement. It left Neil the only one with any maneuverability. Despite knowing he could ride Scott fast and hard and get to his completion with ease, he preferred a slow pace. He watched Scott's face, seeing frustration and bliss compete for dominance.

He's the most beautiful thing I've ever seen.

Neil bent down, uncaring that it disrupted his rhythm. He pressed his lips to Scott's, needing to kiss his lover. Scott made a small sound but kissed him back. It didn't last long. They were both too aroused to delay their release for long.

When Neil started again, he sped up his motions, taking Scott deeper and clenching his muscles around the man's hard shaft. Sweat was beading on his brow, but Neil ignored his erection, determined to make Scott come first. Yet each drag of Scott's cock made it harder to concentrate. He gritted his teeth and continued to slide down on Scott's cock with determination.

Scott fought against the confinement of his jeans to try to thrust into Neil. When Scott changed his angle as

Neil bore down, they got it perfect, and Neil cried out at the deep, penetrating thrust. He clenched hard around Scott's shaft. It was all it took for Scott to shout a curse. He jerked rapidly and spilled inside Neil.

Neil braced his arm on Scott's chest and grasped his erection. He closed his eyes and stroked quickly, biting his lip to muffle his cry. He was so close that he came with only a few passes of his hand. Neil was still catching his breath when he felt Scott start caressing his back. He shifted enough to see Scott's smiling face.

"I could get used to a gift like this when I win a game."

"Well, I aim to please."

Unfortunately, his legs were feeling the strain of his position. So Neil pulled off Scott, only to collapse beside him. Neil closed his eyes and spread out on the bed. He heard Scott kick off his pants before shifting off the bed. Neil cracked open an eye.

"Bathroom?" he asked.

Neil lifted his arm and gestured vaguely. "Door off the living room."

Scott disappeared, but he took less than a minute to come back with a wet cloth. Neil smiled at the now-familiar routine. When he finished cleaning Neil's stomach, Neil caught his wrist and tugged him toward the bed.

"I hope you aren't planning to go anywhere tonight."

"Just the bathroom to get rid of this," Scott said, gesturing with the cloth. He bent down and kissed Neil. "You want to watch something else or go to bed?"

"What time is it?"

"I'll find my phone," Scott replied.

Neil let him go, but Scott didn't go for his pants. He padded out of the room. Neil stretched, feeling content to enjoy the afterglow of a spectacular orgasm. Scott came back with the towel. He had a small smile as he read something on his phone.

"What's got you in a good mood?" Neil asked. "Well…besides me."

Scott put down his phone to crawl up the bed to rest half over Neil. He kissed him lazily.

Pulling his mouth away, but lingering over him, Scott answered, "You think highly of yourself."

"I think I've lived up to my promises," Neil answered, stroking Scott's chest. "Now, what's got you smiling?"

"I got a text."

"Oh?"

"You're invited to a family dinner."

Neil froze, his good humor disappearing.

"*What?*"

"Don't be surprised." Scott kissed his cheek before dropping to lie beside him. "I told you everyone would like you. Lisa clearly does."

Neil didn't respond. He was too busy swiveling between fight or flight. Scott, seeming to finally notice his panic, touched Neil's chest.

"Hey, don't freak out. It's not a set time. It's just an open invitation."

Neil gave a sharp nod, but relaxation wasn't coming any easier. He didn't know why it was so worrying. He'd passed at the baseball game with flying colors, but meeting one sister was a far cry from Scott's *parents*.

And you like him. You don't want to mess this up.

"Neil?" Scott asked, concern in his voice as he stroked Neil's chest in a comforting gesture. "Talk to me."

Neil swallowed. He couldn't look at Scott, choosing instead to stare at the ceiling.

"I don't want to mess up."

"You won't," Scott insisted. "You've never done anything to make me doubt that."

Neil still couldn't believe it.

"I've never been in a proper relationship, Scott. I've met so many people and I..."

Neil didn't know what to say. Or rather, he didn't know *how*. Miraculously, Scott seemed to interpret what wasn't being said.

"Okay," Scott said. "We'll put it off."

Neil turned to him, feeling worried, but Scott didn't look upset or offended. In fact, he looked concerned. *For me.* Neil rolled onto his side and kissed Scott. He hoped it conveyed his gratitude and the wealth of emotions he was feeling. Thankfully, like it had in the past, it seemed to work. Scott cupped his cheek and their kiss slowed until they were just trading gentle pecks. When they finally stopped, they stayed close enough that their noses still brushed.

"It's not even nine o'clock and we don't have to be up in the morning," Scott said. "I'm sure we can find another movie on TV."

"Another terrible old film?" Neil teased, slowly calming down. "Black-and-white and full of bad dialogue?"

"If you've got popcorn, we can make a proper night of it."

Neil finally started to smile. He ran his hand over Scott's chest, simply enjoying the intimacy of the moment.

"You know. I think I do have popcorn."

"Perfect."

And, despite the dinner invitation that he wasn't ready to think about, Neil had to agree. It really seemed perfect.

Chapter Ten

Movement and soft conversation woke Neil. He came to awareness slowly, frowning even as he blinked open his eyes and rolled to look over his shoulder. Scott was sitting up on the edge of the bed. His back was to Neil and his phone was to his ear.

"Yeah," he murmured, "I'll be there soon."

Neil had clearly missed the beginning of the conversation. Scott hung up and turned to better see him. He looked apologetic.

"Sorry to wake you."

"What's wrong?" Neil questioned. His voice was still heavy with sleep.

"I've been called in. There's a nasty cold going around, and they need someone to cover." Scott shifted forward and brushed his knuckles over Neil's cheek. "I'm sorry to ruin our morning together."

Neil felt a swoop of disappointment, but he knew what work could be like.

"You can't help it." He yawned and covered his mouth. "Want me to make you a coffee?"

Scott grinned. "Thanks, but I'll be fine. We've got coffee at the station."

Neil nodded. Scott already sounded far more awake than Neil could manage in the morning. He supposed it came from working in an industry that needed its people on high alert.

"I'd say go back to sleep," Scott said. "But you'll need to lock up behind me."

Neil groaned softly but nodded.

"Do you need a shower or anything?"

"No, I'll be fine."

Scott moved his fingers into Neil's hair, stroking gently and making Neil lean into the touch. All too soon, he was climbing off the bed and hunting for his clothes. Neil had really hoped for some morning sex.

Guess you can't have everything.

They'd watched *Vertigo* on the TV the night before, eating popcorn and discussing Hitchcock films during the ad breaks. They'd then moved to the bed and fallen asleep cuddling.

Neil was only wearing boxers and didn't bother to pull anything else on as he stumbled out of bed. He rubbed a hand over his face and tried not to run into the wall.

When Scott leaves, I'm going back to sleep.

It was his last chance to sleep in for six days. He wasn't giving it up.

They walked to the front door together. Neil deviated to get his keys, but once the door was unlocked and open, Scott paused. He wrapped his arms around Neil's waist and drew him into a hug. Neil closed his eyes and rested his head on Scott's shoulder.

He *really* wanted to go back to sleep, preferably with Scott at his side.

"I'll message you when my shift's over," Scott promised.

"You better," Neil muttered, not thinking to curb the petulant demand.

Scott laughed and dropped a kiss to the top of his head. He then drew back and untangled them. Scott gave him a final peck to the cheek before stepping out of the apartment.

"I'll see you later, Neil."

"Yeah, see you."

Scott lingered, looking like he wanted to do something else. Neil frowned, not sure what it could be.

He looks like me when I didn't want to leave the other morning.

The thought jolted Neil a little more awake.

Is that what it is? He'd rather be in my crappy apartment than go to the job he loves?

Neil understood why people would skip work for sex, but to be the place Scott wanted to relax and spend his day off? It was a lot more special. It was something that Neil, for the first time in his life, related to. He'd rather spend his weekend with Scott rather than apart.

Before he could dig too deep into that realization, Scott sighed and stepped backward.

"Sleep well, Neil."

"Uh" — he still felt a little thrown by his thoughts — "have a nice day."

Scott placed a hand on the doorframe and ducked back in for a quick kiss. He then flashed a smile and left. Neil waited until he was out of sight to shut and lock the door. He stared at the wood for a long moment before shaking his head and walking back to the bedroom.

I don't want to think about that right now.

He'd need coffee and he wasn't yet ready to wake up.

Flopping down on his mattress, Neil shifted to Scott's side, breathing deeply to catch the lingering scent of Scott's cologne. Closing his eyes, Neil dozed off, imagining Scott was still in the apartment, only moments from coming back to bed.

* * * *

The second time Neil woke up, it was because of insistent messaging from his phone. Neil groaned and rolled onto his back, searching blindly for where it was charging. He had five messages from Denise. He squinted to read them, his eyes trying to adjust to the light.

Neil?

Neil? Is Scott okay?

Are you okay?

Neil? Please text me.

Neil????

He frowned and looked at the clock. It was almost midday. Scott had left for work hours ago.

I'm fine. Scott's at work. Why?

The answer was immediate.

People are talking about this big warehouse fire. I wasn't sure if he was fighting it?

Neil sat up abruptly, no longer feeling tired. There was a growing fear coiling in his stomach. He checked for any new messages from Scott, but there was nothing. His last text was from before the baseball game. Neil's mind flooded with memories of Scott — his smile and the way Scott's fingers felt carding through his hair. He'd gone to sleep knowing Scott would message him when his shift was over.

What if something happens to him?

Neil's heart felt twisted by a vise. The softer moments with Scott were replaced by roaring fires and shouts of alarm. Every movie scene with a terrible fire was playing through his mind. Neil's fingers flew over the keys before he could think.

Are you okay?

He stared at his text to Scott, yearning for a response to soothe the mounting panic growing inside him. But if Scott was fighting the fire, he wouldn't be able to reply. His phone might even be back at the station.

He messaged Denise again.

What have people been saying about the fire?

Not much. Just that it's big. They think it might take out a few warehouses. It's supposed to be bad.

Neil quickly did an Internet search, hoping for more details. There were a couple of news articles, but they only stated that the fire existed and that the fire department was attending to the situation. Neil wanted to call Scott's station and find out what was happening. He wanted to get in his car and drive down to the warehouse to check on him. Neil knew both urges were stupid and wouldn't help anyone, but the fear of Scott being injured hung over him like a dark cloud.

Neil had always known what Scott did, but this was the first time he'd been faced with the reality.

He suddenly found it impossible to stay in bed. Neil threw back the sheets and pushed off the mattress. He went to the kitchen but froze at the sight of their unwashed dishes from the previous evening.

All he could think about was Scott—watching movies with him, having Scott's arms wrapped around him, the way Scott *liked* every order and scathing remark.

What if I never have any of that again?

Neil swallowed. He'd never felt like this before. He felt worried and helpless. He felt *afraid*. Neil hadn't known how much losing Scott would wound him until the true potential of it was laid in front of him.

Neil closed his eyes and gritted his teeth.

"For fuck's sake," he hissed. "It's probably not even a big fire. It's just a day at the damn office for him. Pull your shit together."

His phone buzzed and Neil snapped his eyes open. His heart leaped, but when he saw it was just Denise, the frustration and disappointment hit him hard. Neil almost snapped at her but had enough sense not to fire off the text.

He looked around the apartment for a distraction, but everything reminded him of Scott. He needed something separate and untouched by the fireman. Neil walked back to the bedroom as he selected a different name in his contacts. He hit the call button as he sat down on the edge of his bed.

"Why the hell are you calling me? I'm a goddamn chef. I don't do before two p.m. shit—not even for my brother."

"Then why did you answer?" Neil quipped. "You're getting too kind-hearted in your elder years, Adrian."

There was a moment's silence.

"What's wrong, Neil?"

Neil tensed. "Nothing."

"I know you better than that," Adrian said, his agitation having changed to concern. "You rarely call, and you *never* sound like this."

Neil stared at the floor. He didn't talk to his brothers often. The last time they'd seen each other had been two years ago. Adrian was the eldest. He was the one who'd always throw an arm around Neil's shoulder when he was in a foul mood. He'd force Neil to do something until he forgot or worked through what he was mad or sad about.

Maybe he'd called Adrian for more reasons than his worry for Scott.

"I'm..." Neil hesitated on the description, not yet ready to call them *boyfriends* out loud, "seeing someone."

"Holy shit," Adrian murmured. "You're actually dating. Is he a unicorn?"

"Shut the fuck up," Neil snapped, feeling tense and defensive.

"Okay," Adrian said, sounding surprised. "I hit a nerve there. I'd get better control over that before telling Jackson. He'll tease you a lot more than I will."

Neil grimaced. He *knew* his brothers would tease him. His mother would probably throw a party, too. It would be the spectacle of the year seeing him in a relationship. He could handle all their lighthearted ribbing. It would never normally have him lashing out, but some friendly teasing wasn't the real problem.

Neil closed his eyes and admitted, "He's a fireman, Adrian."

"So?"

"There's a warehouse fire."

"Shit," Adrian breathed. "How bad is it?"

"It's a goddamn fire. Isn't that bad enough?"

"Not what I mean and you know it," Adrian said, keeping his voice calm and level. "Is this your first fire while you've been dating him?"

Neil opened and closed his mouth. The answer was simple, but he didn't want to say it. Listening to his brother's even tone made him feel like an overreacting fool.

"God, I'm being an idiot," he whispered. "Forget it."

"Neil—"

Neil hung up, feeling stupid. He had called his brother out of the blue to panic and seek comfort over something that was probably little more than a minor inconvenience to Scott. God, he'd just confessed he was *dating* someone to his brother and all because of a little scare.

He rose from the bed but paused when his phone rang. It was Adrian. He sighed.

"Adrian—"

"Shut up—and don't you dare hang up on me again."

Neil winced but didn't end the call.

"You're not being an idiot," Adrian continued, his voice gentling. "You're allowed to be worried about your boyfriend."

Instinctively, Neil wanted to protest the label of 'boyfriend'. He also wanted to deny he gave a damn. But both of those ships had sailed.

"He's probably fine," Neil eventually muttered.

"But you'll worry until you know for sure. That's pretty normal, Neil." Adrian chuckled. "But, since this is the first person you've dated and cared about, it probably seems weird as hell."

Neil groaned and dropped back onto the bed. He stared at the ceiling before quietly admitting, "I've never felt like this, Adrian."

"Worried?"

"Not just that."

"That serious, huh?" Adrian remarked. "You must care for him a lot."

Neil huffed a breath and smiled wryly.

"I went to his baseball game and met his friends and sister."

Adrian whistled. "Damn."

"He wants me to meet his family. Christ." Neil laughed loudly. "I'm actually in a relationship." Yet, all too soon, he sobered, as he remembered what Scott was doing. "I don't want anything to happen to him, Adrian."

"I'm sure he knows what he's doing and so does his team. They won't take any unnecessary risks."

Neil nodded. The words helped even if they didn't completely quell his worry. Nothing but seeing Scott unharmed would do that. Adrian understood. He'd never offer false platitudes of '*he'll be okay*', but he *would* stay on the phone, despite his earlier complaints, just to give Neil a friendly ear and some comfort.

For the first time in a long time, he really *missed* his older brother.

"Thanks," he mumbled. He also cleared his throat and changed the subject. "How's work?"

There was a pause and Neil wondered if Adrian would let the conversation drop so easily, but thankfully, he did.

"I'm sick of making gluten-free, yeast-free, dairy-free, meat-free hamburgers. Why do you even order a hamburger if you can't eat anything on it? It's not even a hamburger. It's an insult to cooking."

Neil laughed, finally managing a smile. His brother was gruff and could curse like a sailor, but he was also perceptive and able to understand what Neil needed. The complaints continued about the menu, his fellow chefs, management, the clientele and even the cutlery. There would be several hours before he could expect to hear from Scott. Neil was grateful to spend some of it talking to his brother.

* * * *

They spoke for an hour, bitching concerning their respective jobs before running out of things to complain about. Silence fell between them, and Neil knew one of them would hang up soon. Adrian seemed to notice it, too.

"Neil," he said, his tone turning serious, "make sure you tell this guy how much the fire worried you."

"What?" Neil felt a cold sweat break out. "*No.*"

"Neil, the longer you're with him, the more chances this will happen again. You've got to tell him how much it scared you. That way, he can help you through it in the future."

Neil shuddered, not wanting to think about it happening again — not wanting to imagine *worse* blazes Scott could be fighting.

"There might not even *be* a future," Neil mumbled.

"I've never heard you talk about anyone the way you talk about him," Adrian said. "You already told me you don't want to lose him. I can't imagine you letting him slip away easily. That's why you need to talk to him. You can't ignore the risks of his career, especially if you're falling for him."

"I am *not* falling for him," Neil declared hurriedly.

The statement was a knee-jerk, panicked reaction. Admitting to being in a *relationship* was one thing. But falling in love? Neil couldn't be. He wasn't ready for anything like that.

"Uh-huh," Adrian said, clearly not believing him. "Well, either way, you should tell him. His career doesn't change, no matter what you don't or *do* feel for him."

Neil felt uncomfortable just imagining the conversation with Scott, but he felt even worse knowing it wouldn't be the only fire he'd watch Scott fight. He didn't want to do it again as an outsider with no one to tell him what was happening.

"I'll talk to him," Neil finally muttered.

"Good," Adrian replied. "Let me know how it goes." He could hear the smile in his brother's voice. "I can't wait to see Mum's reaction to this."

"Don't say a *word* to her."

If his mother learned about Scott, she'd be driving up within a month in order to meet the mysterious boyfriend.

Adrian laughed.

"Fine, I'll stay quiet. What's the guy's name, anyway?"

"Scott," Neil admitted.

"Last name?"

"Don't social media stalk him."

"You don't give me many chances to be a protective older brother. I have to take the opportunity."

"You're an ass."

"Whatever. Now, what's that last name?"

Neil rolled his eyes. He was smiling even as he hung up. Immediately after, a text message came, demanding the information. Neil's grin grew, even as he continued to deny his brother. Neil knew he would remain worried until he heard from Scott, but he'd calmed down after speaking to Adrian.

He still continued to monitor the news for any updates. Adrian continued to text him, as did Denise, but Neil only relaxed when the fire was extinguished and no one was reported injured. When a text from Scott came in the early evening, Neil let out a breath heavy with relief.

I'm fine. We're all fine. Sorry. I've just finished my shift and I didn't see this. It was a busy day.

Neil slumped against the kitchen counter where he'd been making coffee. The tension that had been building all day drained from his shoulders.

Are you at home?

Just about to leave the station.

Adrian's words were thundering in his ears, and he sent the text before he could overthink it.

Do you mind if I come over?

I'll never mind, but I'm really tired. Was going to order takeout and crash.

That's fine.

Neil grabbed his keys but paused outside the door.

I just want to see you.

He received a reply as he was unlocking his car.

I'd like to see you, too.

Neil smiled.

I'll be there soon.

Scott sent him a smiling emoji and Neil pocketed his phone before taking the now-familiar route to Scott's house.

He was impatient during the drive, just wanting to be with Scott and check him over for any bruises or burns. When he arrived, the lights were on, but the blinds were drawn. Neil parked in the driveway and walked up the path. Scott opened the door before he could knock. Neil ran his gaze over his lover, searching for the smallest injury. He was in sleep pants and a T-shirt with wet hair. He wasn't favoring his side or sporting bandages. Scott looked tired but unharmed.

"Hey," Scott said, smiling. "I'm glad you came over."

Neil closed the distance and cupped Scott's neck. He pulled him into a kiss. Scott wrapped an arm around his waist and Neil relaxed under Scott's touch. When they broke apart, Neil turned his head, pressing it against Scott's damp hair and breathing in the scent of his shampoo.

"You all right, Neil?" Scott asked, rubbing his back.

Immediately, Neil's embarrassment hit him like a truck. He tried to move away, but Scott held him close.

"Neil?" he questioned again. "What's going on?"

Neil felt like an idiot all over again. While he did still want to retreat and avoid admitting the truth to Scott, it wasn't as strong as his desire to stay in his lover's arms.

He compromised by asking, "Can we go inside?"

"Sure," Scott agreed.

He let Neil go, and Neil averted his face, hoping to hide any evidence of an embarrassed flush. Scott stepped to the side and Neil walked through the doorway. Scott's hand came to his back after he shut the door. Together, they walked into the living room and took a seat on the couch. Their thighs touched they were so close, and Scott took one of his hands, cradling it.

"What's wrong, Neil?"

"I was worried about you," Neil said, forcing out the words. "I hated not knowing if you were okay."

Scott was quiet, and Neil felt ready to crawl out of his skin. When Scott started stroking his hand, Neil twitched, but didn't pull away.

"I'm sorry to worry you," he said.

Neil scoffed. "As if you had a choice."

"No, I didn't," Scott agreed. "But you're allowed to be worried, and I'm sorry that you were."

He squeezed Neil's hand and Neil finally dragged his gaze to Scott's face. His lover remained concerned. Fighting the fire would have exhausted him and yet he was still putting Neil's unfounded fears first. It got Neil speaking, saying things he'd never planned to confess.

"I called my brother, admitted I was dating you. He'll have a goddamn field day teasing me once he knows you're okay." Neil closed his eyes. "I just felt like such an idiot. You do this all the time, but I spent the whole day worried something would happen to you."

"You're allowed to be worried," he repeated.

Neil opened his eyes, hearing the smile in Scott's voice. He glared, but Scott's grin spread wider.

"I'm sorry, but it's nice seeing that you care."

Neil tried to yank his hand back, but Scott didn't let him. His lover leaned forward and kissed him. Neil only lasted a few seconds before his scowl melted away and he kissed Scott back. The kiss helped reaffirm that Scott was okay.

When it ended, Scott pressed their foreheads together.

"I'm giving you Cindy's number."

Neil frowned. "Why?"

"So that you can call her if you're worried or want more accurate information."

Neil closed his eyes again but agreed, "Okay."

Scott's hand remained linked with Neil's but his other one came around Neil's back, stroking over his shirt in comfort. Neil felt undeserving of it. He wasn't the one who'd fought a fire today, and yet, every stroke of Scott's hand unwound the tension in his back. It made him want to offer something in return.

He licked his lips but whispered, "I do care about you, Scott."

Scott's hand paused for a moment before quickly starting up again.

"I care about you, too," Scott replied. He slipped his hand under Neil's shirt, the touch remaining more comforting than sexual. "Stay the night?"

Neil felt a pure yearning, but he'd been vulnerable enough tonight. He couldn't let it show.

"Only if you've ordered enough dinner for two," he said gruffly.

Scott chuckled. "Luckily, I did."

"Then, okay."

Scott laughed again, and Neil knew Scott understood him. He wasn't staying for the food. He wasn't even staying for the prospect of sex. Neil was staying for *Scott*. But he wasn't able to say it yet, and Scott didn't make him. It was one more reason he didn't want to let the man go.

It was also why, as his brother had so accurately pinpointed, he was *falling* for Scott. But nothing, not even wild horses, was going to drag that confession from Neil's lips.

Chapter Eleven

Neil spent the night and, for the first time, they didn't have sex. Scott was tired and Neil found he didn't mind skipping it. They had dinner, watched half of a movie before Scott started nodding off on Neil's shoulder then they went to bed. Scott was almost completely asleep by the time his head hit the pillow. Neil pressed against Scott's back and curled his arms around the man, holding him close.

The next morning, he woke up late, having forgotten to set an alarm. Neil had to rush out of the door without coffee or breakfast in order to get to work on time.

After that, everything returned to normal, as if the fire had never happened. The only differences were that Scott texted him Cindy's number and Adrian kept pestering him for information on Scott. They scheduled their next date for three nights' time and Neil had felt hopeful that they could spend an uninterrupted evening and *morning* together.

But when he woke up on the day of their date, he felt like someone had beaten him up in his sleep. His muscles ached, his throat felt like shards of glass were sliding down it and he had a blocked nose. Scott had said a bad cold was going around the station. It seemed Neil had caught it.

He fumbled for his phone and sent Denise a text. They were both on all day. He was sure she'd be able to arrange one of their casuals to do a cover. There was no way he was going into work feeling this awful. He almost fell asleep by the time her reply came.

You poor thing! Get your sexy fireman to come over and cook you soup. I'll work something out. Feel better!

He ignored her tease about Scott and shot back a simple reply.

Thank you.

Neil knew the last thing his lover would want to do on his day off was look after Neil. It was still disappointing. He'd been looking forward to seeing Scott. Pulling up Scott's name, he messaged him.

Can't come tonight. Sorry.

He dropped his phone on the mattress, already feeling exhausted. Neil dragged the covers up to his shoulders, fighting down a shiver. He needed to get medicine, tissues and some honey for his throat. Unfortunately, all that involved moving. He wasn't sure he could climb out of bed, let alone navigate his apartment.

Closing his eyes, Neil hoped to summon enough strength to get up. Instead, he fell asleep, only to be roused awake by his phone. He blinked open his eyes and grudgingly removed his arm from under the blankets. It was from Scott.

Is everything okay?

I'm sick. I blame you and your cold-harboring fire friends.

Are you at work?

Called in sick. Feel like crap.

Neil was struggling to keep his eyes open.

I can come over. Do you need anything? I can go to the chemist.

Neil huffed a laugh. He regretted it immediately when his throat burned.

Yeah, right, he thought. *That's just what our relationship needs — him seeing me as a sweaty, disgusting mess.*

Yet even though he really didn't want Scott finding him like this, a part of him yearned to be taken care of. The last time someone had helped him when he was sick it had been his parents.

Normally, the indecision would plague him, and he'd flood with self-doubt. But he felt like *shit*. He didn't have the energy to fight it.

You can come if you want. I think I have everything. Haven't looked.

You're in bed?

Yeah.

Stay there. I'll be around in fifteen minutes.

Neil's stomach fluttered and his yearning to see Scott doubled.

Okay.

He closed his eyes, almost falling into a doze, when something occurred to him and he jerked awake.

You don't have a key.

We'll worry about that when I get there.

He instantly pictured Scott in his fireman clothes knocking down the door in order to get to him. Neil smiled, drifting off to sleep on that very appealing thought. He didn't know how long he was out for, but he awoke to the sound of knocking on his front door.

Neil forced open heavy eyelids and fought down a tired groan. It took considerable effort to push out of bed. He wrapped the blanket around him, already shivering as he trudged to the door. He shuffled through his apartment and unlocked it with leaden fingers. When he opened it, he was greeted by Scott. His lover was in jeans and a T-shirt and he had a canvas shopping bag in his hands. He looked nothing but concerned.

"Hey, Neil," he said. "How are you feeling?"

"Like shit."

Scott winced in sympathy. Neil shifted to the side so Scott could enter.

"I didn't know what you might need. I brought lemon tea, some DVDs and chicken noodle soup."

Scott shifted the bag to one hand before lifting the other to Neil's forehead. Neil almost groaned. He felt blessedly cool.

"You've got a temperature," Scott said, lowering his hand. "Have you had anything?"

Neil shook his head.

"Is your medicine in the bathroom?"

Neil nodded, but Scott didn't go directly for it. He put down the bag and wrapped an arm around Neil's waist. He helped guide Neil back to bed. Neil relaxed into his lover's firm hold. When Scott got him settled back under the covers, his lover disappeared. Neil closed his eyes, listening to him bustle around the apartment.

When he returned, Neil opened his eyes. Scott had a box of tablets and a cup of water. Neil could hear his kettle boiling in the background. Neil took the packet and popped out two pills. Swallowing them, he ignored the way it felt like nails scraping down his throat.

When he lay back down, Scott surprised him by running his hand through Neil's hair. The touch was soothing, and he automatically leaned into it.

"I'll make you some tea. Do you want me to add honey to it?"

Neil nodded. "Yeah. Thanks."

Scott smiled. He moved his hand from Neil's hair to his cheek, brushing a thumb over it before standing from his crouch and heading back into the living room. Neil pulled the blanket closer. When Scott returned, he had a mug. He encouraged Neil into a sitting position so he could drink the tea. The tartness of the lemon was almost drowned out by the sweetness of the honey. It still hurt to swallow, but Neil kept drinking. It would be better for him in the long run.

Scott took a seat on the edge of the bed beside Neil's hip. He started stroking Neil's thigh through the blanket.

"Can I get you anything else?" Scott asked.

Neil paused with the mug against his lips. He stared at Scott.

How the hell is this guy real? How is he with me?

Slowly, Neil shook his head. Scott smiled and squeezed his thigh.

"Okay. How about you finish your tea and try to sleep for a bit? I'll be out in the living room."

Neil's disbelief doubled.

"You're staying?"

"Yeah." Scott frowned. "Don't you want me to?"

"I thought you'd want to go? I'm sick and this is your day off."

"I'd rather spend my day off making sure you're okay." He squeezed Neil's knee. "I brought some movies to watch. I'll be fine."

Neil stared at him. He felt completely blindsided by what Scott would do for him.

"How are you even *real*?" Neil asked, only to feel mortified a moment after.

Scott's smile turned bashful, and he gave an awkward laugh.

"I just want to look after you. Is that so strange?"

It is for me. No one has ever done that.

Neil wanted to kiss Scott and curl into his embrace. He wanted to close his eyes and rest his head against his lover's chest. But he was sure there were limits to how far Scott would go when Neil was sick and possibly contagious. It was a miracle the man had risked coming here at all.

Neil's gaze dropped back to his tea.

"Thanks, Scott," he mumbled, his voice rough not just from sickness but from building emotion.

When Scott leaned forward, Neil stiffened. But his lover pressed a tender kiss to the top of his head. He lingered there and Neil relaxed.

"Finish your tea," Scott said upon pulling back.

Neil complied, swallowing down the last of it. The pain in his throat had grown after talking, but he didn't regret it. When he finished, Scott took it from him and helped him resettle under the covers.

"I'll be in the living room. Text me. Don't strain your throat."

"When I'm better, I'll strain my throat for you," Neil mumbled.

It took Scott a moment to get the innuendo. When he did, he laughed.

"Focus on getting better, Neil — not getting into my pants."

Neil grinned. "But I like getting into your pants."

Scott chuckled. "Get some rest."

Neil closed his eyes, but his grin didn't fade. Scott ran a hand over his head and around his temple in a soothing motion. Neil sighed softly.

He almost makes being sick bearable.

Neil could feel his exhaustion taking hold. He drifted off to sleep, being lulled into rest by Scott's gentle caresses.

* * * *

Neil woke up to an empty room, but he could hear the faint sounds of the TV through his partly open door. He still felt absolutely horrible, but knowing Scott hadn't left twisted his insides pleasantly.

Getting out of bed, he didn't take the blanket this time. He shuffled to the door and pushed it open. Scott was on the couch with a cup of coffee and a movie. Unlike on their date, he noticed Neil's presence immediately.

"Neil," Scott said, putting down his coffee and pausing the movie, "how are you feeling?"

"Like crap," Neil admitted, his throat hurting with each word.

Scott looked concerned. "Want me to make you some more tea?"

"I'm going to shower," Neil said. "Make it after?"

"Okay," Scott agreed. "Do you need any help?"

"I'll be fine, but thanks."

"Just let me know if you need anything," Scott insisted.

Neil nodded before turning back into his bedroom. He hunted around for a spare change of clothes then went to the bathroom. He was already feeling tired, but his determination kept him pushing through. When he stepped under the water, the heat instantly soothed his muscles and made him feel less disgusting. The steam was helping his nose, too. Neil didn't spend too long under the spray. Each minute was draining his already-depleted energy reserves.

Climbing out of the shower, he shivered at the temperature difference and dried quickly. He changed into his sleep pants and shirt but ignored the siren call of his bed for the living room. Scott was in the kitchen waiting for the kettle to boil. Neil dropped onto the couch and closed his eyes.

"Do you want me to make you some soup?"

Neil didn't feel hungry, but he knew food would help him get better faster.

"Yeah," he croaked out.

"Chicken noodle coming up."

Neil pulled up his feet and curled onto his side. He didn't bother with dignity and lowered his head to the couch's armrest. The kettle boiled, but Neil didn't open his eyes or sit up. He listened to Scott pour the water and stir a spoon, occasionally hitting the side of the cup. The smell of soup made his stomach give a faint sound of interest. Neil only opened his eyes when he heard Scott walking toward him. He placed down a cup of soup and a second cup of tea. Scott then disappeared into Neil's bedroom before coming back with the blanket, which he placed over Neil's legs. Neil rearranged into a sitting position and grabbed the soup. Scott took a seat beside him on the couch. His hovering could have been annoying but only made Neil feel fond.

When his arm came around Neil's shoulders in a comforting embrace, Neil wanted to melt into it, but he resisted.

"What if I get you sick?"

"I've probably already caught it," Scott replied, tugging gently.

Neil gave up and relaxed into Scott's embrace, feeling comforted by his warmth and presence. He brought the cup to his lips, sipping the soup. He glanced at the TV but didn't recognize the movie.

"What are you watching?"

"*African Queen*," Scott answered before shifting enough to reach the control. "Would you like me to put it back to the start?"

"You've already seen it, and I'll probably just fall asleep."

Scott threaded his fingers through his hair, rubbing soothing circles. "That's okay. I don't mind watching it again."

How the hell did I get this guy?

He'd thought it before, but this time it came with a wave of pure affection. Scott was perfect, and for some reason, Scott had decided *he* was the one worth dating and caring about. Neil wanted to keep him and make Scott happy. He suddenly realized what he could do to show that.

"I'll have dinner with your family."

He felt Scott shift and knew the man was looking at him. Neil kept his gaze on his soup.

"What?" Scott asked.

"When I'm better," Neil clarified. "I'll meet the rest of your family."

"Yeah?" Scott asked, already sounding thrilled.

Neil snuck a glance at him, seeing Scott's blinding grin.

"Yeah," Neil confirmed. His heart raced but he ignored it. "It's what a...uh, boyfriend does, right?"

"It is," Scott answered, seeming to get even happier. "We might be able to do it next weekend. I'll find out."

Neil nodded and took another sip of soup. He also wiggled a little farther down the couch, resting his head on Scott's shoulder. Scott shifted to help accommodate him, wrapping an arm around his waist to keep him supported.

Neil closed his eyes. He heard Scott fiddling with the remote, and after a few seconds, the movie started again. Neil didn't bother to watch it. He continued to drink his soup and only listened to the TV with half an ear.

He'd just called Scott his boyfriend and agreed to meet the man's family. Maybe it was because he was sick, but he didn't feel as anxious about it as he'd expected.

* * * *

Scott stayed the night and the next day, keeping Neil company and taking care of him. By the third day, Neil finally felt close to normal. Scott, insisting that the fresh air would do him good, convinced him to go to the park for lunch. Scott made sandwiches and they took a blanket to sit on. When Neil got tired, he lay down with his head in Scott's lap, enjoying the sun on his skin and the fresh air in his lungs. Neil returned to work the next day, trying not to feel guilty that Scott had used all his days off caring for him. Scott had merely kissed away his frown and promised to see him for a date soon.

Denise had quickly noticed his good mood and didn't let it go unremarked upon.

"You look happy for a sick person," she said. "Did your sexy fireman kiss everything better?"

Neil snorted. "I wouldn't go that far."

"Oh?" She looked surprised. "But he made it better?"

Neil smiled just thinking about it—Scott acting like a giant mother hen and bringing him tea and lozenges at the slightest hint of a cough. It had been nice, being so well cared for.

"Yeah," Neil admitted, "he did."

"Aw," Denise cooed. "You really are lucky, Neil." She winked. "I better get an invitation to your wedding."

Neil's breath caught. He knew she was only teasing, but it was like a punch to the gut, especially considering he'd agreed to the family dinner. He'd felt too crappy to think much about it at the time, but now it came back full force. He'd called Scott his boyfriend, and he'd agreed to meet even more of Scott's family.

The scariest part was that he didn't want to take any of it back. He wanted to be a bigger part in Scott's life. He wanted Scott to have a larger part in his.

Holy crap. I think I might... I could be... Am I actually falling for him?

"Neil?" Denise asked, obviously noticing his reaction. "Are you okay?"

Neil planned to dismiss her question, but he stopped at the last moment. He'd worked with Denise for a few years. They'd joked about each other's love lives a lot, and outside his family, she knew better than anyone about his habit of picking up flings and leaving them within hours of sunrise.

"I'm not used to dating someone," he admitted, feeling uncomfortable just broaching the subject. "He wants me to meet his family. I agreed to do it."

He glanced at Denise. Her eyebrows were high on her forehead.

"Well, that's not what I expected," Denise said. "Usually, it's nothing but jealousy-inducing tales of marathon sex."

Neil grimaced. "I know."

"So, he really is different, huh?"

Neil nodded. He glanced at the front of the store, half-hoping someone would show up and force them to end the conversation. No one did. He looked back at Denise to find her watching him curiously. She was waiting for more.

Just get it out. Maybe she can help.

"I don't know how to be in a relationship. I'm going to make a mess." He ran a hand through his hair. "But I don't *want* to make a mess."

"Well, making a mess doesn't mean it's over," Denise pointed out. "It just means you have to fix it if you do."

Neil grimaced. "Knowing me, I'll just shatter it even further."

"There's no guarantee of that," she said. She also stepped closer and squeezed his arm. "Try not to overthink it or you'll ruin what you already have. Just let it happen naturally and enjoy being with him."

Easy for you to say.

Because it wasn't just his own fear of inadequacy. It was the more tangible worry about Scott's job. Fighting fires wasn't safe and now that he was growing to care for Scott, it made his lover's career more than just a sexy uniform. It came with risks and consequences.

He wanted to be with Scott, but every time their relationship deepened, the shield around his heart lowered further. There was nothing to keep him safe if Scott walked away — or into a fire.

Chapter Twelve

Neil tried to follow Denise's advice and let things happen naturally. He hoped that because he actually cared about the result and was invested in their relationship, it would make a difference.

Despite his resolution, their conflicting schedules meant they spent the next week texting. Work was busy for both of them, and they were both too tired to go out to a loud, busy restaurant. No matter how much he wanted to see Scott, Neil was equally ready to fall face-first into his mattress.

He climbed up the stairs to his apartment on heavy feet after another long, exhausting day. He paused in the hallway, astonished to find Scott by his front door with a hessian bag at his feet.

"Scott? What are you doing here?"

His lover had been looking at his phone, but he glanced up with a smile.

"Neil...hey."

He walked over and greeted Neil with a quick kiss. Neil returned it, but his frown of confusion never faded.

"We've both had a really busy week, and we've kept saying we're too tired to go out."

"We have," Neil said, uncertainly.

"Well," Scott said, walking back to the door and picking up the bag, "I cut out the restaurant." He grinned and lightly shook it. "I got takeout from the Italian place near my house. Now we can have dinner without the crowds."

It was the perfect solution. He didn't even mind the encroachment on his solitude. He was too happy to have Scott. Closing the distance, he kissed Scott, hoping it showed his enthusiasm for the idea. When Scott wrapped an arm around his waist, Neil felt the stress from work falling off his shoulders.

"Come on," he said, unwinding his arm. "We don't want the food to get cold."

Neil unlocked his door and they walked in. Scott went to the kitchen and started unloading the food onto the counter.

"Do you want it now?" Scott asked. "Or do you want to shower and change?"

"A shower would be good," Neil agreed. "Give me five minutes."

He dropped his keys, phone and wallet on the table and headed to the bedroom where he grabbed fresh clothes before going into the bathroom. His stomach was already rumbling, and he was in and out of the shower in record time. Neil yanked on his sleep pants but ended up forgoing his shirt.

He joined Scott in the kitchen. The plastic containers were open, and Scott was piling food on their plates.

There was lasagne, lamb ragu and fresh sourdough bread. Neil's stomach rumbled again, and he located a knife to cut them each a slice. When everything was dished up, Neil grabbed them each a beer from the fridge while Scott brought their plates to the couch.

"I think we're supposed to drink wine with this," Scott remarked, nodding at the takeout.

"I don't keep wine." Neil held out the bottle. "Take it or leave it."

Scott accepted with a chuckle while Neil placed his beside his plate. He then lowered onto the couch with a relieved groan. Scott picked up his plate and handed it to him. Neil took it with a grateful smile. He swirled the pasta onto his fork and closed his eyes at the first delicious mouthful.

Damn, that's good.

"It looks like I picked the right meals," Scott remarked, sounding pleased.

"You did," Neil agreed. "But you could have shown up with a microwave meal. I would have been happy with that."

"You might have low standards, but I don't. I'm going to feed you properly."

Neil grinned. "If you're concerned by frozen food, you shouldn't look in my freezer. The contents won't impress you."

"I guess I'll just have to keep bringing you good food."

Neil paused with his fork halfway to his mouth. The words had seemed more serious than their previous teasing. He glanced at Scott and found his gaze earnest. Neil lowered his fork slowly.

"How often do you plan to do that?" Neil asked.

"Whenever we can manage it," Scott replied, remaining serious. "I'll come here, or you can come to my place. We can cook or order in, whatever we feel like. As long as we're getting some time with each other."

"Even if it's only a few hours?"

"Any time together is better than none."

He really means that.

Scott was happy to sit on his ratty couch talking about their days, watching a movie or just silently eating. He'd then climb in his car and go home—or maybe he'd stay the night, even if there wasn't any prospect of sex. He just wanted them to be together.

This is what a relationship feels like. This is what it would be like coming...home to Scott.

Neil poked at his food. He wasn't like Scott, who could express what he was feeling with ease. It was hard for Neil to admit it, let alone actually *say* it to his lover.

"I guess we could make that work," he mumbled.

Scott laughed softly before he shifted on the couch. He placed a kiss on Neil's cheek and Neil closed his eyes and leaned into it.

Scott pulled back too soon, but he didn't go far. Neil opened his eyes. They were pressed more fully together, and Scott had gone back to his meal. Neil did the same. They didn't speak further as they ate their dinner. The quiet was peaceful and comfortable.

Neil finished first. He put down his plate, opened his beer and took a deep swallow, savoring the taste. Scott finished soon after and grabbed his drink. Scott's body was a line of warmth against his side. He could feel each shift as Scott raised his beer to his lips. Neil had missed him over the last few days.

"You don't work this Saturday, right?" Scott asked, breaking the silence.

"No." Neil smirked. "Why? Do you plan to come over and cook me dinner?"

"Well, I can promise a home-cooked meal, just not from me."

Neil's stomach dropped and he tensed as he realized what Scott meant. If Scott noticed, he didn't comment on it.

"So, how does six at my parents' house sound?"

Like a disaster in the making.

He'd known it was only a matter of time until Scott asked. He'd agreed to it, and just because he was nervous, it didn't mean he would back out.

"Sounds fine," Neil said, hoping to project confidence and calm. "Where do your parents live?"

"On the north side, near the river, but I can pick you up."

"Yeah, okay," Neil agreed.

Scott took his hand and linked their fingers.

"Don't worry. You won't be the only one there. My sisters are bringing their partners."

It didn't make Neil feel any better. While it could mean there was less of a spotlight on him, Neil wasn't holding his breath. If anything, he'd be measured against the already-accepted spouses. Lisa and Leslie seemed to like him, but there were six more people to win over.

"Just let it happen naturally. If you make a mess, it just means you have to fix it."

He just had to remember that one mistake wouldn't be the end of everything. Hell, Scott would probably only *smile* at his screw ups. Looking at their linked hands, Neil focused on what it meant to Scott. He could do this. He could pass with *flying colors*, because it meant something important to his boyfriend.

"Neil?"

Neil blinked back to the room and focused on Scott. He looked concerned. Neil smiled, hoping to reassure him.

"My mind drifted. I'm fine."

"You're sure?"

Neil doubted Scott had believed him. He had a good idea Scott would pester him with questions until he got a genuine answer. He'd want to make sure that Neil wanted to attend the family dinner. His worry only furthered Neil's resolve.

"Yeah." He squeezed Scott's hand. "Told you, I'm fine."

Scott eyed him for a few moments more, searching his expression, but in the end, he smiled and nodded.

"All right. Do you want to watch something or head to bed?"

"I'm not tired enough to sleep. How about you find another terrible old film?"

"Brilliant," Scott insisted. "A *brilliant* old film."

Neil rolled his eyes but he let Scott's hand go so his lover could grab the remote and start searching for something to put on. Neil sipped his beer and watched Scott fondly. A family dinner really was a small price to pay to keep this man at his side.

* * * *

The weekend came around too fast for Neil's liking. Denise found out about the dinner but instead of teasing him, she offered tips on how to get through it and come out with a positive family opinion.

Neil still didn't feel remotely prepared when Scott knocked at his door to pick him up. Neil straightened his blue dress shirt, trying to brush out nonexistent wrinkles before opening the door. Scott was in jeans and the purple shirt from Hardgroves.

"You look great," Scott said.

"You, too."

He already had his phone and keys, but he ducked back into his apartment for the bottle of wine he'd bought. He'd figured a gift couldn't hurt his chances.

"Neil," Scott said, grinning fondly, "you didn't have to get something."

Neil shrugged, feeling awkward and trying not to show it. "I figured no one would say no to a sweetener."

Scott shook his head, but he was still smiling.

"You really will be fine. They're going to love you."

"I'm going to remind you of that platitude if my family ever visits."

Scott laughed and some of Neil's tension eased. He locked the door behind him, and Scott held out his hand. Neil took it as they walked down the stairs together. They didn't speak until they were in the car and Scott was pulling out onto the road.

"Now, you've met Lisa and Leslie," Scott began. "Mum's name is Angie, and my stepdad is Donovan. The eldest of my sisters is pregnant and will bring her husband, but he's a contractor, so they're sometimes late, depending on when he finished his last job."

"Okay," Neil replied.

"My middle sister will already be there. She's always the one to pop in early so she can help Mum cook. Her boyfriend will be with Donavon, staying out of the way."

"Do you have a lot of family dinners?"

"Once a month," Scott agreed. "Sometimes more often. We all try to pop over and have dinner when we can, even if it's only one or two of us."

"Oh."

"Your family isn't the same?"

Neil shook his head. "Even when I lived only a half hour away, we only got together for specific occasions. My older brother Adrian is a chef, so he's always busy. I was usually out at clubs and Jackson lived at home while he did his university degree."

"You didn't have dinners while your younger brother lived there?"

"Not really. I mean, if it was a birthday or there was a promotion, we got together. The rest of the time we did our own thing."

"That's so different to my family," Scott said. "We're always together." His expression turned thoughtful. "But I guess your way makes it special when you are."

"Yeah, I suppose it does."

Neil felt a small pang of homesickness.

Maybe I should give my parents a call? Maybe I should tell them about Scott?

Neil squashed the idea the moment it formed. He wasn't ready to admit his relationship to them. His mother's enthusiasm would leave him uncomfortable. His father, at least, would be content as long as Scott could make a good steak and preferred AFL over rugby.

"Is there anything I need to know about your family?" Neil asked.

"I don't think so," Scott said. "We're all easy-going." He flashed Neil a smile. "I've told you. You'll be fine."

Neil ignored the reassurance. He couldn't believe Scott right now. It was better to change the subject before he decided to cut his losses and call the night off.

"How's work been?"

"Good," Scott said. "Everyone's finally back and healthy."

"That must be a relief."

"Yeah. We can work on a skeleton crew, but it's really not recommended. Good thing it's not bushfire season."

A spike of fear went through Neil. He'd watched news reports as terrible fires tore through towns and nature reserves. He didn't want to imagine Scott in the middle of those blazes, trying to keep people and animals safe.

"How about you?" Scott asked. "You've had a busy week."

"Ridiculously busy," Neil agreed, happy to stop thinking about fires. "I'm glad I've got the weekend off."

"I don't have any plans tomorrow. Why don't you stay at my place tonight?" He winked at Neil. "I can make pancakes in the morning."

Neil chuckled. "Well, with a temptation like pancakes..."

"I might have a surprise for you, too," Scott said.

"Oh?"

He didn't expect Scott's cheeks to go pink.

"Yeah."

Neil sat up straighter and eyed Scott curiously. The red on his cheeks only intensified.

"I am *very* interested in what this surprise is now."

"You'll find out tonight," Scott replied, "*after* we get back."

Neil raised his eyebrows and repressed a smirk. He had a feeling this surprise was going to involve the bedroom.

But what about it makes Scott blush?

Neil could think of several interesting ideas, but he tried to halt his wandering thoughts before they went any further. The last thing he wanted was to get an erection just before meeting Scott's parents.

"Okay," he said. "I'll be on my best behavior."

Scott cleared his throat, still seeming a little embarrassed. Neil's curiosity would normally be difficult to ignore, as would his desire to tease Scott until he either revealed the surprise or they ended up making out in the back of the car. But a glance at the car clock sobered him. It was approaching six, and they'd be arriving soon. Neil anxiously turned the wine bottle in his lap.

"What do your parents know about me?"

"They know we met in Brisbane then again by accident at the store you manage. I know Lisa filled them in on everything that happened at the game. I also told them you were a great guy I was lucky to have met."

"I'm sure you tell that to all the boys," Neil muttered, hoping he wasn't flushing.

"I don't see any other boys in my car," Scott countered.

Neil looked out of the window and swallowed around his suddenly dry mouth. They lapsed into a brief silence.

"See that park on the right?" Scott announced. "My sisters and I used to visit it as a kid."

"You did?"

"Yeah. We used to ride our bikes and race. Whoever won got out of doing the daily chores."

Neil sniggered. "That's certainly an incentive to win."

"Oh, it was."

He followed it up with additional stories of races long past. He made it entertaining and didn't hesitate to admit the many times he'd fallen off his bike or lost to his sisters. Neil almost forgot where they were going as he chuckled at every story of a teenage Scott.

It was only when they turned down a well-maintained suburban street that Neil's humor faded. Scott parked in front of a large, two-story house. There was a car in the garage and another one behind it. Scott turned off the engine. Neil stared at the house, feeling a combination of dread, nerves and resignation.

Well, no turning back now. Sink or swim.

"Ready?"

"Absolutely," Neil lied.

He unbuckled his seatbelt and opened the door. Neil forced confidence into his movements and hoped everyone would buy it. He stood outside the car, holding the wine and waiting for Scott to join him. Scott took his hand and led him across the lawn and toward the front door. They were only halfway there when the door opened, and a middle-aged woman emerged. She was short and plump with straight black hair and a friendly smile.

"Scottie!" she called, coming forward to meet them.

She opened her arms and Scott let Neil go to accept his mother's hug. She released him and turned to Neil. Her smile was as open and kind as Scott's.

"And you must be Neil."

"Yes, ma'am," he greeted politely. He held out the wine. "Thank you for inviting me to dinner."

Her smile deepened and she took the wine in one hand while her other arm pulled him into a hug. He startled but quickly and uncertainly hugged her back. When it ended, she kept her hand on his arm.

"Thank you, Neil, but you really didn't need to do this. I hope Scott didn't make you feel you needed to bring something."

"No, he didn't, ma'am."

"Please, Neil," she said, already leading him toward the house, "call me Angie. None of us are formal around here. Now —"

The front door opened again and a new voice cut her off.

"I think Dad's burning the capsicums."

"Donovan!" Angie shouted, letting Neil go and hurrying inside the house.

The woman let her pass and waited by the door. She was obviously Scott's sister. She was as short as her mother with a pixie cut and a nose ring. She looked Neil up and down before grinning.

"Lisa was right. You *did* pick a handsome one, Scottie." She winked at them. "Anyway, I'm Tess." She held open the door so they could step through. "And you boys better come inside. No one else is here yet, and that means you'll be helping make sure Dad doesn't destroy something."

"Donovan can do a lot of things," Scott explained. "But if you ask him to cook anything more basic than eggs on toast, you're asking for a fire."

"And that is why I blame Dad for you becoming a fireman," his sister added.

Stepping inside the house, it didn't surprise Neil to find family photos all over the walls and the mantelpiece. He could even see one of Scott in uniform with other firefighters. Scott had said his family was close, and the evidence was all over the walls.

"But, darling," Neil heard a man insisting, "they aren't even *brown*."

"Out!" Angie said, her voice good-natured but firm.

A gray-haired man trudged out of the kitchen with a dramatic slump to his shoulders. He was in a plaid shirt and jeans, and a man around Neil's age was waiting for him with a grin. He had brown hair in a ponytail, two eyebrow piercings and was wearing a band shirt and ripped jeans. He handed Donovan a beer. The man took it before looking toward them. Donovan's expression quickly brightened.

"Ah, Scott! And you must be Neil!"

He walked over and held out his hand. Neil hurriedly shook it.

"It's nice to meet you," Neil greeted.

He slapped Neil's shoulder and encouraged him forward.

"Come on. Let's get you and Scottie a beer. Angie might have said, but we're very relaxed here. Just a nice meal and a couple of drinks. Maybe a burned capsicum or two."

"If any of them are burned, they're going to *you*," Angie declared.

"You see?" Donovan remarked. "None of them are burned yet!"

A collective sigh could be heard from everyone. Neil was sure there was an inside joke he was missing. Yet, despite being out of the loop, he didn't feel excluded.

The family was welcoming him in with open arms, just like Scott's company of fireman.

Glancing over his shoulder, Neil caught Scott's gaze. His features were soft with fondness and delight.

Maybe this won't be so bad after all.

Chapter Thirteen

Thankfully, he didn't spend the evening being grilled for information. Everyone was curious about him, which Neil had expected, but he wasn't the center of attention. Community gossip held the family's focus, only to be replaced by Scott's pregnant sister once she and her husband had arrived. Everyone was excited about the approaching due date, which quickly turned into childhood stories. It was easy to chuckle over everyone's antics. He didn't feel like an outsider, but they didn't pressure him to be involved, either.

When they sat down to dinner, he was between Scott and Tess. She could talk a mile a minute and barely let him get a word in edgewise. Scott was a warm presence at his side, quietly explaining any backstories that he was missing. There was a large amount of teasing regarding the meal and Donovan's past kitchen failures.

After eating, they moved to the back patio to drink beers and continue their conversations. His stepfather pulled Scott away for a chat, but Leslie came over to discuss their next round of pool. Lisa was quick to join his side, already planning a double date for the four of them. It made Neil realize he didn't have to win them over. They were already accepting him as part of the family.

It allowed him to open up a little more. He didn't even notice the time flying until it was nine-thirty and everyone was leaving. The sisters all gave him a hug while the men shook his hand or gave him a backslap. Angie hugged him, too, and kissed his cheek. She got a promise out of him to attend the next family dinner. He didn't even regret agreeing to it.

When they drove away, everyone was still congregating on the lawn and saying their last goodbyes.

Scott waited just long enough for them to clear the house.

"What did you think?" he asked, uncertainty obvious in his voice.

"Your family is just like you." Neil smiled. "I had fun."

Scott let out a heavy, relieved breath before pulling the car over. It confused Neil until Scott leaned across the divide and kissed him. Neil instantly tried to get closer. The position was awkward, but Neil happily put up with it. He'd only had car sex once before, but he'd happily do it again with Scott.

However, when the kiss broke, Scott rested their foreheads together. He took Neil's hand and linked their fingers.

"I'm really glad you came," Scott said. "I knew they'd love you."

"Well, that remains to be seen."

"They did," Scott assured him. "I could tell."

Scott kissed him again before he could offer any more protests. Despite Neil being more than willing to keep it up and move to the backseat, Scott broke them apart and started them back toward Scott's house. Neil surreptitiously rearranged his pants.

I hope we don't stay this chaste when we get to Scott's. It reminded him of their earlier conversation. *I wonder what my surprise will be?*

He glanced at Scott. The darkness of the car shadowed his lover, but the occasional streetlight bathed him in a glimmer of light. His desire only grew as he traveled his gaze over Scott's body. He couldn't wait to strip the man and get his hands and mouth on Scott's skin. They'd been deliberately light on their affection while at Scott's parents' house. He wanted to make up for all the time they'd missed.

Maybe we'll finally spend the entire morning together.

It amazed Neil that not too long before, the idea of spending *more* time with a lover wouldn't have appealed. But with Scott, he wanted to share breakfast, complain about the man's wardrobe choices and get kissed in the middle of a home-cooked meal.

Next thing you know, I'll want to wake up with him every day.

Neil's breath caught, because unlike the dismissive laughter the thought should have prompted, he felt something else. The idea of being around Scott constantly, of having a *future* with him didn't seem bad.

It sounds like something I could…maybe…

Scott spoke, pulling Neil from his tentative, heart-racing thoughts.

"Neil? You're not falling asleep, are you?"

"No," he deflected, hastily smiling. "I'm just wondering about the surprise that you promised me."

Scott cleared his throat, which had the desired effect of distracting him.

"Try not to get your hopes up," Scott muttered. "It might not be that good."

"Your downplaying is only making me curiouser."

Scott shifted awkwardly and changed the subject.

"Lisa mentioned us getting together for pool?"

Neil's lips twitched with amusement, but he let it occur.

"Yeah. Leslie wants us to team up against the siblings."

"I think he's getting an unjust advantage," Scott complained. "Lisa is terrible at aiming."

"Then you should have arrived sooner. You might have had me on your team."

"That's not fair," Scott grumbled. "He cornered you when I was roped into a discussion about baseball."

"I can't blame a man for taking advantage."

Scott shot him a wounded look. "Choosing another man over me?"

Despite the joking nature, Neil found that even in jest, he couldn't say it.

"I wouldn't do that, Scott."

The words came out more serious than he'd intended. The statement rested in the air like a promise. Scott knew about his habit of cycling through men. He didn't want his lover to doubt him. But when Scott looked at him, his expression was gentle and fond. He took one hand off the steering wheel to grab Neil's and give it a quick, soft squeeze.

"I know," he said.

The softness of the moment left Neil eager for a subject change. He coughed and said, "So, what terrible new movie do you plan to watch next?"

Scott laughed and easily began chatting about his next 'classic'. Neil relaxed into the familiar sound of his lover's voice. He also brought his hand down to absently rub where Scott had squeezed. It still felt warm, even after he'd let go.

* * * *

When they arrived at Scott's house, his lover glanced around and Neil half-expected to see a nosy neighbor peeking out of their windows, but there was nothing. When Scott looked back at him, Neil raised his eyebrows.

"My neighbors keep asking about you," Scott admitted.

"Are they scandalized you keep having a man over?" Neil teased.

"They're scandalized they only know your name. They've been hinting at throwing a street party for days."

Neil shook his head, feeling bemused. "Aren't we running out of people for me to meet?"

They were almost at the front door, and Scott wrapped an arm around his waist.

"Getting close," Scott admitted. "But I can't help showing you off. Everyone's been wanting me to get a nice boyfriend for years." He grinned. "Now, I have one."

Neil felt a burst of warmth, even as his stomach squirmed. He tried to keep both out of his tone and remain flippant and unaffected.

"Flattery will get you everywhere."

"I hope so."

Scott followed it with a wink before opening the door and letting them inside. He turned on the hall light and unwound his arm. Scott shut the door, but Neil didn't let him go far. He curled his arms around Scott's waist and pressed his front to his lover's back. He leaned in until his lips were brushing Scott's ear.

"I think I'm due my surprise."

"Feeling impatient?"

"I've been very patient." Neil slid his fingers under Scott's shirt. "I've waited through two car rides, dinner and hours of conversation. I want to know what my evening has in store."

Scott tilted his head back to rest on Neil's shoulder. Neil turned his head and kissed Scott's neck just below his three moles. He then scraped his teeth over it while he teased around the waistband of Scott's pants. Scott groaned softly and Neil removed his mouth.

"So," he questioned, "where's my surprise?"

Scott groaned again, but this time it sounded more embarrassed than aroused. He pulled away from Neil, forcing him to let his lover go.

"Okay," he said, "I'll show you."

"Show me?"

Scott's blush was reappearing.

"I want to make sure you'll like it before we, um…"

Neil frowned as Scott trailed off. His curiosity was only growing, and he followed close behind as Scott entered the living room. Scott turned on the light before going to the couch. He picked up something plastic before turning it around to show Neil. He immediately burst out laughing. Scott scowled at him.

"You said you wanted it!" Scott complained, his cheeks darkening.

"I did," Neil gasped. "But *why* did you buy a fireman costume? You *are* a fireman!"

"Well, I'm certainly not doing it in my *actual* work clothes."

Neil's amusement faded as he realized *exactly* what the costume meant. He'd offered to play 'my hero' if Scott would don his uniform. Neil swallowed around a dry mouth. His voice lowered to a soft murmur.

"You said you wouldn't do that."

"I also said you'd be the only one to change my mind."

Despite Scott's embarrassment, Neil could see he was interested in the idea. Just the thought had Neil's lust growing. His cock was hardening as he pictured his lover in the yellow costume. He desperately wanted Scott to put it on. He then wanted to rip him out of the clothes.

No, keep him half dressed. Let me take his cock when he's still geared up. Fuck. Have him push me against the wall and take me from behind.

A thousand fantasies were fighting for dominance in his mind, but he liked the latter one a lot. God, he *hoped* he'd be able to get Scott in the outfit again so he could cycle through them all.

Stepping forward, Neil ran his hand over Scott's arm. He dragged his attention from the packaged costume to meet his lover's gaze. Neil swallowed again, but his voice remained rough.

"I've never been prouder to change your opinion."

"Good. Now go into the bedroom, and I'll get changed."

Neil hesitated to follow the order. He rarely let someone else tell him what to do, but something about it sent excitement through him. He'd never thought how sexy it would be for Scott to be in control. If Scott was playing along with the clothes, maybe, in return, he could let his lover be in charge.

Running his fingers teasingly up Scott's arm, he murmured, "I better do what my sexy fireman says."

Scott's breath caught and his eyes darkened further. Neil couldn't resist ducking in and kissing Scott. It was partly in gratitude, but mostly because he *needed* to. Scott dropped the uniform and cupped his cheeks. The kiss was searing, and Neil was quickly groaning against his lover's mouth. When Scott broke them apart, they were both panting.

"Go to the room," he ordered.

Neil grinned and parroted the word Scott used on him. "Yes, *sir*."

Scott barely stifled his moan before pushing him away. Neil tried not to laugh, even as he obeyed. He hurried toward the bedroom, desire and eagerness flooding his body. When he reached it, he turned on the lamps and kicked off his shoes and socks. He also grabbed the lube and condoms from the drawer and threw them on the bed. He didn't want *anything* to impede Scott from getting his cock inside him.

Neil waited at the foot of the bed, fidgeting with impatience and anticipation. It seemed to take forever to hear Scott's approaching footsteps. His breath caught. The darkness of the hall left him in shadow, but when he got close enough to see, Neil's pulse skyrocketed and he almost moaned.

The outfit wasn't a perfect replica, but Scott had chosen something as close to the real thing as possible. There was a baggy yellow jacket with matching pants. The helmet was on his head and he was even carrying a fake ax. Neil could see a hint of the navy shirt underneath his buttoned jacket.

"Hello, sexy fireman."

Scott didn't speak. He walked forward confidently, sending a thrill through Neil. When Scott reached him, he hooked an arm around Neil's waist and yanked him forward in an unexpected, rough gesture. Neil gasped but the sound was quickly lost against Scott's lips.

Neil wrapped an arm around Scott's neck and pressed against him. He hastily opened a button with his free hand so he could slip his fingers beneath Scott's yellow jacket to run over his thin shirt. He went farther up to rub over one of Scott's clothed nipples. His lover groaned, and Neil broke the kiss to trail his mouth over Scott's jaw.

"How can I make my fireman's day?" Neil murmured.

"I thought this was *your* surprise present?" Scott said hoarsely.

"All good deeds deserve a reward," he answered. "I'm happy to be *your* reward."

Scott groaned again. He heard the thump of the ax hitting the ground before Scott threaded a hand through his hair and tugged him into a kiss. Scott *devoured* his mouth. He was like a man unleashed. Neil moaned, his toes curling as he melted against his lover, and his body flooded with desperation to get *more*.

He broke the kiss to pant, "Fuck me."

Scott started kissing his jaw. He used his hold on Neil's hair to turn his face away to gain better access. It sent an unexpected bolt of arousal down Neil's spine. He shuddered and closed his eyes.

"*Fuck me*, Scott," he said again. "Push me against the wall. Get into me. *Fuck*."

Scott paused. "That's what you want?"

"*God*, yes," Neil replied. "Make me. Take me as a goddamn *prize*."

Scott's next groan came from deep within his chest. He yanked Neil back in for a kiss. Neil took his hands to Scott's shoulders, bunching in the fabric of his fireman jacket and holding on. Scott kept an arm around his waist. He broke the kiss to yank Neil across the room. He stumbled but used Scott's shoulders to keep upright. Scott didn't falter once.

Neil shivered. *This* was a fireman. Scott was strong and determined. Neil would bet that the panic and disorientation of someone he was rescuing wouldn't phase Scott. He would get them out and go back in to save someone else.

Now, in a *sexual* context, it meant that Scott could be in control and move Neil wherever he wanted. Neil's breath was coming heavier at the prospect. When his shoulder knocked against the wall, he shuddered, and his cock throbbed in his jeans. He leaned his back against it and looked at his lover. Scott's jacket was unbuttoned and creased from Neil's ministrations while arousal flushed his cheeks with heat. Neil dragged his teeth over his bottom lip.

He snuck his hands to Scott's jacket. He unbuttoned it until it fell open over his navy shirt. Neil then moved to the pants, unbuttoning them and getting a glimpse at the boxers hiding Scott's thick, hard length. Neil pushed them down to reveal the man's cock. He groaned before scrabbling for his pants, unbuttoning and yanking them down around his thighs. He yanked out his shirt, which had been tucked in, not caring that his cock would smear the edges.

Scott moved to shrug off his jacket, but Neil shook his head and grabbed his arm.

"No, don't," he said. "Take me like that—like you just got home."

Like you couldn't wait to get inside me.

"*God*, Neil."

Scott kissed him, and Neil arched into the touch. He felt hot all over, and his yearning made the kiss frantic. Scott jerked away and hurried to the bed to get the condom and lube. Neil spun around and braced his arms against the wall. He spread his legs and rested his forehead on his wrists. His body trembled with anticipation. Every step Scott made sounded loud in the room. Neil's breathing was heavy, and his cock was ramrod hard.

When Scott touched his hip, Neil shuddered and bit down on a mewl. However, when Scott brushed against his entrance, the sound escaped. His fingers were coated with lube and pressed their way inside. Neil spread his legs farther and pushed back. Scott directed the motions of his hips and Neil wished he had better leverage and could take more of Scott inside him.

"Scott, hurry up," he whined.

"No," Scott replied.

His tone was firm, and Neil's breath caught. He opened his eyes but didn't move his head. He suddenly felt overly aware of their positions. His back was to the room. Scott was in complete control, and while Neil knew he could easily break away or call quits, the awareness of exactly how much trust he was giving Scott both unnerved and excited him.

When Scott curled his fingers that little bit deeper. Neil gasped and his body spasmed with pleasure. He forgot all about his discomfort.

"*Fuck*," he cursed. "Scott—"

Scott did it again and Neil rocked back. His lover kept it up, tormenting him with slow stretches and unexpected brushes to his prostate. He would remove his fingers, but only to add more lube. Neil was sweating and trembling within minutes. He wanted more, but he also didn't want to call 'stop'. He knew he could push away and tackle Scott to the bed and ride him to completion. Scott would laugh and let him. But Neil didn't want this to end. He felt *good*. Neil couldn't pinpoint why this mattered, but he wanted to see it through.

When Scott removed his fingers, Neil expected them to come back. He *didn't* expect a touch to his cock. His entire body jerked, and he bit down on a shout. Scott leaned his body against Neil's, and he could feel Scott's hard length sliding beneath his ass, teasing him.

"You're so good, Neil," Scott whispered. "So beautiful. Never thought I'd be so lucky to have a prize like you."

Neil let out a strangled noise, half because of the words and half because Scott was still teasingly stroking his aching cock.

Scott pressed a kiss just below his ear on the small part of his cheek that he could reach. He only remained for a few strokes before he let Neil's cock go and stepped back. Neil made a soft inquiring noise and almost lifted his head, but when he heard ripping plastic, he sucked in a breath. Neil tried to spread his legs even wider and make his eagerness obvious.

When Scott stepped up to him again, he caught Neil's hips and angled him. The head of Scott's cock brushed his entrance and he bit down an unmanly whine.

"I'm going to fuck you now," Scott said.

His voice had an edge to it. He sounded as wound up as Neil was. Not wanting to make a noise that would embarrass him later, Neil nodded frantically.

When Scott pushed the head inside, Neil choked out a gasp. Scott grunted but kept sliding in. His preparations made Scott slip in easily, but Neil still felt incredibly full. He *loved* it. The position made him feel overly aware of his lover — the heat of him at Neil's back, the scratch of the fabric on his thighs and the stretch of being filled by a hard, erect cock.

Scott worked his way in until he was fully sheathed. He panted for breath by Neil's ear. Neil wanted to stay in the moment for eternity. Scott seemed to surround him. He'd never been so content.

Yet, the moment Scott pulled out, Neil remembered exactly why movement was *good*, especially when he followed it by thrusting back inside. Neil moaned loudly and braced his feet. Scott held his hips and pulled him down onto each thrust. It only took two strikes before Scott's aim came true. Neil jerked like a live wire. He shifted his head off his forearms and braced his hands on the wall. It allowed him to better move into every thrust. Scott was picking up speed, and every time he pounded inside him, Neil gained another firework of pleasure.

Everything was rushed and frantic — a desperate climb to completion — and yet, it didn't have any of the detachment Neil would have expected. He experienced an even *deeper* connection to Scott. Neil couldn't see his lover, was following his sounds and movements. He *trusted* Scott to make it good and to keep him safe.

"Scott," he whispered.

"Neil," his lover replied.

When Scott slid a hand down to his cock, Neil cried out. He felt over-sensitive and ready to combust at any moment, and Scott seemed to realize it.

"Let go," he murmured, pumping gently. "I've got you."

Neil came. It took him by complete surprise. His voice cracked on a moan, and his body shuddered through intense aftershocks. Scott was still inside him — panting and groaning and giving small, rocking thrusts. He came without fanfare, pressing his lips to Neil's shoulder and moaning his name.

Neil panted and rested his forehead on the wall. He was sweaty and exhausted, but also incredibly satisfied and content. Neil didn't understand how rough wall sex had turned into something that made him feel so *good*.

Scott kissed him through his shirt, making Neil smile. When he trailed his mouth up to Neil's neck then to his ear, Neil laughed and jerked away. He turned his head and looked at his lover. Scott was grinning. He also leaned forward and Neil met him halfway to share a brief kiss.

"I suppose the surprise was a success," Scott said.

Neil chuckled. "Yes. I expect it to make a repeat appearance."

Scott snorted but his eyes were twinkling. "Yes, *sir*."

Neil's smile returned their usual equilibrium. It also, unfortunately, meant Scott pulled back and slipped out of him. Neil bit down on a groan of displeasure at them being parted. Despite the regret, Neil was soon straightening and stretching muscles that were beginning to cramp. Scott placed a hand on his back and directed him toward the bathroom.

It was a quick and easy cleanup. Scott dumped the costume on the floor and Neil did the same with his clothes. They had a perfunctory wipe-down before Scott tugged them to the bed. They lay down under the sheets and Scott tugged him close so that he was lying in the man's arms, his face near his chest. Neil closed his eyes, finding it easier to relax into Scott's embrace. Scott trailed a hand up and down his back in a slow, affectionate caress.

Neil was already hoping that with so much skin touching, they would *finally* be able to have morning sex. His plan was to straddle Scott and ride him until they came. Maybe after, he'd fuck Scott again. Neil grinned, already looking forward to it.

"What are you smiling about?" Scott asked.

Neil opened his eyes. Scott was already watching him.

"How I'm going to make you come tomorrow morning."

Scott barked out a surprised laugh. "Just finished and you've got the next round already planned?"

"Mm-m," Neil hummed.

He also shifted and placed a kiss on Scott's chest. He then dared to dart out his tongue to flick Scott's nipple. Scott groaned and touched his head, directing him away.

"Stop it," he protested lightly. "I'm tired. We can do more tomorrow."

Neil swallowed down a laugh but relented. "Fine. But you'll owe me two rounds."

"I can accept those terms," Scott said, sounding amused.

Neil closed his eyes and grinned again. He felt light and *happy*. He didn't even want to fight the feelings.

Neil just wanted to accept and enjoy them. He'd just had a great round of sex, and he had two more to look forward to—along with breakfast and a night curled naked around his gorgeous lover.

Scott started playing with his hair, and Neil relaxed further. They were quiet for long enough that Scott's movements stopped. Neil thought his lover had drifted off. It surprised him when he spoke.

"I'm so glad you're here, Neil," Scott said, his voice loose and relaxed. "S'nice."

Neil opened his eyes and shifted a little to look at Scott. His lover looked ready to fall asleep. Neil's heart rate picked up. Something about the moment seemed weighted. He tried to remain casual.

"Where, um…else would I be?"

Scott smiled faintly, his eyes were closed and his face was serene. "Don't know. Just want you here, always."

Neil sucked in a sharp breath, his eyes wide and his heart beating over time.

"What?" he asked, his voice small.

"Mm," Scott hummed, sounding even sleepier. "Miss you when you go away."

Neil was certain he was misconstruing things. Hell, Scott looked seconds away from falling asleep, but Neil *had* to know.

"You want me to move in with you?"

"Mm…yeah."

For a few seconds, shock fought with warmth and elation, but then *panic* took over. He was frozen for the longest time. When Scott's breathing turned even, he squirmed away from Scott and sat up. His lover didn't stir. Neil stared down at him, feeling overwhelmed and *afraid*.

He'd never lived with anyone. He'd never *wanted* to live with anyone. Scott made him think about it. Scott made him...

But Neil couldn't finish the thought. He wasn't ready for what it meant about his feelings or Scott's. He wasn't ready for *any* of this.

I need to get out of here.

Neil slipped out of the bed with a racing heart. He went to the bathroom and grabbed all his clothes and changed into them. It was his old routine with thousands of flings, but it felt so *wrong* to do it to Scott. Neil hesitated by the doorway and looked back at his lover, sleeping peacefully under the glow of the lamps. Scott meant so much more to him than any man he'd ever let into his bed.

And he wants you to move in with him.

Neil flinched. The terror he felt was too overwhelming. He hurried down the hallway and grabbed Scott's keys. Neil didn't care if he was running away. It was too much, and he just couldn't stay.

Chapter Fourteen

Neil hadn't been at his apartment for fifteen minutes when Scott texted him. Neil had been in the kitchen, staring at the tea that Scott had left at his apartment after he'd been sick. Guilt for leaving had warred with discomfort and fear over what Scott had admitted. The feelings only doubled when his phone rang.

It was Scott.

Neil swallowed. He looked at his lover's name and felt a wave of emotions. It was all too overwhelming, and he let the phone ring out.

Closing his eyes, Neil rested his elbows on the counter and put his head in his hands.

Looks like I do fear commitment after all.

Neil laughed hoarsely. It wasn't a realization he'd wanted to uncover. He also felt *worse* the longer his phone went without a text or a phone call. He'd hurt Scott, he was certain.

Finally, he's worked out I'm more hassle than I'm worth.

It *ached.* He'd blown things with Scott—made the mess he'd always known he'd make. They were clearly better off apart.

So why does it just make me feel worse?

"Fuck," he growled.

Neil shoved away from the counter and moved to one of his rarely used cupboards. It had a half empty bottle of Bundaberg Rum. He grabbed it and a glass. Neil poured a large amount in and went searching for Coke. He cursed when he didn't find any. There was *nothing* to mix it with at all.

"Goddamn it."

He slammed the fridge then kicked it for good measure. He turned back to the shot, but one sniff of the liquor had him opening the bottle and pouring it back inside. Neil put it back in the cupboard and went out to his living room.

He dropped onto the couch with a groan, his nose getting squished against the cushion. He didn't move away, just groaned again. Neil's mind cycled through their relationship and Scott's words. It was an unending loop, showcasing the way Neil had sabotaged a great thing.

He didn't know how long he lay there, but knocking on his door made him lift his head.

"Neil? Come on, Neil. Open the door."

Scott.

Neil's heart traitorously sped up.

"Neil? *Please.*"

Neil pushed off the couch without thinking about it. When he was on his feet, he hesitated for a moment before going to the door. He paused once more with his hand over the knob.

"Neil? I'm sorry. Please, just—"

Neil opened it. Scott's hair was a mess and he'd hastily thrown on his clothes. He looked fearful and apologetic. When he saw Neil, relief flooded his features.

"*Neil,*" he murmured.

"Hey, Scott."

"I'm sorry about what I said," Scott immediately began. "I didn't mean to make you uncomfortable or feel like you had to respond." He grimaced and ran a hand through his hair. "I was half-asleep and got carried away."

Neil swallowed. "But you meant it."

Scott winced but still nodded. They fell into a tense silence. Neil didn't know what to say or how to respond. There were feelings catapulting around inside his chest, but he didn't know what they meant or how to express them. He wasn't sure he *could* say them. Scott had always been the one to do that, not him.

"It doesn't mean we have to do anything about it," Scott said, his expression and tone earnest. "I like what we have. Yeah, I want you around more, but I don't want to lose our relationship because I said something stupid while I was so tired."

Neil chewed on his bottom lip. He still felt the clawing edges of panic at the prospect of *'moving in'* and deepening their relationship, but Scott's assurances were making him feel less likely to bolt.

I don't want to lose him. If we stay as we are, what do I have to fear?

"We can stay as we are?" Neil clarified cautiously.

Scott's expression brightened. "Yeah. Absolutely. You set the pace, Neil."

Neil let out a relieved breath. He also nodded. Scott hesitated but stepped closer. Neil opened the door farther and Scott enfolded him into a hug. Neil immediately relaxed and wrapped his arms around Scott. They both let out a breath of relief at the same time. Neil squeezed his eyes shut.

But just because they'd sorted things out, it didn't mean the guilt wasn't still twisting through him.

"I'm sorry I left," Neil forced out around a lump in his throat.

Scott just gave him a comforting squeeze.

"It's all right. I shouldn't have put you in that situation. I know you're new to a lot of this."

Neil huffed an awkward laugh. "I walked out on you in the middle of the night. How the hell are *you* the bad guy?"

"*Neither* of us are bad guys," Scott said. He pulled back to catch Neil's gaze. "We're just different." He smiled and brought up a hand, brushing Neil's cheek. "Just because I want you around all the time—just because I'm falling—it doesn't mean I expect you to do it at the same speed."

Neil sucked in a sharp breath, his eyes flying wide.

Falling.

Falling in love.

Scott might not have said the words, but the implication was clear. Hell, they'd implied their mutual affection and interest many times, but this inched them closer to a word Neil rarely said, even to his *family*.

Yet, unlike the half-asleep request to move in, this one felt a little less daunting. Maybe it was because Scott was holding him tenderly and smiling. There was no obligation in his gaze. There was just warmth and fondness. Neil felt like fidgeting. The feelings inside him were becoming too much.

So, he kissed Scott.

His lover kissed him back and Neil felt the last of his tension unwinding.

When they broke apart, Scott brushed their noses together.

"Do you want me to go?" Scott asked. "I don't want to crowd you. I just wanted to make sure we were on the same page."

Neil shook his head and clenched Scott's shirt. He might not have worked out everything, but Neil knew enough to make his answer certain.

"I want you here tonight."

Scott smiled and kissed him again. Neil sighed and loosened his grip.

It didn't fill him with the same soft contentment he'd felt earlier in Scott's house, but he would take a slight awkwardness rather than send his lover away.

* * * *

Scott stayed the night, but they didn't go straight to bed, choosing to put on a movie. Scott wrapped an arm around his shoulders and held him close. Neil closed his eyes and tried to focus on what has happening rather than the confessions Scott had spilled.

But he kept thinking about them.

"Just want you here, always."

"Miss you when you go away."

"Just because I'm falling."

He couldn't shake them, and when they finally went to bed, Neil lay awake for a long time. When he eventually dozed off, he didn't feel anymore settled.

When he woke in the morning, it was to soft kisses being placed along his shoulder. He turned his head and opened his eyes. Scott stopped and shifted to hold his gaze.

"Morning," he said quietly.

Neil grunted and peered at the digital clock. It was past ten. He was surprised Scott hadn't woken up earlier — or woken *him* up. He'd learned enough to know the man was an early bird.

"Want me to make you some coffee?"

Neil nodded and buried his nose back in the pillow. Scott chuckled and kissed the top of his head before climbing out of bed. Neil relaxed into the bedding with a soft sigh. He could hear Scott walking through his apartment and getting out cups from the kitchen.

Finally got my morning with him.

Unfortunately, the thought reminded him of the night before. His eyes opened and he stared across the room at his wall. His blinds were keeping out the light, but Neil wouldn't have cared if it was beaming in. Their conversations woke him up better than any caffeine. He rolled onto his back and rubbed his eyes.

It was all he'd been able to focus on before falling asleep, and it had only curled him into a tight, uncomfortable knot. Scott had said they would go at his pace. He *should* feel fine.

So why does this keep haunting me? He's not asking me to say yes or confess back. Why then can't I let it go?

Neil didn't know. His mind was so preoccupied that he almost startled when Scott re-entered the room. He was in boxers and had two coffees in his hands. Neil shifted into a sitting position and took his. Scott sat down beside him on the bed. Their legs touched...but nothing else.

Neil sipped his coffee and Scott did the same. For the first time, the air between them felt uneasy. Scott sighed.

"Do you want me to go home, Neil?"

Neil's head jerked up. "No!"

Scott looked unsure. "You don't seem comfortable with me here."

"I'm fine."

He wasn't, but the last thing he wanted to do was have a heart-to-heart about it. He couldn't run away this time. He didn't actually *want* to flee from Scott's life. Neil just wasn't sure how to handle things, and he didn't want to look at his emotions too closely — which meant he needed a new coping mechanism. His best option was sweeping it under the rug and forgetting about it.

A great way to do that was with sex.

"Besides," he added, forcing a smile, "I thought you owed me two rounds?"

Scott observed him. "I wasn't sure that would still be on the table."

"Of course it is," Neil insisted.

He followed the words by leaning forward. Scott met him halfway. They kissed softly at first, but when Neil's confused feelings intensified, he quickly deepened the kiss. Scott hesitated for only a moment before following suit.

They only broke apart to put their coffees aside. Swiftly after, Neil pinned Scott to the bed and straddled his hips like he'd fantasized about the night before. It wasn't exactly how Neil had planned it, but when Scott cupped his hips and grinned up at him, Neil hoped that despite Scott's words and his panic, things would still be okay.

* * * *

Neil never truly regained his equilibrium. He faked it, but sometimes, he was sure Scott saw right through him. Denise seemed to, as well. She kept asking pointed questions about how he was. When that elicited no reaction, she asked how *they* were. He always changed the subject.

Neil knew she might be able to help him if he confided in her, but he couldn't do it. Just thinking about it made him uncomfortable, and he knew it would be worse to talk about it.

Frankly, Neil wished he could erase it all from his mind. He didn't want to think about what he felt or what Scott wanted. Anytime he turned his mind to it, his chest got both warm and tight while his stomach felt like a ball of snakes. He just wanted things to go back to the way they were. It had been *easier* like that.

But everything seemed to have changed overnight.

Scott still texted him, but each message felt different. It was like Scott was holding back or over-thinking. Neil had no *proof*, but something in the phrasing screamed discomfort.

Or maybe he was just projecting.

Because Scott never mentioned what had happened. He still texted asking about Neil's day and fired back amusing quips. He organized their next date at a restaurant. Scott acted the same—and that agitated Neil.

Because if it wasn't Scott with the problem. It looked like it might be *him*, and he didn't know how to deal with it.

For three days, everything continued in an awkward standoff Neil didn't know how to fix. But it all came to a head when they met up at the restaurant. Scott was waiting out the front. He smiled and came forward. He touched Neil's wrist and kissed him. It was just like normal, only Neil's skin prickled with unease.

"It's great to see you," Scott said.

"You, too," he responded instinctively.

Scott clasped his hand and drew him into the restaurant. They were at a Thai place tonight. The restaurant was full of packed tables and loud conversations. The place was warm and smelled of spices. Neil vaguely remembered trying to order food while drunk. The group he'd been with had left without a meal, but he'd gone home with one of them. The reminder of his old lifestyle was a sharp contrast to his current one with Scott.

His lover gave their names to the waiter, and he directed them to their reserved table. They took a seat and ordered beers.

When they were alone, Scott asked, "Have you been here before? They do one of the best chicken curries."

"No, I haven't."

It was safer than giving Scott his drunken hook-up story.

"All their food is incredible."

Scott picked up his menu and Neil did the same. He skimmed over the lists, seeing several things he knew, but there were others he'd never heard of. It all sounded good and the smells in the restaurant combined with how packed it was only further backed up Scott's statement as to its quality.

"So, I was talking to Leslie today. He wanted to arrange a time to play pool. Lisa suggested inviting a few others, too."

Neil shot his focus from the menu to Scott. His earlier unease came back with full force. Unlike in the past, it wasn't nervousness to be around Scott's friends and family. Now, it brought the similar flare of panic that had made him flee Scott's house. He swallowed it down.

"*Oh.*"

"Yeah." Scott glanced up from his menu and smiled. His expression dimmed as he noticed Neil's reaction. He reached across the table and placed a hand over Neil's. "There's no rush. We don't have to go."

In the past, that had been comforting. Now, something new sparked to life inside him. *Annoyance.*

"I agreed, didn't I?" Neil questioned, his voice turning sharp.

"You did, but things can change."

"What *things*?" Neil insisted.

Scott seemed to notice the growing edge to his voice. He frowned.

"Well, anything. I told you we'd go at your pace —"

"*My* pace. As if I haven't been agreeing to every meeting you've suggested. As if it hasn't been *your* pace the entire time."

Scott blinked, looking shocked.

"I never once meant to pressure you, Neil. I've told you that."

"But that's just it, isn't it?" Neil argued. "You keep pushing and *asking* and I keep *agreeing* and —"

I've liked every second of it — until you asked me to move in and it scared the hell out of me.

The realization drew him up short, and he stopped talking. He also yanked his hand from Scott's. He felt exposed and uncomfortable.

"Neil? What's going on?" Scott asked.

He wasn't angry, he only looked *concerned* — and that was too much. Neil abruptly stood. He needed to get away. All his emotions were building inside him. This time, he wasn't sure he could keep them back.

Turning on his heel, he walked out of the restaurant. Scott called after him, but he didn't stop. He didn't care how many people were looking at him. He just needed to get out. The restaurant was making him overheat, and Scott was too fucking *nice*.

He got out of the door but only a few buildings down before a hand caught his arm.

"Neil! Wait! Neil, talk to me."

He tried to jerk his arm free, but Scott wasn't budging.

"Neil —"

Neil whirled on him. His panic switching to anger in a single, furious moment. His urge for flight had gone, and now he wanted to lash out and *fight*. The pent-up emotions bubbling under his skin were finally going to be expelled.

"What the hell do you want from me, Scott? A goddamn husband to tend the fucking garden and walk the dog?"

Scott reared back at his sudden statement. Despite his shock, he didn't let go of Neil's arm.

"What are you talking about? Neil, I just want to get to know you…to date you. Yeah, maybe down the line if we work out, it might turn into something like that, but —"

"So, you *do* want that?" Neil demanded.

Scott let out a frustrated breath. "Of course, I want a lifetime relationship."

"And you want it with *me*?"

His tone was harsh and accusatory, but somehow Scott's expression softened. He squeezed Neil's arm gently.

"Yeah, Neil. I thought that was obvious by what I said the other night."

Neil shuddered. A war was going on inside him. He wanted to lean into Scott and soak up the warmth of being *wanted*. He also wanted to shove Scott away and cut all ties with the person who made him think about a future he'd never imagined having.

Neil was teetering on the edge, his destress being banked by Scott's calming words and affectionate touch.

"Come on, Neil," Scott coaxed. "Talk to me."

Neil laughed roughly.

"I don't know what I fucking want, Scott."

"Neil—"

"I'm meeting your friends and your family and staying at your *house*," he spat. "This shit isn't me. I'm not some domestic fantasy." He laughed again. "I sleep around, and I piss off the next day. I'm not cut out for this crap."

"Neil, calm down."

"Why?" He finally yanked free from Scott's grip. "Isn't this what *you* want?" He held out his arms. "Neil Farris in all his relationship glory? Making a scene and freaking out because you want a *future* with him?"

Scott's expression looked pained and concerned. There wasn't a *hint* of embarrassment or annoyance.

He only gives a damn about you.

A noise caught in Neil's throat, something wounded and emotional, but he swallowed it down. He put his head in his hands and scrubbed his palms over his face.

"Fuck," he said. "I'm not ready for this."

"Neil," Scott tried, sounding dismayed.

He touched him, but Neil jerked away. He didn't know what he'd do if he allowed Scott close to him.

"Neil," Scott said, hurt obvious in his voice.

"I'm not the right guy for this," Neil forced out.

It was harder than he'd expected, and it ached. He immediately wanted to take it back, but everything was too confusing, and he just wanted *out*.

"Neil, you *are* the right guy," Scott tried desperately. "I know you are. Maybe it's soon, but that's what I've always believed happens when you meet the right person. Everything clicks, and you can't imagine anything more comfortable than being with them. I wouldn't be feeling this way if we weren't compatible." He didn't touch him again, but Neil felt his body heat and heard Scott step closer. "It wouldn't mean so much to you, if you weren't feeling something, too."

Neil's heart skipped and his stomach twisted into a painful knot. He raised his head and caught Scott's dark, emotion-filled gaze.

"You're wrong. And this should have been over a long time ago."

Scott's expression crumpled and he looked like someone had struck him. Neil turned away rather than watch. When he left this time, Scott didn't follow him.

Neil had never broken up with someone. He'd never realized it could hurt so much. He felt like he'd left his heart back on the pavement, but he didn't turn back.

It was better for everyone if he cut the cord. He was an asshole who was bad at relationships and forever destined to be single. That was where he was comfortable. That was where he'd been *happy*, and he'd make it work again. A future with Scott Fields wasn't meant to be a part of his life.

Chapter Fifteen

Neil couldn't remember a time he'd felt worse than the morning after their breakup. After returning home from the restaurant, he'd drunk a good amount of the rum in his pantry, along with a bottle of wine. He'd woken up hungover and needing to throw up. He'd then swallowed down two painkillers and gone to work with a throbbing headache, nausea and an ache in his chest that he couldn't blame on the alcohol.

When Denise arrived an hour later, Neil was leaning his elbows on the counter, rubbing his temples and trying to will away the pounding in his skull.

"Well, that's a sight I haven't seen for a while. You look like something the cat threw up."

"Screw you," he muttered.

"And I thought we'd seen the last of the party days," she teased, moving toward the backroom. "Something go wrong with your sexy fireman?"

Neil flinched, unable to stop it. Denise stopped moving and her teasing immediately switched to concern.

"Wait! Neil, did something happen with you and Scott?"

Neil knew there was no use keeping it from her. She'd work it out eventually.

"We broke up."

"Oh, *Neil*."

She came around the counter with open arms. He shifted away from her.

"I don't need a hug. I didn't get drunk because of him. They're unrelated."

Denise scowled. She also darted forward and wrapped him in her arms before he could avoid it. Neil stiffened. She squeezed him gently.

"I don't believe you," she mumbled. "I know you liked him. I'm sorry."

A lump formed in Neil's throat, but he tried to ignore its existence. He was relieved when a customer arrived, and he could get away from her and attend to the man. He felt her hawked gaze on him throughout the morning, but he stayed busy to avoid having to speak about Scott.

But it was only a matter of time before she cornered him.

She slipped out of the shop to do the banking and returned with two cups of takeout coffee. He took his with a murmur of gratitude, but she didn't move away.

"Neil," she began, "I know you said you're fine, but it really helps to get it all out." She touched his arm and squeezed. "I'm always willing to listen."

"I don't need to talk about anything."

Denise sighed but she dropped her hand.

"Well, if that changes, I'll be here." She smiled. "I'm great at cussing out assholes who hurt my friends."

Neil startled and almost spilled his coffee. He'd never considered Denise a friend, just a fun co-worker. He'd always assumed she'd categorized him the same.

And now she's ready to defend me against Scott.

"He's not," Neil blurted.

Denise turned to look at him, seeming puzzled. Neil knew he shouldn't have spoken, but he couldn't have her thinking Scott was in the wrong. It was all on him. He'd pushed Scott away and put that pained look on the fireman's face. Neil had always been the disaster waiting to happen. Now, he'd finally struck.

"He's not the asshole, Denise," he said quietly, shame and guilt prickling his neck.

Her expression softened. "If he's not the asshole, then maybe there's time to fix things."

Neil shook his head. This wasn't something to mend. He was destined for strings of one-night stands and Scott was better off looking for someone who *could* be Mr. Right.

Thankfully, Denise didn't press him any further. It allowed Neil to focus on the day rather than Scott. He managed it until his lunch break. When he checked his phone instinctively, he felt a sharp ache. There weren't any messages. Normally, he'd have at least one from Scott. The silence felt deafening.

Neil hovered his fingers over the screen. Yearning fought with fear. He still didn't know what he wanted, but he knew staying the hell out of Scott's life would be simpler for both of them. Scott might think he was the guy to grow old with, but he was wrong. He had to be.

Closing his eyes, Neil shoved his phone resolutely in his pocket. But out of sight, out of mind wasn't working. His thoughts couldn't be held back.

If this is better for both of us. Why do I feel so bad? Why do I want to take it back?

Whenever he closed his eyes, Neil relived the moment outside the restaurant. He kept seeing Scott's hurt face. He'd walked out on dozens of men. Some had even looked disappointed when he'd picked up his clothes. Neil had never given a damn—until now.

Scott had convinced him on a date. Then to meet his family and friends. Scott had made the whole prospect of a relationship seem *good*. But moving in? Getting married? That caused a cold sweat to break out.

But is it fear of doing it — or fear of messing it up?

Neil shoved away the thought, just like he'd been shoving away his emotions since Scott had sleepily confessed. Because, if he acknowledged exactly how he felt or what he wanted, Neil wouldn't have any defenses left. He'd be opening his heart completely to Scott, and Neil didn't know if he'd ever be ready for that.

* * * *

Three days.

They'd broken up three days before, and the pain in Neil's chest hadn't receded. Instead, it had only become worse. He'd tried going back to his old clubs, but after stepping inside, he'd realized he couldn't go through with it. There were dozens of available men on the dance floor, ready for a good time and a fling, but it felt like a betrayal to Scott. Worse than that, the idea of sleeping with any of them turned his stomach. He didn't *want* them.

Neil took a seat at the bar and nursed a beer. He shot down anyone who tried to flirt with him. It didn't matter how hot they were, they just weren't *right*. When he caught his thoughts drifting to how quickly he could reach Scott's house from the club, he called it a night. It was only when he was hailing a taxi that he saw he'd missed a call from Scott.

Neil's heart skipped a beat and he stared at his phone. His thumb hovered over the touchscreen. Scott had phoned forty minutes before. He could call back, see what he had to say.

Maybe I could go over...

Neil clenched his jaw and closed off his phone. He would *not* go back on his decision and open a door to more frustration and confusion for both of them. Scott deserved someone better.

He probably realized it was a bad idea and hung up. That's why he didn't leave a message.

Neil went to shove his phone in his pocket, but when he glimpsed red hair entering the bar he paused, briefly mistaking it for someone he knew — someone who would be perfect for his current mood.

I don't need to hook up with someone to stop thinking about him. All I have to do is find people to drink with.

Opening his phone, Neil scrolled down for a different contact. He dialed and waited for them to pick up.

"What the shit?" a loud voice shouted over pounding music. "Thought you'd gone and pissed us off."

"Been busy," Neil answered. "Where you at tonight?"

"Old Bar." He heard laughter then. "Bundi's next."

Neil was just down the road and started walking toward the club.

"Be there in five."

There was more laughter on the line and Neil hung up, knowing the man wouldn't care about his manners. He might not even notice. It was all about drinking with him, and that was exactly what Neil wanted.

When he arrived at Old Bar, Neil grabbed a beer before making his way toward the back of the club. He found the group with ease. They were sitting around a table with Harry Walsh in the middle. Everyone knew him as Walshy and he could always be found at the center of a party. He had red hair, a thick beard and the start of a beer gut. Despite his growing weight, he had a girl on each of his arms. Five other people were at the table, along with a sizeable number of empty glasses. Walshy noticed him and pointed.

"Ralph Lauren finally shows his goddamn face."

Neil rolled his eyes. The group all looked at him. A girl squinted. "He isn't Ralph Lauren."

"He's always dressed like he's going to a fucking fashion show."

The group laughed and Neil tried not to grimace. He usually smirked at the nickname, but now it only brought to mind Scott and his terrible clothing choices. It reminded him of the times Scott had *let* him choose what his lover would wear.

For God's sake, stop thinking about him.

Slotting in beside one man he recognized, Neil took a large drink of beer. He didn't know the name of half the people around him, and he probably wouldn't find out. This wasn't like a meeting with Scott's friends. This was barely even social. Neil wanted company and alcohol. These people would provide both.

* * * *

Neil woke up on a mustard-colored couch that had seen better days. *Walshy's*, his mind sluggishly supplied. He'd passed out on it multiple times before. There were three people sleeping on the floor and leaking beer bottles were making more stains on the already-filthy carpet. He was the first one awake. He rolled onto his back and covered his eyes. Bits and pieces of the previous night were resurfacing, but once he'd joined Walshy's group, it had been a steady stream of drinks.

His clothed state proved he hadn't had sex, which was unexpectedly relieving. He also had no memory of drunk-dialing Scott.

Thank God for that.

Clambering off the couch, Neil held a hand to his head while stumbling his way through the living room to the kitchen. He was grateful when his stomach didn't revolt on him. Neil fumbled open a cupboard for a glass and poured some water from the tap. He had three glasses before he felt willing to tackle the ride home.

Taking his phone from his pocket, Neil looked at the screen, only for his stomach to twist and his heart to pound. Scott had called again. It was from two hours before and this time, he'd also left a voice message. Neil felt torn. He wanted to hear Scott's voice, but he was worried about what he would say. It also felt wrong to bring Scott even remotely into this part of his life.

Neil looked over the filthy state of the kitchen and living room. He felt a prickle of shame. This was a place of hungover strangers who slept around.

"Neil Farris in all his relationship glory."

He winced as his old words came back to haunt him. Neil left the kitchen and went to the bathroom to relieve his bladder and splash water on his face. He also found the painkillers Walshy always had on hand for headaches. When he was done, he sent for a car and leaned against the wall. He closed his eyes but all he saw was Scott.

He remembered when Scott had taken care of him when he'd been sick. Neil wanted that so desperately that it *ached*. The phone felt like a heavy weight in his pocket. Neil felt like shit, and he *missed* Scott.

It was a terrible combination and it found him opening his phone. He knew he'd likely regret it, but standing in Walshy's messy bathroom, all Neil wanted was to hear Scott's voice.

"Hey, Neil."

Neil's heart clenched. Scott sounded so tired and upset.

"I haven't wanted to pressure you. I know I've done a lot of that already, but I wanted to talk to you. I'm called out to this big fire, and I don't want to leave things the way we did."

Neil stood straighter. His eyes flying wide as fear flooded his body.

"I know a relationship is new to you and that I messed things up by going too fast, but we can work this out if you want to. I really care about you. I know you might have changed your mind about being with me, but I really want to try again."

Scott sighed. His voice got lower and softer.

"I miss you, Neil. I miss texting you and having dinner. I want to show you more movies and hear you call them terrible."

Scott laughed roughly.

"I want to kiss you again, too. But mostly, I just want to hear your voice and know I haven't fucked everything up."

Scott paused.

"I hope I'm not the only one missing us. I hope you'll give us another chance. Call me back?"

He sighed.

"If you don't, I guess I'll have my answer."

The message ended, and Neil felt like his heart was in his shoes. He was clutching the phone so hard that his knuckles hurt. He immediately hit the redial button, not even thinking the action through. His heart ached, his stomach felt worse than when he'd woken up and his worries had tripled. The only thing he cared about was wiping the sadness from Scott's voice.

But Scott didn't pick up.

It went to message bank. He hung up and tried again. It did the same. This time, Neil stood with his mouth open but no words escaping.

I miss you, too. I screwed up, not you. I'm sorry. Please don't get hurt. I lo —

Neil cut off the thought and shut his eyes. He ended the call with a harsh jab of his finger. But it didn't stop the swirling pit of panic.

He knew it was a bad idea, but he googled information on the fire. It was big, and it was nasty. There were all the wrong weather conditions — a strong wind, dry grass and plenty of kindling. Every news report sounded more alarming than the first. A cold sweat was breaking out. All he wanted was to hear Scott's voice telling him everything would be okay.

But he didn't have Scott, and before he could think better of it, he was making a new phone call.

It connected after only a few seconds.

"Neil."

"Cindy."

She sounded as tired as Scott had. Neil didn't know if she was aware of his and Scott's break up, but he spoke quickly, not wanting her to refuse him out of anger on Scott's behalf.

"Scott called me, but I missed it." He swallowed, his voice rough and not just from the hangover. "I just. I heard about—"

"You heard about the trapped truck."

Neil almost dropped his phone. "Trapped truck?"

"Oh, God," she whispered. "You didn't know?"

"What do you mean?" he asked, his voice rising in pitch. "What the fuck? Is Scott—? Is he—?"

"I don't know," she admitted, and Neil finally registered the strain to her voice.

Her husband is with Scott.

"Oh shit. Cindy, I didn't— I'm sorry. I'll go. I'll—"

"No." Her voice turned firm in an instant. "No, don't you dare, Neil."

She sucked in a breath and Neil realized his own breaths were coming in sharp gasps. He tried to get back under control but felt the panic claw at his chest. He just wanted to be in Scott's arms. He *needed* to know his lover was safe.

What if he's trapped and he thinks I don't care? That I didn't call him back and never missed him?

Tears pricked at his eyes and he pressed his fingers in the corners, wanting to stop them from falling. He felt guilt and shame add to his fear. It found the words spilling out of him.

"I-I had a fight with Scott. I missed his call, and he thinks I don't want him back. I d-didn't want to move in, but I still *want* him, and he doesn't know and—"

"Neil," Cindy cut in, her voice soft and compassionate, "I'm sure he knows."

"But—"

"And I don't think you should be alone. Come to my house."

Neil gave a choked laugh. "I went out last night. I'm a fucking mess."

"Come anyway. No one will care."

"Cindy—"

"I could use the company, too, Neil."

All Neil's protests disappeared. He might have a lover battling a fire, but she had a *husband*. He wasn't the only one who needed someone to lean on.

"Okay," he mumbled.

She told him the address and he nodded and hung up. When he used his phone a second time, it was to check how long his ride would be. His fingers trembled over the keys, but he tried to keep it together.

It might not be Scott's truck. Everything could be fine. The report could be wrong.

Yet, regardless of what encouragement he tried to give, Neil could feel nothing but fear. Not only had he ruined everything with Scott, but he'd let his lover go off to fight a fire all while thinking that he didn't give a damn.

Chapter Sixteen

Cindy and Paul didn't live far from Walshy's. It took almost no time to arrive, but the difference between their lifestyles was stark. Their house was in a great neighborhood and they had a well-maintained lawn and garden. Walshy's was an old weatherboard that had seen better days and resided in a street that was equally rundown.

Neil felt out of place arriving at their driveaway. He looked and probably smelled like crap. He wasn't the ideal boyfriend for a respectable, well-loved fireman. Neil was a hungover interloper who had screwed up with Scott and just didn't *belong*.

But God, he was scared. He didn't know what was happening to Scott. He felt guilt and shame over their breakup. The prospect of being alone in his apartment with no one to turn to was the final straw. Cindy had told him to come, and he wasn't going to turn down support, even if he didn't think he deserved it.

He climbed out of the car, feeling grateful the driver hadn't complained about his hesitation. The man was already paid, and he left without a word. Neil walked up the front path to the door. He lingered for a moment with indecision before knocking on the wood.

He heard movement and a murmured voice before it opened. Cindy was wearing a simple dress. Normally, she was vibrant and cheerful, but she looked as tired as he felt.

"Neil," she said.

A moment later, she hugged him. Neil closed his eyes and slumped against her. He hugged her back, feeling a small amount of his tension ease, knowing he wasn't alone. She was the one to break the embrace, but she kept a hand on his arm as she led him inside and shut the door.

They walked into the living room where Peta was lying on the floor with a coloring book. She looked up and frowned at him.

"Why is Uncle Neil here?"

Uncle Neil.

He hadn't expected to hear that again. He'd have thought they would have told her he was no longer with Scott. No longer *welcome.*

Yet, here you are, and Cindy isn't turning you away.

"He's just stopping by for coffee like your daddy's friends do."

She looked past him and toward the door. Her frown deepened and she looked back at her mother.

"Is Uncle Scott coming, too?"

Neil sucked in a sharp breath, feeling like he'd been punched in the stomach.

Of course, she doesn't know he could be in trouble. She's a child. They won't tell her unless something happens. Right now, there's nothing to say.

"No, sweetie. He's off fighting fires with your dad."

"Oh, okay."

She turned back to her coloring book, allowing Cindy to direct him into the kitchen. She made him sit down on a chair at the counter. Cindy moved away but Neil stared at his hands. His mind was overrun with images of bushfires. He kept seeing a truck in the middle, helpless against an intense blaze. He kept picturing Scott and never seeing him again. His thoughts were a painful spiral, making him feel gutted and lost. He only jerked out of them when Cindy took his hands.

He glanced up to find her gaze sympathetic but firm.

"Neil, you can't keep thinking about it."

He laughed harshly. "How can I *not*? He's out there and I fu—"—he glanced at the living room, only to lower his voice—"messed up. What if it's his truck? What if he d-doesn't come back and I—"

"If you think like that, it will break you apart," Cindy interrupted. "Nothing is certain. It could be their truck, but we don't know. We can only hope and hold them close every time they come home."

Neil pulled his hands from hers and covered his face.

"I'm not going to be *able* to do that anymore, Cindy. I screwed everything up."

"How did you do that?"

There was no reproach in her voice, just a gentle prompting. He found all his emotions pressing against him, and with one look at her compassionate face, it broke out of him like a dam.

"He wanted me to move in, and it wasn't even *now*. It was just the prospect. He wants to have a *relationship* with me, and I couldn't handle that." He chuckled weakly. "All he wanted was *more*, and I've never had a guy want that. Never had a guy *deal* with me and think I was still worth it. Like, what the hell? How goddamn low are his standards, anyway?"

Cindy didn't answer. She just waited patiently. He could feel her gaze on him, but Neil stared at the countertop.

"He never pushed," Neil admitted. "Never made me come to outings or stay over. Always let me back away like it didn't even matter. And I never... I didn't..." Neil gritted his teeth. "I always said *yes* — and now he's not around and everything was supposed to be easier without him but it's *not*." He scrubbed his hands through his hair. "It just *hurts*, and I miss him all the time."

"He clearly misses you, too."

Neil couldn't contest it, not after the voicemail he'd received — and Cindy wasn't finished.

"And he called you. I can't speak for Scott, but I don't think you've done something that can't be fixed."

"But should I fix it?" Neil questioned. "I'm not a catch. Scott could do better and — "

"And isn't that for Scott to decide?"

Neil fell silent. He dropped his hands from his head and just looked at them. It was the root of so many of his problems and worries. He'd been avoiding the issues for days — longer, maybe, since before Scott even brought up his wish to deepen their relationship. Finally, he was giving it voice.

"What if he does decide it?" Neil asked quietly. "What if he works it out in a few months?"

"Oh," Cindy breathed, realization sinking in. "You're not worried about committing to him. You're worried that after doing it, he'll leave you."

Neil flinched, hit hard by something he'd tried so hard to deny.

All those years of people saying I was scared of commitment. And it turns out they were closer than they thought.

"Neil," Cindy continued, taking his hand again and squeezing it, "that's the risk we all take when we let someone into our heart." He met her gaze once more. "But Scott is loyal. He won't give up just because there's a bump or two in the road. He likes you and you like him. That's all anyone can hope for when they start a relationship."

I don't know if I'm ready for a relationship.

Yet, even as he thought it, Neil knew it wasn't true. He would be willing to try for Scott. He *wanted* to try it with him, and he knew that Scott would take him back. He *could* fix this, as long as he was willing to take a chance with his heart.

As long as Scott comes home.

Neil closed his eyes and took in a shaky breath, trying not to think about it. Cindy was right. If he kept thinking about the '*what if's*', he'd be unable to function. Scott could be gone for hours or days. He needed to pull it together.

"When Scott gets back, I'll talk to him."

Cindy smiled. "Be honest, Neil. That's the best way to make any relationship work."

Neil snorted, feeling a stab of wry amusement.

"Honesty is rarely my problem. I'm surprised he let me near his closet."

Cindy let out a startled laugh. "I *had* noticed his wardrobe has expanded." She lowered his voice conspiratorially. "And he always had a secret smile when he wore his new shirts, like they reminded him of something special."

Neil sucked in a sharp breath, his heart flipping. Cindy's smile was knowing. Neil wished desperately that Scott were nearby so he could hug and kiss the man. He wanted to press his face into Scott's neck, smell his cologne and apologize for how *stupid* he'd been.

But just because I've made a mess doesn't mean I can't clean it up.

Denise and Cindy had both assured him it was possible. Scott's phone call had only backed that up. He just needed to explain exactly why he'd bolted. The idea formed fresh discomfort, but he refused to let it win. If Scott could fight a goddamn bushfire, he could man up and admit what he felt.

It didn't have to be a romantic movie confession. It just had to be *real*.

He stayed at Cindy's house for a little over an hour until the report came through that the fire truck was free and no one had been injured. They'd both breathed a heavy sigh of relief. Although she'd been happy for him to remain longer, he'd decided to go home. If he was going to date Scott and *commit* to Scott, he had to be able to handle the man's job.

Despite his conviction, it was *hard*. He couldn't get his mind off the fire. He stalked news reports, and although Cindy told him to think positively, he couldn't help worrying. When he went to bed, he had *nightmares* and woke up gasping and wishing Scott were beside him — or only a short drive away.

Once, he turned on the TV and found a black-and-white movie. He watched it with a lump in his throat and a cup of tea in his hands. But he didn't break down again like he had with Cindy.

She kept him updated via text, and he was beyond grateful. She also invited him into a group chat with a number of spouses and family members. He'd been awkward at first, but everyone was kind and ready to offer a friendly ear or sympathetic shoulder. Lisa was there, and she offered to send Leslie over with beer.

No one seemed to know about his fight with Scott, and if they did, they didn't hold it against him. Their support helped keep him going. Their tips on distraction allowed him to function. Even when Adrian called to check on him and Denise hugged him tight at work, he didn't crack open with the force of his worry.

He kept it together for four days — until Cindy called him at work. He'd been with a customer but when he saw it was her, he'd given an excuse and answered.

"Cindy? What's happening?"

"The fire's contained." She sounded joyful. "They're coming *back* and are en route to their station."

He was almost knocked over with the force of his relief.

"Shit. Fuck. *Thank you.*"

"Scott will want to see you. I'm on my way there now."

"I'm coming."

He didn't wait for a response. He hung up and turned back to Denise. She was watching him with nerves and hope. The customer just looked confused.

"He's on his way back. I have to go."

"Oh, thank God," Denise breathed. "Yes, go. Get out of here. I'll sort something out."

"Thank you," he said before rushing past her and the customer.

As he left, he heard her explain, "His partner is a firefighter. He's been battling that big blaze."

My partner.

Neil felt a surge of pride and determination. Because that was what Scott *was* and Neil wouldn't let fear keep him from holding onto his lover. He'd spent four days wavering between guilt and worry. He had to make it up to Scott. He just hoped Cindy was right and Scott *would* want to see him.

When he arrived, the station was packed with people. There were all kinds of uniforms. Police and emergency services, along with people wearing volunteer name badges. He didn't know where to go or who to ask, but Cindy found him and dragged him to a group of awaiting spouses. He'd spoken to most of them on the group chat, and they all either shook his hand or pulled him into a hug. There were a few children around, waiting at their mothers' feet. He could see Peta playing some kind of hand clapping game with another girl.

He hadn't been there more than ten minutes when the fire truck pulled into the station. Neil's breath caught and his muscles strained with a longing to rush toward the truck. When it parked and the firemen climbed out, there was clapping and backslapping and words of congratulations. The moment Neil saw Scott, he moved.

He didn't pay attention to who he pushed to the side. All he cared about was getting to his lover. Scott looked exhausted and his smile wasn't as bright as Neil was used to as he nodded to an SES who was talking to him. Neil had almost reached him when Scott turned and finally saw him. His eyes widened, and his lips parted.

Neil closed the last remaining distance and threw his arms around Scott's shoulders. Scott gasped before his arms came around Neil's waist. Neil closed his eyes and breathed in deeply. Scott smelled like sweat and smoke. He was *alive,* and Neil felt ready to burst with relief.

"Neil?"

"I'm so sorry," Neil whispered.

"What do you mean?" Scott asked, stroking his back soothingly. "What for?"

Neil pulled back and looked at his perfect lover — the man who looked worried and concerned, who'd just fought a *fire* but was still putting Neil first.

"*Everything,*" Neil whispered. "For making you think for *one goddamn second* that I don't love you."

Scott's eyes went wide, and Neil kissed him. He cupped Scott's cheeks and poured everything he felt and feared into the press of their mouths. Scott gave a small, shocked noise, but he kissed back. He held Neil close and stroked his back.

Neil didn't even realize he'd started to tremble until Scott broke the kiss. He pressed their foreheads together, but Neil kept his eyes closed. He felt a different fear as he recalled what he'd just blurted.

Scott had never even talked about love, but he'd thrown it down without any cushioning.

"Hey," Scott said, moving a hand into his hair and stroking it gently. "It's okay. Everything's okay."

Neil laughed harshly. "No, it isn't. I made a mess, then I made a *bigger* mess and bombarded you when you just got back and —"

"I couldn't have wished for a *better* way to return home," Scott interrupted seriously.

Cautiously, Neil opened his eyes. Scott looked earnest, and he also seemed *happy*. His smile was bright, and his eyes were filled with the soft warmth Neil had missed seeing so much.

"What you said earlier. Did you mean it?"

Neil's throat dried up on saying it again. *I love you.* The words had spilled out, but they weren't wrong. He'd had days to work that out, even if it had taken *this* to admit it. He nodded jerkily. Scott smiled.

"I love you, too," he confessed.

Neil sighed shakily and closed his eyes. He wrapped his arms back around Scott and turned his face to hide it against Scott's neck once more.

"Does this mean we're back together?" Scott questioned.

Neil snorted and mumbled, "What the hell do you think?"

Scott laughed back. "Well, I just wanted to make sure." He played with Neil's hair. "I don't want to invite you back to my house if you don't want to come."

Neil lifted his head and caught Scott's gaze. His lover was still smiling, and his gaze was hopeful. The last time he'd been at Scott's house had been the catalyst for their breakup. Now, after the last few days, he might be nervous about moving in with Scott, but he didn't fear it.

"I want to," Neil admitted. "I... I also wouldn't mind, uh, *more*. Later. Down the line. I mean. You know. What you offered."

Scott's smile grew even wider, and Neil felt vulnerable and exposed, but this time, he didn't turn away or hide. He held Scott's gaze, despite the pounding in his heart and churning in his stomach.

"Then we'll work toward that—however fast or slow it comes."

Neil felt relief. He also smiled, and when Scott ducked in to kiss him again, Neil closed his eyes and relaxed completely.

He knew it wouldn't always be simple and that their relationship would no doubt have bumps in the road, but Neil wasn't going to let fear keep him from holding on to what he wanted. He'd spent a week without Scott in his life, and that was a week too many.

If Scott could risk his life every day, then Neil could take a chance and risk his heart. Because no matter how terrifying it might seem, Neil was certain it would prove worth it.

Epilogue

Neil was just locking up the shop when his phone rang. He juggled the items in his hand as he wrangled it from his pocket. He smiled at the caller ID and pressed it to his ear.

"What's up?"

"Did you want to grab some of those fresh rolls for dinner?"

"Are you talking bakery rolls or the little tiny ones in the oven?"

"Oven ones."

Neil narrowed his eyes. "You're making a pasta dish, aren't you?"

There was a pause.

"Maybe."

Neil snorted, but he was grinning. Several months of dating made his lover a little predictable.

"Whatever it is has a red sauce, doesn't it?"

Another pause.

"If you keep this up, dinner won't be a surprise."

Neil laughed. He also finished locking up and started heading for the supermarket which was, luckily, only a few shops down from where he worked.

"I didn't know dinner was *meant* to be a surprise. Did I miss an anniversary?"

"Can't a man cook a surprise meal for his partner after his hard day of work?"

Neil shook his head, but his smile couldn't be contained. "That almost sounds like you're trying to butter me up for something, Scott."

"Well, Lisa did mention a sibling versus spouse bowling competition."

"I fail to see why I need buttering for *that*."

Since he'd become a regular fixture at Scott's side, he was often tugged into the lighthearted rivalry that existed between Scott's siblings and their partners. It was all in good fun and always ended with humor and a good time had by all.

"Well," Scott said, "she's angling for it to be, um, next week."

Neil's steps faltered. "*Oh.*"

Next week. *The* week. When Neil had invited his parents to come and meet Scott for the first time.

Scott's family functions meant Scott's parents would be present. They'd track the scores and probably have their own lane for competing against each other — or maybe even with the kids. It would be a *family* event, and clearly Lisa wanted to make sure *his* parents could be involved.

"We can tell her no," Scott said. "Put it off another week and — "

"No," Neil said. "It's okay. I'll ask them. They'll probably want to come."

"You sure, Neil?"

Neil smiled again. The same concern that Scott had always shown for their relationship and his comfort was shining through. It always made his heart melt.

"I'm sure," he insisted. "I'll run it by them and message Lisa tomorrow."

"Okay." There was a slight pause before, "I was actually making you dinner before she called."

"Yeah." Neil smiled. "I know."

Scott had never pushed or bribed or tried to influence him. Scott only ever wanted him to be happy and comfortable — the same thing that Neil wanted for Scott. It was why they *both* made dinner for each other whenever they were able.

"Okay." Scott sounded relieved. "I better let you go."

"Do we need anything else from the shop?"

He heard Scott moving and the fridge opening. "Maybe another milk?"

"Okay. I won't be too long."

"See you when you get home. Love you."

Neil's chest flooded with warmth, and after eight months together, it was easy and natural to say the words he'd once been so afraid of.

"Love you, too."

The call ended and Neil slipped the phone into his pocket. He stepped into the supermarket with happiness and excitement to get home. Because two months ago, that's what Scott's house had become. *Home.*

He'd moved in, and while he'd been nervous at first, he'd never wanted to take back the decision. Living with Scott might mean grumbling when Scott woke him climbing out of bed for his morning run or feeling lonely when Scott was away on a training course or fighting a fire—but it *also* meant coming home to someone.

Being with Scott had opened his life and heart to something he'd never imagined and now couldn't live without. He had a new family, a community of friends and a contentment he'd never expected. He'd never been more grateful for taking a chance and risking his heart.

A text message drew him from his thoughts, and he looked down. It was from Scott.

Hepburn A or Hepburn K?

Neil grinned and his gaze traveled to the plastic bag hanging from his wrist. It held a DVD collection he'd ordered a few weeks ago that had finally arrived. They were five black-and-white movies that Scott didn't have. He knew Scott had been curious to see one of them but had never found a copy.

I've actually got something else in mind.

He knew Scott would love the gift, and he couldn't wait to see his excitement or hear his gushing about the movie's reputations.

While it might have been a long day at work, Neil's evening was setting up to be a perfect one. He had dinner, a movie and his lover all waiting for him at home. Who could ask for anything more than that?

Want to see more from this author?
Here's a taster for you to enjoy!

Enemy Territory:
Dangerous Ignition
Elizabeth Hollows

Excerpt

Rico Hanthorn found few pleasures greater than riding his Harley. He loved his bike as much as he loved his family. The purr of the motor beneath his thighs defied words as she rumbled with power with every rev of her engine. The feelings and the freedom it gave him were unmatched. She was his pride, and she carried him through the city with the respect and fear gained by his station.

His father, John Hanthorn, was the leader of the Angels of Mercy bike club. Their club had run the west side of the city for forty years. The Angels had fought bloody wars when he had been a child—his father disappearing at odd hours only to come home with the smell of oil on his hands, soot on his clothes and grim satisfaction in his eyes.

The Angels had hard control over the import and export of weapons, while high-quality drugs were theirs to disperse. Rico was one of their best enforcers and well regarded to eventually take his father's position. Leadership wasn't a blood right, but Rico had the respect of his peers. He had sacrificed his time, body and life to the Angels. He'd more than proved his worth, and no one would ever doubt his allegiance to the club or his fellow members.

Through years of toil and grit, they had squashed any incursions into their borders. The west was theirs. But on their eastern outskirts, an unending rivalry had waged. The Demon Riders had a chapter on that side of the city. They were slightly smaller, but they traded in the same enterprises and were just as ruthless in maintaining their power.

The Angels' most violent altercations had occurred with the Demons.

In more than ten years as part of the Angels, Rico had only faltered once when faced with the rival club.

It wasn't during a bloodied battle or a moment of unexpected compassion. It was during a cease-fire in a part of the city controlled by neither club. Rico's job, like many at the time, had been to stand quiet and menacing behind their leader. The Demon Riders and the Angels of Mercy had been clashing so often and so ferociously that the police were not only arresting sizeable numbers of their members but also manipulating their animosity against them.

The clubs had always hated each other, but they'd always detested the cops more.

Utilizing a tentative truce, they'd met in the dead of night in an empty parking lot to discuss options and territory boundaries. Rico had only been three months initiated but had been eager to be involved and please his father.

He'd felt confident and calm—until he'd scanned the Demon Riders and seen a familiar face. Their gazes had locked, their eyes widening, Rico had felt the sinking realization of a grave mistake. As an Angels of Mercy member, he shouldn't have felt fear when surrounded by his club—but he had. Rico had felt certain everyone would realize what he had done.

Although he had escaped the encounter without the revelation of his youthful stupidity, the terror had lingered under his skin for months, sinking into his dreams and everyday life. It had hammered home the need for discretion and to keep his liaisons within the safety of his territory.

It was a lesson Rico had hoped to never need to teach his sister.

Angelica was ten years his junior—seventeen, arrogant and reckless. At his father's request, she was to be kept as far from the club as possible.

"She's young and impressionable," his father had insisted one evening.

John Hanthorn's bald head had shone under the porch's backlight. He'd held a smoke in one hand and a beer in the other. Even when at rest, with no club members to control or impress, John Hanthorn had a barely leashed ferocity.

"Your mother wants her behaving. I want her nose out of business that doesn't concern her. You'll get her back in line?"

"Yes."

"Good." He'd taken another long drag, letting it out in a heavy cloud. "And, for God's sake, get her hair back to normal."

"That's more difficult."

His father had turned his head slowly, his gaze flat, his voice cold. "Did I stutter on my order?"

"No," Rico had immediately corrected. "It will happen."

"Good."

His job had been made clear. Unfortunately, Angelica had refused to listen to him. His sweet, brunette sister had turned platinum blonde. Her dresses, floral shirts and jeans had become revealing crop tops, ripped pants and a tight-fitting leather jacket.

Rico had spent more time chasing after her than at the club's headquarters or doing work with his fellow members. He was a glorified babysitter, and it was only fear of his father's anger and retribution that kept him from complaining about the situation.

Every day, Rico waited to hear a tale about her stupidity. She acted like an unruly child who wouldn't stop until she'd made her point. He had enough faith to believe her actions wouldn't be life-threatening. His goal was to keep the extent of her rebellion and the fallout from their parents.

Today, he hoped, would be a little bit peaceful.

He'd dropped his sister at the house of another club member whose daughter was a friend. It meant he had most of the day to focus on other more *important* tasks for the club. He'd ridden across town and parked his bike outside Carson's Gym. He had one arm resting casually on his leg while the other stayed on the handlebar of his bike. He stared into the establishment.

A week ago, the Angels had gained word that a dealer had been working from inside the gym without permission and with no dues being paid to the Angels. His operation had only been small, but the Angels had never tolerated competition. He'd been found by enforcers who had left him bloodied but alive. Rico's presence outside was a reminder to the owners that they were no longer trusted.

He'd been there for almost an hour, his gaze following everyone who came in and out. He'd seen the son of the owner flinch at the sight of him before rushing inside. Rico was almost ready to leave when his phone rang. He pulled it from his pocket, seeing his sister's number.

"What?" he demanded.

"I'm sorry!" she said, sounding panicked. Her voice was thickened with tears. "I'm sorry, Rico!"

"What happened?"

She gave a tearful, fearful sob and Rico heard a muffled sound as something covered the speaker. Rico was on edge, his teeth gritted as he tried to hear anything to give away what was happening. When the noise stopped, Rico's every muscle was tightly coiled.

"Angelica?" he asked.

The answer didn't come from his sister.

"Hanthorn."

He knew the voice. It sent a complicated rush of emotions through him. Pearce Walton — a Demon Rider and someone who had been causing Rico grief for more than a decade.

"Walton," he bit out, "what have you done to my sister?"

"You should come here."

"Where is she?"

"Pine Hotel on York Street. Room 6A. Come *alone*."

The call ended.

Rico turned on the engine and swung his bike around, going toward York Street. He felt a tight ball of anger and worry form in the pit of his stomach. Their gangs notoriously fought over York Street. It was currently on the Demons' side, and while it wasn't the heart of enemy territory, it was still far from a safe zone.

Why the fuck is Angelica in a hotel room with a rival gang member?

Rico would *kill* Walton if he'd laid a finger on her.

He sped and cut corners to get to the street quicker, his tension only mounting as he crossed their borders.

He expected to see Demon Riders lining the street or to ride into a trap and have numerous guns pointing at his face, but the streets remained free of enemies, and no one stopped him. When he arrived in front of the Pine Hotel, there was only one Harley present. He came to a stop beside it. The bike was in prime condition and accented in red. He knew it was Pearce Walton's.

Rico climbed off his bike and walked into the hotel lobby. He scanned the space, his hand twitching with the desire to grab a weapon. The receptionists were busy behind the counter and a few guests sat with suitcases. No one seemed suspicious, but his worries didn't ease.

He crossed the lobby to the elevator and hit the floor number. The hotel was simple enough that he didn't need a key card to access the upper floors. Rico cracked his knuckles in the lift while running through a plan. He had a knife and a handgun. If he needed to, Rico could shoot Walton and get Angelica back to their side of the city. The consequences could be dealt with once his sister was safe.

The elevator doors opened, and he scanned the room numbers before walking toward the letter he needed. Not far down the hall, he spotted Pearce Walton leaning against a door. The man had a slimmer build than Rico, and although his enemy was slumped, Rico knew the Demon Rider was as tall as he was. His sleeveless black vest had many patches displaying his allegiances. His heavily tattooed arms were crossed, but the bright colors of his skulls and flowers were unmissable. His blond hair, which stopped at his shoulders, was brushed and slicked back behind his ears. His beard was thick but well-trimmed and maintained.

This brings back too many memories.

Angelica was in danger. The past should have been the furthest thing from his mind, but Pearce Walton had always been complicated. He was entangled in things Rico couldn't easily pull apart. He was a cold, standoffish Demon Rider now, but ten years ago, he'd been clean-shaven with his hair falling loose. His smile and touch had been rife with flirtation, and his moans had been unguarded and interspersed with Rico's name.

"Hanthorn," Pearce greeted.

He then turned, opened the door and walked inside the room. Rico placed a hand on his gun but followed warily. The room was small, and the sheets of the bed disturbed. Angelica was sitting in the middle, while at the foot was Benny Walton. He was Pearce's cousin and the son of the Demon Riders' leader. He had an eyebrow and ear piercing. His jet-black hair was spiked, and his leather jacket had no insignias, making it clear he wasn't yet fully initiated. Benny looked cautious. Angelica, despite her tear tracks, looked stubborn. She reached out and took Benny's hand in her own.

Fuck, Rico thought.

"We have a problem," Pearce stated.

No shit.

"We're not a *problem*," Angelica exclaimed. "We're a *couple*."

Rico knew that tone. He'd been dealing with it for the last few weeks as he'd argued with his sister and told her to stop sneaking into the clubhouse. The club's members tolerated her, but that was only due to respect for their father. Rico knew how quickly respect could change to animosity. If the Hanthorns couldn't control a teenager, were they fit members to run the club?

Rico had tried to explain that to Angelica, but she'd only crossed her arms and turned away from him. When he'd persisted and forced her to look at him, she'd just argued more.

Rico could tell from her mulish expression that she wouldn't be giving Benny Walton up without a fight. And a fight was the *last* thing he wanted, especially if it involved the Demons and the Angels going to war.

He glanced at Pearce. The man had his arms crossed again and was leaning against the wall. When they locked gazes, Rico knew Pearce had worked out the problem as swiftly as he had. They couldn't force the teenagers apart. It wouldn't work. But if they left them alone, they'd only end up getting caught by someone less willing to be discreet.

Rico made a gesture with his head toward the door. Pearce nodded and followed him out into the hall. He shut the door and leaned against it once more.

"He won't change his mind," Pearce stated.

"She won't either."

Pearce nodded. "We can try keeping them away."

"But they'll slip out," Rico acknowledged.

"Kids," Pearce agreed.

His statement had been flat, but when their gazes locked, electricity ran down Rico's spine. Because *they* had been kids once — stupid teenagers who'd liked men more than they'd ever liked women.

At least we weren't dumb enough to fuck someone we knew *was from a rival gang.*

"We'll still need to do something about this," Pearce continued.

Rico rubbed a hand over his mouth. He would have liked the luxury of pacing, but he wouldn't turn his back on an enemy, no matter that their objectives currently aligned.

"Whatever we do, they'll fight against it," Rico acknowledged.

"Unless we give them what they want."

"*Let* them do this?" Rico demanded, outraged. "They'll be found out."

They both knew what that would entail. The Demons would be harsh against Benny. Angelica might gain some lenience from being a woman and non-club member, but she would never wash away the disgrace. She'd be ruined and sent away. John Hanthorn would never accept such a betrayer living under his roof.

And that was only if the *right* people found them. If they got someone harsh, uncaring and determined to make a statement, then there was no limit to the viciousness that could be unleashed. If an Angels member thought Benny had been taking advantage of Angelica, he'd be killed. But if a Demon Rider thought she was up for grabs and willing to spread her legs...? The thought sickened him.

"We won't let them be found," Pearce explained. "They're not going to stop. So, we have to do a better job at hiding them."

"You want us to facilitate this and let them betray our clubs?"

"They aren't smart enough to stay away from each other," Pearce answered. "They'll get over it. We just have to wait."

Get over it, like we *got over it?*

It had been too many years to hold anything resembling affection for Pearce, but back when it had happened? When he'd realized his lover was an enemy that he was meant to hate on sight? It hadn't been so simple. He'd once stood so close he could count the flecks of green and gray in Pearce's hazel eyes. He'd seen laughter and fondness crest the man's youthful face.

Get a fucking grip. You locked those memories away for a damn good reason.

He couldn't afford anything tugging his attention away from the club and the safety of his family.

"If they don't get over it," Rico replied, "and if they're *caught*, this could spark a war."

"Stupid teenagers won't start a war."

"My sister might pull off being a stupid teenager. Your cousin will garner a heftier price than a lecture."

Pearce straightened and lowered his arms to his sides. It took those few posture changes and he looked larger and more intimidating. Rico knew all the tricks. He'd been taught by one of the best in his club.

So different from the past.

When he'd known Pearce, the man hadn't tried to take control. He'd seemed to like Rico grabbing him and pushing him down. Now, he was all grown up and used to giving commands that were readily followed. Pearce might be a nephew of the leader, but, like Rico, he would have climbed up the ranks through tenacity and displays of loyalty.

"No one will find out," Pearce said lowly, his eyes narrowing. "I'll make sure of that."

Rico stiffened, sensing the change in tone.

"Is that a *threat*, Walton?"

"If you don't cooperate."

Rico closed the distance but allowed enough space to draw a weapon or throw a punch. Pearce smelled of bike oil and cigarettes.

"Don't threaten me, Walton."

"Don't threaten my cousin."

"That wasn't a threat. It was a *statement*. Your club is as ruthless as mine. He's an aspiring member, for fuck's sake. There's a reason you don't *do* shit like this. He'll be gunned down, and Angelica will be ostracized."

Frankly, if Benny were his cousin, he would have slapped the man upside the ear and tore through him about learning where to put his dick. Knowing it was happening with *his* sister made Rico's teeth grind. He would happily punch the man for daring to touch Angelica, but he knew his sister could handle a flirtatious teenager. If she couldn't, she'd only need to say a word and the Angels would brutalize whoever treated her wrong. Her insistence that they were a *couple* only proved that violence would not solve the problem. He'd *never* harm his sister, and he couldn't risk beating Benny Walton.

"What do you suggest instead?" Pearce asked, his tone clipped.

Rico tried to devise something better, but there was nothing that came to mind. Anything he considered left Angelica open for punishment or discovery. She'd also never back down if he confronted her directly. She'd run into the arms of the Demons if she thought it would give her what she wanted. Pearce's suggestion seemed to be the only solution. If they let them have their time together, the attraction of bedding an enemy would hopefully run its course.

"I don't have a better solution," Rico admitted, grudgingly.

"Then take her back to your territory. I'll take him to mine. We'll arrange something for them."

If I can't convince her to use her fucking brain.

Rico knew he had a snowball's chance in hell of succeeding, but he would try anything before committing to this insanity. It was more than just her skin on the line if the Angels uncovered their deal. Protecting family wouldn't be enough to keep him from the club's disgust and wrath. They'd make sure he left the clubhouse in a body bag.

"I'll take her back," Rico replied. "But I swear to you, Walton, if you betray us, no one will find the pieces I'll cut you into."

His hand had never been far from his gun, and he pulled it out, pressing the barrel to Pearce's stomach. The man barely reacted. He kept his gaze locked on Rico's. He even leaned forward until there was barely a sliver of space between their lips. Rico could almost feel the scratch of his beard and wasn't prepared for the sudden and intense desire he felt.

It had been too damn long since he'd been so close to a man.

His club was staunchly heterosexual, and he'd always had to hide his lovers. He'd strip off his insignias and travel to areas of the city where no gang member would ever go. It was difficult to be discreet, but after the stupidity of his youth, Rico had adopted a state of paranoia and anonymity. So far, no one had uncovered his secret meetings in gay clubs. Hell, he'd even slept with women when out with his fellow club members, just to keep the Angels off his scent. But Pearce was not only the forbidden fruit hanging before his lips—he was also a fruit Rico had sampled thoroughly. Pearce had been his first time, for Christ's sake.

It was no wonder he could never fully push the man out of his mind.

"Threaten me again, Hanthorn," Peace murmured, "and I'll make you regret it."

Pearce's menacing tone should have infuriated him, but it didn't. Instead, Rico felt a crashing wave of desire. He *wanted* him. People didn't speak to him like that. The Angels knew to follow his commands and never dare disappoint him. His lovers rarely had the guts to ask for his name. Yet, he had a goddamn *gun* to Pearce and the man wasn't backing down. Rico had never wanted to devour a man's mouth more — to shut him up not with fists or bullet wounds but with lips and tongue.

Does he kiss any better than he did years ago?

Rico shifted the gun, trailing it up the man's stomach and over his chest. It wasn't a threat anymore. His motions were too languid, his grip too lax. Pearce could have shifted away or yanked the gun from his hand. He didn't. Their actions were still the height of idiocy. Rico hadn't flicked off the safety, but it was still live. The first rule of owning a gun was to never point it at anyone unless you planned to shoot them. Pearce let him do it without a bead of sweat. It was addicting. *Erotic.*

How many people have the balls for this? All my other lovers would run screaming at the sight of my gun.

"I'll threaten you as much as I like," Rico said lowly, "until I know you'll obey."

He wasn't sure if it was a threat or a promise.

"I don't obey many, Hanthorn," Pearce answered, his voice rough. "What makes you think I'll obey *you*?"

Rico's need intensified. He held Pearce's gaze and saw matching heat in it. Pearce wanted it, too. An urge to pin the man to the wall nearly overwhelmed him. Rico wanted to put Pearce in his place until he did what he was told. But a sound of movement behind the door had them stiffening.

The snap back to reality was sudden and sharp.

I'm using my gun like a fucking sex toy, flirting with a goddamn Demon Rider in their *territory.*

He stepped back and holstered his weapon. Pearce noticeably swallowed. That and the desire in his eyes were the only signs that Pearce seemed affected by what had happened. Rico felt shaken. His heart was pounding and his cock already showing interest. The scent of oil and smokes had never been so alluring.

A goddamn disaster.

It was why he'd avoided getting in close contact with Pearce for ten years.

"Neither of us bow to our enemies," Pearce said, his voice returning to its cooler and more disinterested tenor. "But our clubs made a truce before, so we'll make one now. You don't tell the Angels. I don't tell the Demons. Our priority is keeping these kids from ending up dead."

"Agreed."

"Good." Pearce stepped away from the door and his voice sharpened and raised to a loud bark. "Get out here, Benny."

There was no reaction at first, but slowly the door opened. Benny exited first, clasping Angelica's hand as she followed. They both looked wary but didn't seem to have heard their conversation. Rico hoped the dangers of being caught had sunk in.

"We're leaving," Rico announced.

Angelica glanced between him and Pearce before back to Benny. She placed a hand on his cheek and kissed him tenderly. Rico clenched his jaw. He was already unhappy about them, but his previous interaction with Pearce had left him with an even shorter fuse. He grabbed Angelica's arm, pulling her from the kiss. She made a sound of surprise as he yanked her out of Benny's grasp.

"Contact me," he said brusquely to Pearce.

He didn't dare catch the man's gaze as he pulled his sister down the hall and to the elevator. Rico didn't like turning his back on an enemy. But if Pearce could handle a gun to his chest without a flinch, Rico could endure a few seconds of vulnerability.

He reached the elevator and slapped the button. It was already on their floor from his arrival, and he could pull her in without waiting. Angelica had been silent until the doors closed.

"Rico," she blurted, "I'm meant to be with him. I will stand up to father for him. I love him. You don't understand—"

"I understand that you're a selfish, stupid child who found a person to fuck who would piss us off and get you killed."

"It's not like that!" she argued, immediately flushing with rage. "We're in *love*!"

"You're seventeen, and you don't know what you are."

"I know I want him! I'll *never* give him up."

It was exactly what he and Pearce had expected. They could shout until they were blue in the face, but nothing short of locking the teenagers in separate rooms was going to keep them apart. And anything they did was only going to make the allure stronger. Pearce's solution was the only option.

Rico breathed deeply, trying to calm his temper, but it was harder than normal. His moment in the hallway with Pearce had given him too many emotions to process. He wanted to funnel them all into rage rather than acknowledge whatever else was brewing within him.

By the time he felt moderately calmer, the elevator had reached the lobby. His hand had remained encircling Angelica's arm and he dragged her through the hotel. He glowered at anyone who looked at them for too long. When they were outside and had stopped at his bike, Angelica stared longingly back at the hotel.

"Get on the bike," he ordered.

She finally met his gaze and glared.

"You can't stop us, Rico. We're going to—"

"I'm not going to stop you," he snapped.

Her eyes widened. "What?"

"I'm going to make sure you don't end up disgraced or dead." He pointed at the bike. "Now get the fuck on."

This time, Angelica followed his command. He passed her his helmet before taking a seat and starting the engine. She wiggled into place behind him and wrapped her arms around his waist. Rico left the curb as soon as she was secured. He rode with speed back into Angels' territory.

Rico knew it was only the start of the misery Angelica was going to put him through. He hoped Pearce would let their next conversation be a phone call. He didn't want another repeat of whatever lapse of judgment had occurred in the Pine Hotel hallway.

About the Author

Elizabeth Hollows is an Australian writer of LGBT love stories specializing in homosexual or lesbian romance. Her preferred genres are fantasy, science fiction and contemporary/modern.

She has been writing since she was twelve, but has spent the last few years writing romance stories and discovering a passion for LGBT romance.

When Elizabeth is not writing she embroiders, reads and plots her next novel. She is a fan of the winter months and always has a book in her handbag and a cup of tea nearby.

Elizabeth loves to hear from readers. You can find her contact information, website details and author profile page at https://www.pride-publishing.com

PUBLISHING

Sign up for our newsletter and find out about all our romance book releases, eBook sales and promotions, sneak peeks and FREE romance books!